Sylvan Mist
The MacLomain Series-
Book 3
By Sky Purington

~Sylvan Mist~

Dear Reader,

Thank you for purchasing, *Sylvan Mist* (The MacLomain Series- Book 3)

Sylvan Mist proved to be a story that seemed to want to write itself. The words came so easily. I thought it would be a sad story to tell. After all, I was saying goodbye to the series. But *Sylvan Mist* kept me smiling. I had no idea the hero, William had such a great sense of humor and I also had no idea that any man would have the pure finesse to crack the stern outer shell the heroine, Coira had built around herself.

All the heroes and heroines from the series converge in this novel without stealing William and Coira's debut. If you read *Destiny's Denial* you know well who William is. Though a boy then, he's become a wizard and chieftain of the MacLomain clan in this story. And Coira... she was a little girl in *Fate's Monolith*! No more. Now she's a strong woman with a purpose and a wee bit too much attitude.

I fell in love with this series. For that reason alone, I felt it deserved a re-launch. Tighter, fresher and definitely more sensual, I'm walking away happy. Be sure to purchase your copy of *The King's Druidess* (The MacLomain Series- Prelude), *Fate's Monolith* (The MacLomain Series- Book 1) and *Destiny's Denial* (The MacLomain Series- Book 2) at Amazon, Barnes & Noble and Smashword.

Best Regards Always,
Sky

~Sylvan Mist~

Previous Releases Include:

The King's Druidess (MacLomain Series-Prelude)
Fate's Monolith (MacLomain Series- Book 1)
Destiny's Denial (MacLomain Series- Book 2)

Highland Muse

Darkest Memory
Heart of Vesuvius (Sequel to Darkest Memory)

The Victorian Lure (Calum's Curse- Ardetha Vampyre)
Coming Soon- The Georgian Embrace- Acerbus Lycan)

A Christmas Miracle- FREE READ

What they're saying about Sylvan Mist...

"If you're looking for that great summer beach read that will take your mind off all your worries this one is for you. If you love the time travel romances of Lynn Kurland, this one equals any of hers. "

~Long and Short Reviews

"I have never read any of Sky Purington's books before, but after reading "Sylvan Mist", I can't wait to read more. It is a great book, mixing magic with history and time travel with romance, all following a family line through time. I loved the storyline and the great characters."

~Night Owl Reviews

"This final story in Purington's MacLomain trilogy is an enchanting story of time hopping. Closely connected to the previous stories, the action is intense and the finish is a fine conclusion to the series."

~Romantic Times Reviews

This is a work of fiction. Names, characters, places, and incidents are either the product of the author's imagination or are used fictitiously, and any resemblance to actual persons living or dead, business establishments, events, or locales is entirely coincidental.

Sylvan Mist: The MacLomain Series, Book Three

COPYRIGHT © 2011 by Sky Purington

All rights reserved. No part of this book may be used or reproduced in any manner whatsoever without written permission of the author except in the case of brief quotations embodied in critical articles or reviews.

Contact Information: Sky@SkyPurington.com

Cover Art by *Tamra Westberry*

Published in the United States of America

~Sylvan Mist~

Dedication

This story is dedicated to my sister, Deborah. You've been there for me through thick and thin. Thank you for your endless support in all I do.

I love you, sis.

~Sylvan Mist~

Prologue

"Flesh and blood?" The devil chuckled. "You give yourself too much credit."

She didn't bother struggling. "Do I really?"

He leaned in close until the edge of his mouth skirted hers. "Aye, and I've little use for those such as you."

"I doubt that." She remained still.

"Dinnae doubt, lass." He ran his tongue along her jaw until he seized her earlobe with his teeth. He growled, released his hold, and threw her to the ground. In a flourish of precise, deadly movements, he lodged a knee into her back and withdrew his sword.

She felt the satisfaction in the steady draw of his breath, the purr of domination. So she was to die like this? With a sword driven through her back? Fear rose sharply. She tempered it. What good would it do?

He lifted her dress, straddled her backside, and whispered in her ear, the words more efficient than his blade. "Did you think your death would be so swift?"

To speak would be a waste of time. He'd only become more violent. Again, fear threatened to overwhelm. *God, please don't let this happen. No. No. No.* His hands traveled up her thighs.

"Release her."

It was a dark and dangerous whisper on the wind. She struggled to see, but blinding snow made it impossible. Her teeth began to chatter.

The brute above her chuckled, the sound evil and warped. He threw his words at the unseen stranger. "Interesting that you chose words over action. Do you ken the difference? The result of such foolishness?"

He shoved her face against the ground and leaned back. Then his large hands squeezed her neck. She gasped, arms flailing.

She tried to fight the horrifying fear of helplessness. The clutch of strong fingers dug deeper into her windpipe and made reasoned thought impossible. The alabaster snow released black flecks into her vision. Panic seized. She fisted the icy moisture beneath and struggled for air. Her body grew heavy and leaden.

Milky white ground became foggy gray. She struggled to see, not to lose the last of this reality. Yet fate was not that kind.

Blackness descended.

~Sylvan Mist~

Chapter One

Salem, New Hampshire, 1816

"No more!" Coira jerked awake, slammed her hands down on the secretary, and shook off the dream. Flame still curled in the lantern, the papers she'd been working on scattered about.

Ridiculous, this nightmare of hers; it had started on the first of the year and was nothing but a thorn in her side. She knew well what it meant and wanted none of it. She'd done just fine for herself thus far and had no intention of being lulled into the oddities that plagued her bloodline. Besides, what did he mean "no use for those such as her"? And how did she seem to know what to answer?

She walked to the window, and pulled back the curtains. The moon was a wide eye overhead and sparkled off the oak leaves beyond. Why her? She closed her eyes and banged her palm again the glass. She couldn't deal with this, not now.

"Coira?" She turned and offered her mother a steady smile. "Mama, why are you up at this hour?"

Marie stepped into the room, and candlelight flickered off the traces of silver in her red hair. "It's not that late, child. I thought I heard something."

She walked back and straightened her paperwork. Her mother knew. Secrets such as this did not keep well in the O'Donnell family. "So you know. I'm surprised it took this long."

"I've known for some time." Marie placed a hand on Coira's arm. "There's no shame in it. Let me help you."

"No." She pulled away. "This makes no sense. Remember, I'm the only child who carries no magic. And thus far I've been content with such."

"That does not mean you are immune to the MacLomain call. Magic is not necessary to feel their summons," Marie responded.

Coira sighed and sat. She was an odd being, the child of a witch and sister to two more. Only her father shared her plight, her normalcy. Sixteen years ago, her cousin Arianna vanished. She'd traveled back in time to medieval Scotland, never to return, all because of a MacLomain.

Not her. Coira would not be pulled. "I've a love for England and all things English; somewhere, somehow, someone miss-stitched. No offense, Mother, but Scotland would not appreciate me on its soil."

Marie's back straightened. "Lass, you're half Irish and half Scottish. Will that ever mean anything to you?"

"Of course it does. It's just not my passion." Coira took her mother's hand and squeezed. "Come now, I merely mean that I'm an English history teacher. It's highly unlikely my fate would carry me in such a direction."

Her mother had fled Scotland during the Highland Clearances but remained fiercely proud of both her homeland and her clan, the Brouns. Liam, her father, was proud to be from Dublin, Ireland.

Marie's expression saddened for a moment. "Aye, it does seem unlikely, but fate is a funny thing. There's always a lesson to be learned in its design."

She nodded her head once. "But not a lesson for me. My lessons are only what I teach here in Salem."

Her mother's eyes turned hard and wise. "So you think. I'll leave you to your rest now. Remember, your sister and brother will be visiting tomorrow for the festivities. They will not leave you be about this dream you've been having."

She watched Marie depart and frowned. No doubt they wouldn't. Calum would be returning from overseas having studied in France for the past year, and Annie lived in Hampstead working as a housekeeper. She'd not seen Annie since Christmas, because she was thoroughly engrossed in writing one novel or another when not busy with her duties.

Though twenty-four, Coira remained with her parents. The siblings had decided that one of them would stay to help their parents and watch over them. She didn't mind living here for the most part. Spinsterhood had suited her fine until recently.

Now things would change.

At tomorrow's gathering, Coira and James would announce their betrothal. Her friend would become her lover. She ignored the ripple of apprehension that stole down her spine. There was no reason for it. James was dashing and as British as they came.

She retired to bed and snuffed the candle. As darkness surrounded, she wondered yet again. Who was the stranger who meant to save her in the dream? Did she really care? After all, he was but a Scot.

****

"Come here, you!" Annie lifted her skirts and flew across the drive.

Coira braced for impact. Never was a more spirited woman born than her sister. Annie swooped in for a tight embrace.

"Oh, how I've missed you!" Annie laughed and pulled back.

"And I you." She smiled. Where she'd inherited their father's black hair and blue eyes, Annie possessed the glorious chestnut hair and golden eyes from their Scottish blood.

Immediately, Annie's eyes narrowed. "No?"

Coira grimaced. Not this fast. Annie had only to take one look at her to know about the dream.

"Shush."

Her sister's eyes were saucers now. "You? Who would've thought? My Lord, this is incredible!"

"Shush!"

Annie waved away Coira's insistence. "People are only just arriving, and nobody's paying attention anyway. This just astonishes me. Aren't you getting married? Oh no, that's a bad idea. You should break it off right away. You know how these things—"

She clamped a hand over Annie's mouth and leaned in close. "If you don't stop talking now, I'll tell everyone about what you always wondered and were determined to find out."

If it was possible, Annie's eyes rounded further, and she shook her head.

"That's what I thought." She removed her hand and offered a serene smile. "We'll talk about this later, and I *am* announcing my betrothal."

Annie rolled her eyes and shrugged. "Who am I to argue when you blackmail me?"

"And how have you blackmailed your sister this time?" James had approached unseen.

She welcomed the intrusion. "Would I do such a thing?"

James laughed and took her hand. His sea green eyes twinkled. "In a heartbeat to get your way."

She loved his accent, so crisp and English. Defined and articulate. His sun kissed brown hair was wavy and his height substantial. They had known one another for years, and both taught at the same school. They'd finally decided to marry in that neither had found another who suited. They would live nearby and be available to help Marie and Liam with whatever they might need.

"James, how are you?" Annie gave him a big hug.

"Excellent, now that I've nearly secured your sister as my fiancée."

Annie shot her a look of aggravation. "No doubt, and it's about time, too. She's not getting any younger!"

"You should talk." Coira arched an eyebrow. "You're but a year younger than I."

"And you're still both unmarried, me daughters?" Liam announced on arrival.

Annie rushed to their father and mumbled a tearful greeting into his chest. Liam beamed and held her tight. When they pulled apart, he looked Coira's way.

"My girl, today is a big day for you!" He was a beautiful man, her father. Tall, big boned, and as black Irish as they came.

"I've some sad news, lassies." He frowned and shook his head. "Calum will not make it home for the day. I've received a post that his ship has been delayed. I'm sorry to bear such news."

Both girls deflated. How they missed their brother.

"I'd say everyone else is here. Are you ready?" Liam directed this at James.

"Of course." James pulled her toward the tables where people were gathered. Theirs would be a casual announcement.

She pasted a smile on her face as James gathered everyone's attention. Suddenly, her feet felt like lead. A newborn trepidation swallowed her.

Or was it so new?

James hailed the crowd and smiled widely. "I'm certain you all know why we're here." He turned to her but spoke to them. "I have an important thing to ask of Coira."

The women smiled knowingly from beneath their bonnets, and the men nodded their approval.

James fell to one knee and took her hand in his. He gazed up at her with both approval and finality. "Coira, we have been friends for so long. Would you do me the honor of becoming my—"

His lips continued to move, but something shifted. Time slowed, his form faded, blurred. His hand in hers became a death grip, a force. A fever stole up her arm and wrapped her body in mist. Verdant lightning blinded her with images: diamond eyes, sensual lips, incredible, unattainable, foreign beauty. But where was he? She fell to her knees.

The world was gone. He was not. Moisture prickled her skin and dampened her pores. She was light and alive, alone yet not. Arms of nothing wrapped around her waist and pulled her close. Then there was lust. Like a roll of flaming ice, it churned her womb with potent agony. She reached out and grasped male flesh.

His voice roared, yet whispered. "You are safe."

Her mind rebelled against the thick Scottish burr, but her soul clutched him tighter and pleaded. "I'm not safe. Not from you. Leave me be."

He pulled her close. "Who are you?"

She closed her eyes yet images continued to bombard. Hard skin, thick lashes. "I am no one."

Rich laughter buried her defiance. "Aye, you're someone."

She opened her eyes, and daylight blinded as James embraced her. They knelt before one another on the grass. Applause saturated the lawn full of townsfolk. She pulled away from James and accepted his hand as they stood.

She shuddered at the chill that swept through her. God no, it really was happening.

One look at Annie more than confirmed it.

****

Annie met Marie's eyes in mutual understanding. Coira was being called back. They were both surprised. It was obvious in the distress blatant in her mother's eyes. Coira? Prim and proper and all things English.

This was bad.

They could all have understood it happening to Annie; after all, she loved all things Scottish. The obvious difference between the siblings had always been a bit of a joke between them. When they were children, they would battle with sticks in the woods. Annie would be the Scotsman defending his country, Coira the Englishman determined to bring order and surrender. Yet when the call came from Scotland to a woman of the Broun lineage, it was impossible to ignore.

Literally.

Annie knew the moment she touched Coira she was doomed. Doomed in Coira's eyes, not in hers. Why couldn't she have been called? Blast it! When her sister fell to her knees, she'd seen the magic swamp her. Felt it in her bones. What had Coira just experienced? How she longed to find out. But she knew her sister. She would be tight-lipped to the end. She was determined to marry her Englishman, come Scottish plague or no.

Her mother made it to her side. "We will bring her to the attic, Annie. We must show Coira her wedding gown."

"Do you really think that's wise?"

~Sylvan Mist~

Marie's expression darkened and she murmured, "Aye, it is. Though I wish it were not the case."

She knew the pain her mother was feeling. "Oh, Mama. I'm so sorry."

"No, no." Marie shook her head. "Don't be. This is the way of things, I know that."

Coira walked in their direction, face pale though she smiled for the neighbors. She suddenly seemed to want to avoid them and veered toward the barn. When they caught up with her, Annie linked an arm through one of Coira's and Marie did the same.

Annie spoke softly. "Are you well?"

Coira stopped short, a blank expression on her face. They saw the crisis coming and led her forward a few steps before they closed the barn stall doors behind them.

Then, like a candle flame beneath a heavy downpour, Coira crumpled to the ground.

****

He swirled before her. A man made of mist, beautiful, hypnotizing, and without a face. A hand held out to her in offering through a fog of barn ceiling and hay. Though reluctant, Coira was curious, and she lifted a hand in welcome.

"Sweetheart, are you well?" Her mother's voice drifted through the enthralling haze and sharpened her senses. *Am I well? Am I engaged?* Her eyes felt heavy and overused, as though she'd been correcting papers for centuries. She spoke yet nothing came out.

"Coira, it's Annie." Her sister's cool hands brushed back the hair from her forehead. Slowly, she opened her eyes. Oh, but the dim light of the barn blinded. She shut her eyes and pushed herself to a sitting position.

"I'm fine." She whispered the reassurance more to herself than to them. At last, she opened her eyes and saw her mother and sister kneeling in front of her.

"Are you?" Marie worried.

"Coira?" Annie frowned with concern.

She shook her head and smiled ruefully. "If you could both stop looking at me as though I'm some sort of anomaly, I do believe I would feel much better."

They appeared momentarily chagrined but smoothed their expressions. Her eyes drifted to her left hand. The engagement ring was exquisite, a shimmering diamond that overtook her slender finger. The stone shone brightly in the dim recesses of the barn.

But not nearly as brightly as the small diamond chip within the ring that Annie wore. She again cursed her envy of the ring given to her sister by their parents years ago. Two hands coming from separate directions holding a diamond-centered crowned heart between them.

Why she should envy the Irish heirloom was beyond her. Perhaps because it was one more stone in the wall between her, with no magic, and her mother and sister. An Irish ring would not suit her any more than the Scottish plaid her mother so favored.

She brushed her thoughts aside and stood. "I'm fine."

Marie shook her head. "Nay, lassie. You're about as far from fine as I've ever seen you. Annie?"

Annie nodded. "Aye, Mama's right. You just had a moment with him out there, didn't you?"

A painful rumble of laughter rose in her chest and she waved them away. "You're both mistaken. I had a moment with no one."

Lucky them, witches that they were, that they could so easily see. Still, she didn't mean to give them an ounce of assurance or confirmation.

"Come, lass, I've something to show you." Marie looped her arm through Coira's and reopened the barn doors.

Sunlight overwhelmed and she squinted. Townsfolk filtered around and offered smiles. The smell of apples and cornmeal filled her nostrils, the grass underfoot lush and suddenly so green it was all she could see. The oak overhead flipped its leaves in passing. A light wind caressed her cheeks. Compelled, she stopped a moment and looked up past the tall sturdy trunk to the many branches that forked against the afternoon sky.

"I'll protect you."

She stared at the leaves overhead and heard his voice, clear, intense, and horribly Scottish.

"No, you won't!" She screamed at the oak and shook her head. Through the red haze of anger, she heard her mother command Annie to get her inside, up the stairs into the attic. It was happening too fast.

She tried to speak, tell them nothing was happening too fast. That she was newly engaged, and all was well. All was normal. But they didn't listen, because they couldn't hear her. She saw the doors to their home. Saw the foyer and the stairs, knew that James was behind them but being told to go away.

Then the attic stairs loomed before her, steep and foreign, a place where she'd never been invited for she carried no magic. Breathless, she was led up, yet was so outside herself that she stumbled and fell.

But he broke her fall.

Of mist and muscle and flesh, he cushioned the blow of the sharp wood. His concern washed over, and his words echoed in her ear. *"I'm here, lass."*

She pushed away from nothing and stumbled up the stairs. Everything was happening too quickly. She couldn't get her bearings. The attic rose up, and nausea brought her to the flat planks underfoot. Before she could vomit, Marie brought her to her feet and pulled her close.

The nausea receded. What on Earth was going on? She was shocked when Annie bit off a sob.

Marie pulled back slowly and stared into Coira's eyes. She'd never seen such a sad look upon her mother's face. "I must show you something."

She slowly released her breath. "What do you wish to show me?"

The sunlight streaming through the small windows receded when Marie flicked her wrist, and a candle sputtered to life. It rested on a small three-legged table and cast a glow on what looked to be a tree stump sitting alone in the middle of the attic. On that stump sat the most amazing thing she'd ever seen.

A crown of gold, so glorious it was hard to look at.

Marie lifted and held it out to Coira. "This is a family heirloom."

Instinct shot her hand forward, and she grasped the circular piece between the sharp spikes. Reluctant, Marie released and the crown's full weight took her by surprise. She studied it. "How beautiful!"

Marie appeared confused as did Annie.

Annie spoke first. "So it's not as it seems?"

Marie shook her head, mystified. "It has to be, the wedding dress was not right yet."

Her eyes snapped to attention. "What are you two talking about?"

But they were already too deep in debate.

Annie's eyes narrowed. "Well, why is nothing happening?"

Marie's brow furrowed and distress crossed her dainty features. Before she could utter another word, Annie sprang into action, as was Annie's way.

"May I?" she said to Coira, and wrapped her hand around the crown as if to inspect it more closely.

Coira gasped when the golden headpiece turned to ice. Her arm numbed, and her legs liquefied. Oh dear God, what was happening? Annie was falling, a look of both horror and wonder on her face.

Marie screamed in denial from a great distance away. Coira could barely see anyone or anything as a whip of green moisture encased her body. It crawled over her calves, up her thighs until it encaged her torso. She tried to push it away, but her hands slid through the weightless cocoon. The verdant mist took her torso and head.

All turned white and peaceful.

Then hell was unleashed, and everything fell away. A horrible roar filled her eardrums, and a sugary smell filled her nostrils. The floor let loose, and she fell hard and fast. But she had no fear, only wonder. Was she finally a part of magic? Had she been allowed entrance?

When terror should have seized her, wonder turned to anger. Why should she be shown magic now after all this time? She locked her muscles and flailed in defiance. Darn them all, she was an English teacher, and as such this plight held no interest. As she fought the maddening rush of energy and harsh whips of power thrown, she had only one thought.

She did not want to go to Scotland.

Chapter Two

Scotland 1225

"Take me hand, laddie, I've no use for sentiment. Either ye want this or ye dinnae."

William stared down at Iosbail and didn't know quite what to make of her request. Did he want this responsibility? Aye, for all of his life, he'd craved the honor. That thought didn't make the moment any easier.

He looked to the others standing in the stone chamber. Adlin's face was one of sorrow, Muriel's of consternation. They kept their gaze on Iosbail, for this decision was William's alone without influence.

"I will take the gift you offer, if you will it to be." What else was he to say? He'd just been offered greatness, a position within their clan that far surpassed mere chieftain.

Iosbail's thin fingers wrapped around his hand tightly, and she gave a brisk nod, an amazing feat for an elderly woman on her deathbed. Her words were low, yet louder than a vicious thunderclap. "So ye will become the fourth, a black wizard, one of two to balance four. I give ye my gift."

He felt her lifeblood crawl into his veins. Her memories became his, her waning vitality an addition to his vibrancy. He ran through the meadows of her childhood. Felt her love for a man long gone.

Experienced the pain of the many clansfolk she had lost under her care.

Then he felt no more.

She'd made the transition very easy and peaceful indeed. He opened his eyes to Adlin running his hand down his sister's wizened face. Out of respect, he closed her eyes to the death that had taken her.

It was done.

William was one of them now. He carefully released her hand and stood. His mother, Muriel, lowered her head and left the room. Adlin followed. The moment was to be betwixt William and his mentor. He had known his fate all along, to be one of the four MacLomain wizards.

He also knew it was his fate to become chieftain of one of the most powerful clans in Scotland. Cowal was his now. Iain, his uncle and former chieftain, had relinquished control six months prior when he left to deal with Clan Cochran to the north. After many long years, they still held a vendetta against the MacLomains because of Iain. Now they were led by the son of the Cochran chieftain he'd fought back in the war of 1199. Over time, they had again grown into a formidable power.

The new leader was more ruthless than most, and Iain had gone to investigate, bargain, and perhaps pacify. William knew what would happen and was prepared.

He said one last prayer for Iosbail's soul and left the chamber. Though responsibility weighed heavily upon William's shoulders, he had never been one to dwell on or over think the decisions he'd made in the past. He was a visionary, and to second-guess some of those decisions would drive a man insane.

He made his way to the wall walk and was surprised to find Arianna there. Normally, he would take great pleasure in sneaking up on her unexpectedly, but she was low on humor with Iain gone so long.

"Greetings, lass." He spoke on approach. "'Tis a fine day to gaze on your homeland, aye?"

Arianna turned her face slightly and offered a small smile. "Aye." She leaned her side against the stone wall. "So you've finally graduated, poor Iosbail."

He rested his elbows on the stone and relished the warm salty wind on his face. "I suppose you could call it that, couldn't you? No small thing becoming one of these infamous wizards. Iosbail will be missed."

"I'd say you have your hands full now, but of any man I know, you're certainly capable of everything that's been thrust your way." Arianna touched his arm. "Something bad is going to happen, isn't it?"

He hid behind his eyelashes and slid a glance her way. Arianna had aged well. Her long, reddish gold hair held no silver, and her skin was still smooth. "I've had no such vision. I can tell you, however, that Iain is well."

She sighed. "I know. I would feel it otherwise."

"Yet you still mourn."

"Of course I do. He's my husband, and I've been without him too long. He'll not risk traveling to me with magic. I don't trust the Cochrans. You know their place in our lives." She grunted with disgust.

He leaned back against the wall. "Aye. It still amazes me they are to be a problem for this clan once again."

"Do you think Iain will be able to smooth things?" Arianna sounded concerned.

He would not add to her distress. "I think if anyone is capable of it 'tis my uncle."

"And I think if anyone is capable of looking on the bright side of things 'tis you." Arianna shook her head and looked back to the mountains. "But I thank you for the vote of confidence."

He made to speak when the floor shifted beneath him. Instinctively, he pulled within himself and centered his being. Whatever caught him was powerful, too powerful. He closed his eyes and allowed the horrid transition, the pull of dark magic. He had no choice, for he was pulled by many enemy wizards.

****

"Oh, God." Coira immediately leaned over and vomited. Somehow she retained her footing and stood. How her legs still held her she had no idea.

"Coira, Coira. Stop that now," Annie whispered.

She slowly stood upright. The silence was deafening, her surroundings horribly foreign. Where were they? Foolish question. As reality infiltrated, she knew exactly where they were. It wasn't good.

They were completely surrounded by a wall of long-haired, weapon-wielding men wearing plaid cloaks. The smell of sweat and horse filled her nostrils. No one spoke as they eyed the women.

Annie pulled her closer. "Son of a bitch."

She was in no mood to reprimand Annie's language. In fact, she agreed with her sister's assessment. Yet, in their current predicament, there were more useful things to say. Three men in particular stood out, all cloaked like the rest, yet different.

She was just about to speak to them when the air compressed, then expanded. At first, all she could see was a blur within the circle. Then a faint hum seared her eardrums before another figure appeared.

"Dear Lord." This a faint whisper from Annie.

Coira stood up straighter and took an involuntary step back. Annie couldn't have been more correct in her appraisal. Mere feet from them stood the most beautiful man she'd ever laid eyes on. And that was only his profile. His hair was long and a strange mixture of black with dark auburn highlights. With high cheekbones, a straight nose, and a tall powerful build, his essence nearly toppled her over.

He simultaneously stepped in front of them and turned toward the three clansmen, protecting her and her sister.

His Scottish burr was deep and commanding when he spoke to the three men. "What foolishness is this? Your nerve astounds me."

Her breath caught. His voice was familiar. She knew she'd been called back to this time by a MacLomain, but it couldn't possibly be the man in front of them, could it? That would not be good. He was much too large to dismiss. But dismiss she would if need be.

The tallest of the three stepped away from the others, his platinum hair unmoved by the wind. "Ah, but are we so foolish when you are so sorely outnumbered?"

She was glad she understood Scottish Gaelic, or she'd be left out of all of this. As it stood, she was less afraid of impending death and more enthralled by the stranger's muscled back in front of her. She dared a glance at Annie and found her sister's eyes roaming the back of the clansman with appreciation as well.

Then the stranger responded. "Dinnae tell me I'm outnumbered. As I see it, there are three of you and one of me—fair odds in my eyes."

The blond enemy laughed. "What of the hundreds around you?"

"What of them? If I kill you, they will not stay to fight."

"You always did have a sense of humor, didn't you, MacLomain? For surely you're trying to jest now." The blond urged the other two forward.

MacLomain's hand skirted the dagger at his waist. She kept her gaze focused on that large hand, felt the tension building, and watched it move away from the dagger.

"I want no bloodshed. Take me, release the lasses," he said softly.

How gallant of him. She almost laughed but stopped. What was wrong with her? The man's statement made perfect sense and kept her and Annie safe.

"Excuse me?" Annie lightly tapped MacLomain on the shoulder. Coira grimaced as the three clansmen opposite frowned and focused their attention on her sister.

MacLomain turned his head slightly. "Now is not the time, lass."

Annie nodded but continued nonetheless. "I think that both Coira and I would be more content staying with you."

She rolled her eyes, pulled Annie closer, shook her head, and put a finger to her lips. She had no desire to stay here, period.

The MacLomain clansman said nothing but focused his attention on the enemy.

"So one wishes to speak?" The blond strode forward but MacLomain shifted so that he blocked Annie completely. This left Coira exposed. Oh no.

The blond shifted his target, snatched her arm roughly, and pulled her forward. MacLomain's hand shot out and grabbed her other arm.

She almost lost her footing at the feel of his hand, the exquisite desire it invoked. Her eyes immediately shot to his. His profile did nothing for the whole of his face and eyes. Oh Lord, his eyes. The lightest shade of gray she'd ever seen. Like mist caught in sunlight. And his lips, she knew those sensuous lips. She had seen them before.

His gaze flickered over her face, and he frowned before his lethal eyes cut to the other man. Why had he frowned? She was not considered unattractive by her family and friends. The nerve of the man to disapprove of her!

MacLomain's brogue turned low and deadly. "Release her, Cochran."

"Now why would I want to do such a thing? She's a bonnie wee lass, and I've not had a woman in some time." The blonde's grip strangled her arm.

MacLomain's gaze did not waver. "Because as it stands now, you are outnumbered."

The enemy clansmen's eyes shot to the forest in mild alarm and narrowed. He remained calm, yet one hand rose in the air. "Flee, kinsmen. Avoid war. Now is not the time!"

She pulled back her arm when the Cochran clansman faded and then vanished, as did the other two men behind him. The woods exploded with activity. MacLomain released her arm and ran forward, catching a massive battleaxe thrown to him. He caught it by the hilt and released a roar unlike any she'd heard before.

She pulled Annie close and the sisters huddled together while havoc let loose. Half of the Cochrans tried to flee while the others turned to fight. Dozens of men wearing the same blue and green plaid as their MacLomain champion poured forth. Metal clanged when claymores crashed into each other. She tried to look away from the surrounding death but was unable. Instead, she watched it all through an odd haze of calm.

Blades and men alike became bloodied. Raw power slid off the warriors while they battled their foes. The MacLomain covered the circumference directly around them and cut down an alarming amount of men.

Though it felt like days, within an hour the final enemy lay slain, and the two women stood within a circle of dead clansmen. The air held the sharp tang of blood and sweat, death and defeat. Yet the man who had defended them from the start still stood nearby. She focused on the sound of his breathing, heavy and masculine.

"Coira?" Annie whispered, shakily.

She shook her head, unable to speak. They'd surely been dropped into the pits of hell. Why was it necessary that they see all of this?

"William."

She focused on the tall Scotsman striding toward them. He had spoken to them, or had he? Who was William? The man stood nearly as tall and wide in the shoulders as the man in front of them. He clasped arms with him, hand to elbow.

So their hero had a name. William. She rolled the name around in her mouth. She couldn't dispute it was a good name and certainly not terribly Scottish.

"Iain, glad you made it." William smiled.

She wished he hadn't done that. Too handsome with a scowl, a smile made his face that of an angel. Who would have thought the man capable of possessing dimples?

William's voice turned gruff. "We've company."

Iain turned their way. She judged him to be in his late thirties, perhaps early forties based on the light starburst of wrinkles fanning out from his emerald green eyes. His hair was a mixture of mahogany and black. His eyes were kind when he assessed them.

"Welcome, lasses. You could only be Brouns."

Annie nodded with vigor, but Coira interrupted before she could speak. "Actually, we are O'Donnells. I'm Coira and this is my sister, Annie."

Iain took her hand and kissed the back of it. A very nice courtly gesture, she approved.

"Ah then, O'Donnells." Iain offered the same courtesy to Annie. A devilish twinkle lit his eyes when they shifted to William though he spoke to them. "I take it you traveled far to make it to us, and I see there are two of you, how curious."

"Why is that?" Annie cocked her head, spirit revived by the clansman.

Iain stepped back and shrugged. William gave them his full attention, his expression a strange mixture of discontent and curiosity.

William answered Annie's question. "Do you truly not know the answer to that, lass?"

He lifted Annie's hand to his lips, his eyes lingering on the ring on her finger. William's eyes narrowed and then shot to Annie's face. "Interesting ring."

Annie was too busy gawking, so Coira gave a sharp elbow to rouse her. Her sister stammered for a moment, then regained some wits. "Aye, it was given to me by my father. He's Irish."

William nodded slightly and turned to Coira. The last thing she needed right now was his undivided attention. She was an engaged woman after all. Coira offered him a cool smile.

He cocked his head slightly and took the back of her hand to his lips. Searing fire blazed through her when he kissed the tender skin. She swallowed hard when his eyes rose to hers. Blood pounded through her body in heavy gushes. Flecks of light threatened her vision. Was she swooning? Then the fire flooded below, and her limbs felt as though they blew apart. He didn't release her hand but grasped it tighter. She knew then how close he was to pulling her against him. She also knew how opposed he was to his own desire to do such a thing.

When he spoke, his voice was as sensual as his lips. His eyes flew to Annie's briefly. "Welcome, Annie." Then they flew back to her. "And Coira."

She clenched her jaw and pulled her hand away. William's face broke into a wide smile and he laughed. Laughed! Brute. What was so funny?

He turned to Iain. "Where's Arthur?"

"Back at the castle and none too pleased about it."

William howled with laughter now. "You denied him a battle to appease your wife when you could've sent someone else? He must've loved that!"

Iain laughed as well. "He wasnae happy, but I owed him one."

"I willnae ask what he did to deserve such wrath." William turned his attention to Coira and Annie. "We'll travel a short distance and make camp, lasses."

They said nothing as William whistled. From nowhere, two great warhorses appeared. Iain mounted the black steed and William the dark chestnut.

William brought his horse close and held his hand down to Annie. "Come, lass, ride with me."

Coira ignored the irritation surging through her when her sister stepped forward, took his hand, and swung up in front of him. Iain laughed and shook his head. He offered a hand down to Coira. She could do this. Annie had. She reached up and took Iain's hand, amazed by his strength.

More amazed that she had consented to ride with him.

****

Later that night, William leaned back against a pine tree trunk and watched the low campfire. His eyes traveled beyond the fire to the women sleeping on the other side. They were wrapped tight in MacLomain plaids and both visions.

His gaze settled on Annie. She looked so much like Caitlin. With long platinum-streaked chestnut hair and golden eyes, she could be her twin. He wondered how Caitlin fared. Now married to his cousin Ferchar, they lived in the twenty-first century.

His eyes slid easily from Annie to Coira. Now there was an Irish beauty with a prickly attitude. Her long ebony hair curled around porcelain features. Full, lush lips mumbled in her sleep, and thick black lashes fluttered. Coira's beauty struck him as supernatural, one with the moon.

One with the mist.

He quickly dispelled the thought. She did not wear the ring. Nor did he want her to. It was obvious she had no use for the Scottish, yet his country's blood ran in her veins.

William closed his eyes but knew sleep would not come easily this eve. For one of the lasses interested him. The other made him burn with need.

~Sylvan Mist~

Chapter Three

"We're going to see cousin Arianna again!" Annie's urgent voice drilled a hole into Coira's slumber. She pried her eyes open and bolted upright. Long-haired men in plaids filtered through the tall pines. Some sat around small fires as dawn broke through the forest and ignited the golden needles underfoot.

"Oh Lord, it wasn't a dream." She removed Annie's hand from her arm and stood.

Annie scrambled to her feet and frowned. "You always wake up so grumpy."

She disregarded her sister and smoothed her maroon day dress. She must look a fright. Why on Earth was she here? Obviously someone somewhere had made a mistake. It made sense that Annie was here; she wore the ring. Evidently her destiny was to be brought here by a MacLomain. Apparently Coira's proximity to Annie when they traveled back in time had simply brought her along for the ride.

Those visions and dreams had found the wrong sister.

She made a survey of the men and grimaced. Surely she was not meant for one of these barbarians?

"Good morn to you, lassies." Both women turned at the sound of Iain's voice.

"Good morn, Laird Iain." Annie dipped a curtsy. Coira greeted him without the curtsy.

~Sylvan Mist~

Iain laughed. "Nay, lass, I'm not the laird anymore. I've passed it on to another."

Annie cocked her head. "And who is that? Better yet, where's Arianna, she's here, isn't she? You're the man from the past who took her away when we were wee bairns."

Coira rolled her eyes. Annie loved to talk the way of the Scots.

"You're full of questions, aye?" Iain's verdant eyes sparkled. "My wife Arianna is here and well. How pleased she will be to see you both again. And the laird is—"

"Me." The deep voice came from behind.

Shivers ran down her spine. William stood so closely behind her, Coira swore she felt his breath on her neck. She stepped away, but not before their eyes met. Her heart fell into her stomach. Had she ever met an Englishman as beautiful as William? Surely she must have. She straightened her back and squared her shoulders. "I do believe I've been brought here by mistake."

One of William's dark brows shot up. "Have you now?"

She nodded once. With great effort, she kept her gaze locked with his. "Most certainly. Both Annie and I are well rehearsed in the ways of this connection between the MacLomains and the Brouns. I'm quite sure that I'm not supposed to be here."

William's silver eyes left hers and swung to Annie. "Nay, you're both here for a reason."

When they returned to hers, a mocking gleam burned within. "Fate doesnae make mistakes."

She narrowed her eyes, not trusting him a bit. He was clearly intent on Annie. "Be careful, if I'm here for a reason, then it is without any doubt to protect my sister."

An insolent smirk made love to his lips. "We will see, then, how well you champion your sister."

Coira swallowed hard and kept her gaze steady. "You would be amazed at my strength."

"I'm sure I will be," he murmured.

Annie broke through the battle of wills with her usual good humor. "I need no champion. Who here will have me?"

Iain alone laughed. Coira and William continued to glare at one another.

"We mount, aye, William?" Iain whistled and his horse trotted forth. "Annie, why dinnae you ride with me?"

Both William and Coira started to protest, but it was too late. Iain had already swung Annie up onto his mount.

Coira put her hands on her hips and eyeballed William. "I do not wish to ride with you. May I ride one of the spare horses?"

"'Twould be my pleasure." He smiled and she nearly relaxed. "If I trusted you, which I dinnae."

She bit back a growl. A growl! She was a lady, she didn't growl. Before she knew what had happened, she was neatly plopped in front of William high astride his horse. Her skirt stretched uncomfortably over her legs and her backside nestled far too intimately between his thighs, very strong muscular thighs. She closed her eyes and counted to ten. Ridiculous noticing such a thing!

If that wasn't enough, his hands suddenly covered her thighs. Her eyes popped open in shock.

"Easy, lass." His hands tugged briefly at her skirts and loosened them so as to ease her discomfort.

She whacked both intrusive hands away and refused to thank him. She had no use for his kindness at the moment. Damn him.

The easy canter they set allowed Coira to take in the surroundings. Comfortably warm air blew back her hair. The pines dropped random needles in an array of sunlit spikes. Wild ferns and shadowed moss lined the feet of tree trunks far and wide.

Coira relaxed instinctively. She couldn't deny the beauty around her. Nor could she deny the heat and scent behind her. He smelled clean and fragrant, musky and masculine. Her eyes strayed down to his thigh, the way the tartan rode the muscled skin.

When he spoke his voice was close to her ear. "'Tis mesmerizing, Scotland, is it not?"

She shivered with awareness when his warm breath brushed her cheek. "It is very nice."

She felt the low rumble of his laughter against her spine and her heart thudded heavily. No, absolutely not. She willed her body to ignore the incredible physique at her back. She was about to speak but he did first.

"Tell me about your sister."

She straightened and pulled forward, embarrassed that she'd allowed herself to sink back into his embrace. Her words were clipped. "My sister is none of your concern."

"Ahhh, but she is."

She whipped around and glared up at him. "Then why did you not summon her?"

She regretted the words the moment she spoke them. Was she willingly pushing him to acknowledge that he had accosted her at her betrothal? This was slippery ground and she preferred a solid stance and credible reality in her world.

His eyes fell to hers. At this range, his handsome face swamped her senses. Fire flooded her face, but she didn't shy away.

"I summoned no one." His gaze fell to her lips. "Especially not you, if that's what you're implying."

For the first time in her life, Coira wanted to spit in someone's face. She spit words instead. "Let me down from this horse."

"No."

"Yes. I demand it."

"You demand it?" His drawl was incredulous.

Her temper erupted. "I deplore a Scotsman at my back. Remove me this instant!"

Within a flicker of a moment, Coira was standing on the ground. She didn't miss a beat but threw back her shoulders and continued walking.

William tossed his words down at her just before he spurred his mount. "You've the devil in you, lass; enjoy your walk."

She sniffed with derision as he disappeared into the line of horseflesh in front of her. Fool! Who did he think he was? A man, that's what he was. How could she ever have found him attractive?

After a good hour of walking, she realized the last of the riderless horses was passing her. Her legs were tiring, and it appeared she was going to be left behind. Or was she? No, she wasn't. Her horsemanship was excellent, and she was positive she could mount one of these large horses.

And she did! Almost.

He being a stallion, she was surely a fool for trying such a feat. When he easily tossed her down to the needles underfoot, Coira lay looking up at the trees and scowled.

She scurried to her feet and realized there were but two horses left, one black and one white. The white horse took one look into her eyes and evaded. That left one. And he was large. She readied herself and stood tall, not an easy task at five foot four.

"Come here, laddie, I've a request." She spoke softly and held up her hand.

It appeared the horse appreciated her attempt at a Scottish brogue, for he stopped directly in front of her. She kept calm and patted his muzzle. "I've a need for a ride. Are you up to the task?"

The stallion snorted, his black eyes bordered on wild. She took a step back when he lifted a foot and stomped it down, then lowered his head in unexpected submission. She wasted no time and thanked God there was a hollowed out tree next to him. She crawled onto the log and then pulled herself onto the horse.

Lord, she was high. The great beast between her legs pranced a bit before he released a neigh as loud as a foghorn. She'd never felt such strength. It exhilarated her. On a whim she leaned down and whispered in his ear. "Want to have some fun?"

****

"Someone has to go find my sister!" Annie looked from William to Iain.

Night had fallen and they had drawn camp. Globes of firelight could be seen throughout the woods, burning within throngs of small groups. William leaned back on his elbows and watched the flames play over Annie's face. She was thoroughly stricken and in a near state of panic. Aye, she'd been affable enough through her endless stream of questions, but the anxiety in her voice prompted him to ease her fear.

"She's just on a bit o' a journey, lass. We'll see her soon enough."

Iain nodded and laughed. "Aye, we will."

Annie looked from one man to the other. "Why aren't either of you concerned? Coira is not good at this sort of thing. She doesn't deserve to be left behind. Again, why did you leave her behind, William? You shouldn't have done that!"

William looked to the fire. "She chose to dismount. It had naught to do with me."

"I doubt that!" Annie shook her head.

It wouldn't matter to him if she were halfway to England, bloody insolent lass. He'd almost thrown her from his horse when she declared her disgust of Scotsmen. He also knew that she was still on MacLomain land and safe. Therefore, he was comfortable sitting back and relishing her adventure.

A sound erupted from the forest, half scream and half whoop. The whole of the MacLomain clan rose as did Annie. Iain and William did not.

"No!" The feminine screech broke from the darkness just before the slender woman astride the tall black stallion. William sat forward a bit, enthralled. Aye, but she did make a picture.

Coira's black hair streamed behind her as the horse raced across the way and leapt the fire. Sparks dusted its belly and nearly lit her skirts aflame. For a split second he swore he saw green mist swirl around the horse's feet. When he blinked, it was gone. The horse reared, but the sprite of a woman held tight, her skirts billowing around its flank. He had never seen such a sight. Prim American-English bred blackguard of a lass. Dainty, his arse.

"Bloody beast, enough!" She swore a few more obscenities before the horse calmed and gallantly looked back at her. Coira nodded her head as though she were a queen, back ramrod straight. Then, as though she'd fought the long wars of Ireland, her spine turned to liquid, she melted forward and slipped free from the horse's back.

William moved faster than Iain and caught her before she hit the ground. She was a wee thing, her bones as fine as a newborn larch branch. He turned his thoughts from the way she'd felt earlier on the horse in front of him. Och, but he did well not touching her then. Every move of his mount had brushed her backside against him, and he thanked the gods she was an innocent and knew not the arousing effect she'd had on him.

Damn it all to hell. She was the wrong lass.

Annie hurried over with a frenzy of incoherent words. "Is she well? Oh no. You should have never left her. How did she end up on such a horse?"

William easily tuned out her chatter. The lass could carry on something fierce. He removed another plaid from his horse and wrapped it around Coira.

"What are you going to do with her?" Annie strode alongside.

William stopped at the base of a thick pine and sat, cradling Coira in his lap. "I'll take care of her, Annie. Fear naught."

"Well, I'm lying down right here then." Annie swiftly fell to the woodland floor beside him.

"Aye, lass." William leaned back against the trunk and closed his eyes. Coira would sleep the night.

Before Annie could continue her banter, he held one hand in the air and shook his head. "Sleep, Annie, your sister will be fine."

Thankfully, Annie said nothing and within minutes he heard her breathing shift to the rhythm of slumber. He couldn't help but open his eyes and survey the woman within his arms. Her dark hair covered half of her delicate features. William ran a hand over her forehead and saw that she dreamt only of a tall black stallion and the wildness of the Highland woods streaming past.

He was just about to pull his hand away when the stallion turned to a man, him, running with wild intent through a blanket of white snow, his claymore drawn and fury carving his features to stone.

~Sylvan Mist~

What was this?

Then he saw the feral gleam in his own eyes. He was set to kill a man, and all because of her.

****

Coira yawned and snuggled closer to the fire.

Had she ever been this comfortable? The heavy thud of rain pelted the ceiling overhead. Her mother must be cooking something scrumptious. It smelled wonderful, slightly sweet, apples? No. More like cinnamon and nutmeg melting over a low flame, yet earthy and potent. What was that?

She smiled and opened her eyes. My, it was dark in her room, must be the storm outside. Then the rain became the steady thud of a heart and her pillow became the muscled chest of a man.

Coira froze. Where was she?

"I know you're awake, lass." The brogue was as deep and sensual as smooth whisky.

She jerked up and slammed into the pewter gaze of the man staring down at her. She sat cradled in his lap, both his strong arms and a rough tartan cocooning her. Darn it.

"Release me this instant, you lout!" she hissed.

William did not release her but bared his straight white teeth in a wolfish grin and pulled her closer. "But you seemed so peaceable a moment ago. In fact, if I didnae know better I would have thought you—"

She clamped a hand over his mouth, knowing full well he was about to say something appalling. She narrowed her eyes. "Shush."

"Shush?" He pried her hand from his mouth but did not release it. Instead he turned it over, his eyes falling to the glimmering diamond engagement ring on her finger. "Do you love him?"

She hadn't expected the question and he knew it. "Of course I do."

His silver regard returned to her face. Whatever he saw there pleased him. "As a friend."

She frowned. No. Not as a friend, as a fiancé. "No, as a man."

Were his lips edging closer?

His hand rose to her face and traced her jaw line. "A man who is a friend."

What did he just say? His forefinger and thumb clutched her chin. She would not be distracted and spoke with a level of calm she didn't feel. "A friend who is a fiancé." Lord, that hadn't come out right at all.

"So 'tis to be a marriage of convenience." His throaty declaration brought his lips closer.

Her eyelids became very heavy, and her lips throbbed. "Is it not convenient to marry a friend?" Again, not what she intended to voice.

His lips were within an inch of hers, his burr soft. "Aye, 'tis convenient enough, but what of passion?"

Never impulsive, she was shocked by her own curiosity and closed the distance. When her lips touched his, everything fell away. Searing heat flooded first her face, then neck, until it burned a path to her stomach. Tendrils of pleasure engulfed her torso and magnified sensation when his lips spread hers and dove deeper.

She heard a distant moan and was shocked to realize it came from her. All she could taste was heat and sweetness. When their tongues met, gravity released and her hands wandered without control. She traced the hollows beneath his strong cheekbones, the cords of his muscled neck. Then the threads of tendons that led to the rapid pulse above his collarbone.

His growl filled her mouth and his hands cupped either side of her face. She had no choice but to respond and wrapped her hands into his hair. An eagle overhead tossed a cruel cry into her reverie, and William pulled back.

Then Coira realized what she had been doing. And who she had been doing it in front of.

No one.

The surrounding forest was devoid of man and horseflesh alike. This should have pleased her in light of her slip. It didn't. Some unattainable part of her wanted the kiss with everyone present, especially Annie. Not to hurt her sister but to prove him wrong about where his desire lay. She closed her eyes and muffled a very unladylike curse. What was the matter with her?

"Up, lass." His words matched his actions, and she was lifted and placed on the ground. Coira opened her eyes and glared. She felt like sampled goods.

"Don't kiss me again." She met his eyes with her order.

One corner of William's mouth inched up as he strode past her. "I didnae kiss you. You kissed me, so you best tell yourself not to kiss me again."

She rounded on him as two horses approached. His chestnut mount and the black horse she'd ridden the day before. "I didn't kiss you, and I'm not riding that horse again."

He offered a small smile and swung astride his mount. "Then walk, because you're not riding with me."

Coira tempered her rage. She was good enough to kiss but not good enough to ride with? Then good sense got the better of her. She'd made it clear yesterday she had no desire to ride with him and that remained the same. Or so she tried to convince herself. She eyed the black beast and wondered if she dared to ride him again.

She circled the horse and bought time with words. "Where is everyone? I heard no one depart."

Worry seized her. "Is Annie well?"

William watched her skirt the stallion with amusement. "They left early. I stayed with you to allow you to rest, and aye, your sister is fine. In fact, she's likely reuniting with Arianna at this moment."

She should thank him for his courtesy but decided against it. Though thoroughly aggravated with him, she needed him. "Will you help me mount?"

William snickered. "Nay."

She spun back and planted her hands on her hips. "Foolish of me to think you might have even an ounce of gentleman in you."

He laughed, the sound deep and enticing. "I'm a Scotsman and a barbarian, aye? Why would you now seek me to be a gentleman? Mayhap if I had a wee bit o' English in me—"

"No more, I'll mount on my own. I don't need your help." She turned away from the brute and stepped closer to the horse. She'd done this before and could very well do it again.

There was a hip-high rock mere feet from them. She strode to the rock and turned back to face the horse. "Come here. I wish to mount you."

The horse didn't budge an inch. She spared a fleeting glance at William. He lounged forward, an elbow on the back of his horse's neck, chin resting on a closed fist. Amusement danced in the depths of his eyes.

Forget him.

Coira repeated her request to the beast, but he remained impassive. She knew what he wanted. And she wasn't going to give it to him. Coira strode forward until she stood nose to nose with the stallion. "Please come with me. I implore you."

The horse shook its head and snorted in her face. How ridiculous, the silly horse intended to make her do it. One must comply when cornered. She chose to be discreet and moved until she could stand on tiptoes and whisper into the stallion's ear. "Just a wee favor for an old friend, lad? The rock over yonder, please. I cannae mount you from here."

The horse tilted his head in acknowledgment and then trotted over to the rock. Coira sighed with relief, ran to the rock, and swung onto the horse's back. She had done it again!

She turned the mount and held her head high. "I'm ready."

William grinned, brought his horse alongside hers and winked. "See how well we Scottish males respond to a soft female brogue."

She straightened and glared. He had heard her whisper. "Some of you seem just fine with an American accent."

"American? And here I thought you prided yourself on being English, though you've not a drop of it in you." William kept his grin. "And our kiss was just a kiss, Coira. You lured me with no accent. 'Tis quite obvious you are taken with me."

"I am not. Don't fool yourself!" With that, she urged her horse forward into what she hoped would be a leisurely canter. As was the case before, the stallion broke into a full run.

****

William shook his head as Coira and her black horse raced ahead into the forest. He couldn't contain a burst of fresh laughter and broke into a run after her.

What a contradiction she was, one moment soft and giving, then the next brittle and unyielding! He couldn't fathom why the great stallion allowed her to ride him. Until he heard her Scottish purr meant only for equine ears. Her voice sounded like silk and velvet rolled together in seduction. Surely the horse must be in love. She had a way about her.

And her lips, had he ever tasted anything so lush and pure, sweet and alive? Why would the gods torment him so? Was this a test? She was not meant for him, but he wanted her. He wanted to feel her satin skin beneath him, around him. But fate was fate and his to follow. Coira was not his and never would be.

Yet, was he not allowed a moment of fun?

He gained on her quickly, and his horse skirted the tree trunks alongside her stallion. Coira's face was alight not with fear but with pleasure. Her black hair streamed behind, and the black horseflesh beneath pushed her faster. She looked his way and laughed, the sound as carefree as a fairy's wingspan. No disgust curled her lip now when she saw him, only freedom and challenge.

William roared with laughter; his mount took up the challenge and pulled forward. He flung his words into the wind but knew that they would reach her ears. "Can you not go faster, lass?"

Coira's stallion launched ahead, and her words slapped back. "How can you ask such a thing? I'll always be faster than you!"

So they raced through the forest and covered the distance in short time. When they burst onto the open field before the castle, his breath caught. Her form was ethereal against the backdrop of emerald green and deep blue loch. Splashes of crimson and purple flowers appeared to part before her and bow. A dusting of the same green mist he'd thought he'd seen before seemed to wash back into the trees she left behind. He shook his head against the vision and kept stride.

He heard his men yelling to one another at their rapid approach. As was the way during the daylight hours, the portcullises were raised and the drawbridge lowered. When they drew closer, people stopped the selling of wares, and maidens ceased their gossip.

She didn't slow at all and made the first portcullis before him. The drawbridge shuddered under the thunder of their horse's hooves, and she cut out ahead of him. The blasted lass made the second portcullis and burst into the inner confines in a flurry of flying skirts and a triumphant cry that had people falling back in a wave of awe.

How could she consider herself an Englishwoman when she was so obviously a Scottish hellcat?

~Sylvan Mist~

~Sylvan Mist~

Chapter Four

Coira had never felt more alive in her entire life.

Through a haze of pure joy, she sensed the scenery was fantastic. A wide meadow of startling green, a glorious swath of water, and a castle made in Heaven invited her into its womb. But all she saw was the Scotsman gaining ground on her right rear flank. The wildness in his eyes sparked something inside, and all she desired was to beat him. Show him he did not have her figured out.

And she had!

As her horse came to a grinding halt at the base of the stone stairs leading to the castle door, all she was capable of doing was releasing a cry of triumph. She had bested the laird! Beat him at his own game.

Silence descended as quickly as reality. Hundreds of people in medieval clothing lined either side of her. The women were astonished, the children giggling, and the men curious. What had she just done? She knew well by the heavy panting of the beast beneath her and the warm flush that stole over her.

"Coira!" Annie flew down the stairs. "I was so worried about you!"

At this particular moment, Coira was grateful for her sister's outspoken ways. Ironically, she figured that she had managed to make much more of an impact on the MacLomain clan than Annie had.

"I'm fine." Coira slid down from the horse and used it as a wall between her and eager eyes. "I just...well...I woke up late I suppose."

Annie released a crude snort. "And were you still wrapped in William's arms when you did?"

She blew out a puff of air and readjusted her dress. "None of your business."

"That's what I thought." Annie nodded vigorously. "He's the one, isn't he?"

Coira clenched her teeth when her protective stallion pranced away. She leaned closer to Annie and whispered, "No, he's not. How could you have left me alone with him?"

Annie's eyes went round. "You kissed him!"

"I did not kiss him." Curse her sister's magically enhanced insight. "He kissed me."

"Oh, what was it like? Are you in love with him? You must be. It's your fate, Coira. William's your fate." Annie offered a wide smile.

She wanted to slap some sense into her sister. "You are his fate, Annie, not I."

Annie frowned and bit her lip. "Really? I'm not so sure you're right about that."

"I am." Coira ceased the conversation before the whole clan heard Annie's thoughts on her current situation.

"You've made quite the impression, love."

She jolted at the sound of William's voice. He stood directly behind her. Had he said love? No, she must have mistaken. "I'm thoroughly embarrassed. Just look at what you caused me to do."

Though William wore a straight face, his eyes twinkled. "And what was that?"

"These people—" She kept a steady gaze on his face despite the blood scorching her veins. "Think I'm crazy."

"Nay, lass, they dinnae." He gave a dazzling smile and leaned closer. "But I do."

"Coira?"

She turned toward the sound of the feminine voice, grateful to escape his heat. His power over her.

Coira gasped. "Arianna?"

A lovely redhead raced down the stairs of the castle, her long tresses flying behind. Before Coira had time to assimilate seeing her cousin after so many years, she was embraced tightly.

Arianna pulled back and held her at arms' length. "Look at you. You're fully grown and so beautiful!"

Coira was speechless. She remembered well her role in sending Arianna back to Scotland to begin with, her silly bit of folklore on All Hallows' Eve in the year 1799.

Only eight, she had thought it great fun to tell her older cousin Arianna about the superstition that involved walking downstairs backwards while looking into a mirror. It was said that you only need request who your one true love was, and he would appear in the looking glass. Arianna had. It was that night she saw Iain in the mirror and traveled back in time. Coira had never quite managed to forgive herself for her part in it.

But then, she knew naught about her bloodline at eight years old.

"Can you speak, lass?"

Startled by her cousin's question, she gathered her wits. "Yes, hello, cousin, it's been so long."

"Such a formal greeting!" Arianna cried and pulled her into her arms once again. "I just can't believe you and Annie are here."

When at last Arianna drew away, Coira could only nod. She didn't possess the spirit of this woman. Annie did, of course. They were both outspoken and free with their gestures. She did not have that sort of rebellion in her. Did she? No, definitely not.

Arianna and Annie ushered her up the stairs into a great hall. Though she tried not to gape, her mouth hung open in amazement. She'd never been in such a large room. Hundreds of torches burned along the stone walls. A low fire blazed on the mammoth hearth at the far side of the hall. Fine, brightly woven tapestries lined the walls, and furs, not rushes, lined the floors. It was splendid, inviting, and impressively elegant for this time period.

They sat her before the fireplace where she was greeted by a man and woman who first offered her a goblet and then sat with her, Arianna, and Annie.

The woman smiled warmly. "I'm Catherine. Iain is my brother. This is my husband, Shane."

Coira smiled in return and looked to the man beside her. He was exceptionally handsome with black hair and turquoise eyes. When he spoke, his brogue was not nearly as thick as the others. "Welcome, Coira. I, like you, am not from this time. I am, however, a distant relative from your future. I came here from the twenty-first century many years ago. My sister, Caitlin, who bears a striking resemblance to Annie, married the previous laird and remains in the twenty-first century."

Coira automatically brought the goblet to her mouth—whisky. She never imbibed, but she would now. Shane was a relative from her future? She should speak and tried to. Nothing came out.

He grinned and nodded. "'Tis difficult at first." He made a sweep of the hall with his arm. "But the welcome from this clan will soon put you at ease."

She doubted that. Where was William?

"Isn't this all so wonderful, Coira?" Annie was bubbling over with excitement and having trouble sitting still.

Her muscles were locked so tightly she doubted she'd be able to display even an inkling of Annie's thrill. Where was William? Why did she keep asking herself that?

She knew the reason the moment he entered the hall. Her muscles relaxed, and she felt like herself again. As he strode in their direction, she cursed her sudden need for his presence. When he was near, she remembered exactly who she was. A woman of class who well understood these Scots. Who understood the grand history of England and all the morals it had taught her. Oh yes, it was very good for William to stay close. He kept everything in perspective. And he was a stark reminder that she was engaged. Very well indeed.

Arianna embraced first William and then Iain who was right behind him. "My boys are both home safe, life is good!"

Iain pulled his wife close and kissed her thoroughly. Coira tried not to stare but couldn't help it.

Naturally William would interrupt. "So now we've two more Brouns amongst us, and aren't they lovely?"

She bit her lip when William sat down next to Annie and lounged his arm on the bench behind her. Annie's face broke into a wide grin, and she offered him a mock punch on his shoulder. "You're too kind, sir."

"Nay." William's diamond eyes met Coira's. "Just truthful."

She looked away. Why was he bothering to look her way when his arm was nearly around Annie? Fool. He was quite sure of himself.

~Sylvan Mist~

Arianna's shrewd gaze swept between William and Coira. "I've already shown Annie around the castle. William, in that you're laird, would you like to show Coira around?"

Both spoke simultaneously. William agreed. Coira declined.

Arianna laughed and shrugged one shoulder. "The laird wins, 'tis his castle."

Then he should have been here to show Annie around. Coira kept her opinion to herself and stood, as did William. Here we go again. She had no desire to be alone with the man. Not really. "Greetings, lass!"

Coira almost lost her footing at the sound of the booming voice. The man who accompanied that voice was just as intimidating. By far the tallest man she'd ever met, his long flaming red hair and barrel chest blocked the light of the hall entrance.

"Hello." Her voice was a weak squeak.

"I'm Arthur, first in command to William's warriors. It does me good to lay my eyes on a few more Brouns." He looked at Annie and a wide smile split his face. "Especially one with enough fire to enflame the whole of Scotland."

She was shocked to see Annie's cheeks color. She'd never seen a man make Annie blush before. Except for William. Arthur held out his hand to Annie. "Care to see those horses I spoke with you about earlier?"

Annie bolted from her seat and nodded eagerly. "Aye."

Coira frowned. Arthur had to be at least a decade her senior. But then, Annie was not a child and capable of making her own decisions.

This brought her attention back to William, who now held his hand out to her. She did not take it but followed him toward the stairs. Suddenly, she rethought things. The innards of the castle would most likely find them alone together.

"I'd much rather tour outside." She stopped at the base of the stone stairs. No doubt his private chambers were up there. And his bed. She'd acted loosely enough earlier when she allowed him to kiss her. If she gave him another opportunity, he'd probably take full advantage.

A wry grin teased his lips and he cocked his head. His words were low and tantalizing. "I would not have thought you a coward, Coira."

Her eyes snapped to his. Had he read her thoughts? She recognized the challenge and twisted the ring on her finger. "And I would have thought you capable of keeping your hands off my sister."

Why had she said that? This man made her speak impulsively. Coira was a planner. She didn't have a spontaneous nature, nor would she ever.

William laughed, took her hand, and led her toward the hall entrance. "Are you jealous?"

She yanked her hand away but continued to follow him. "Don't flatter yourself, my laird. I'm simply protecting Annie as I said I would."

"I wish you success in your endeavor. Know this though, sprite, if I want your sister, I'll have her."

She snarled at his back as they walked down the steps into the community below. Early dusk hid the setting sun beneath the towering inner walls of the compound. How long had she slept? The people were prosperous, and the grounds clean. A long armory lay to her left, then stables. It was all so much more civilized than she would ever have thought.

The air smelled of freshly baked bread, salt, and sea. The clansfolk were clean and polite, offering her smiles and nods, likely because she was with their chieftain. Wares were sold without dispute, and good nature and health pervaded her surroundings. No, medieval Scotland was not as she had envisioned it.

The next hour slipped by, and she became enthralled with ancient civilization. This annoyed her on many levels. Scotland had never enticed her before. And she refused to acknowledge that it may be less her surroundings that enticed her and more the laird, who was proving to be a perfect gentleman.

****

William stood in his chamber and debated his next move. The Broun sisters had arrived yesterday, and his clan had welcomed them with open arms. This eve marked the *Fheill-Eoinm* celebration, the longest day of the year. He would have to agree, it truly felt like the longest day of the year.

How could it not, being torn between two lasses?

He recognized he wasn't torn at all. That made no difference. Destiny had its design for a valid reason. Not that he was pleased with the design, he wasn't. But he had no choice.

He departed his chamber, made his way through the castle and onto the field. He looked to the darkened sky and saw not the moonless black night but the clear, startling blue of Coira's eyes. Och, he needed to shift his way of thinking.

But even as he crossed the wide field, he thought back to earlier in the day when Coira stood upon a hill amongst other clanswomen. Many still practiced the ways of the Celts, and she had been urged to participate.

Standing there with the sun in her hair, she had cast handfuls of golden flowers and herbs into the wind. He knew she had been told to appeal for courage and achievement and wondered if she realized just how much courage she was going to need.

The forest ahead glowed, the great fire igniting the leaves in an ambush of iridescent green flame. He made his way through the trees until he came upon a wide clearing surrounded by trees.

"There you are." Hugh met him halfway. "'Tis a glorious night."

William nodded at his father and smiled. "And all the more glorious because we've visitors."

"So I've noticed." William eyed his father. He was grateful to have him in his life. Many years before, Hugh had disappeared on search for William.

William still recalled the time he spent in the twenty-first century. A vision had told him he was to help bring Ferchar and Caitlin together. That had meant traveling to the future. His unexplained absence had cost both his parents a great deal of pain.

Hugh studied William. "You're thinking about what happened the last time a Broun arrived here."

"How well you know me." William grew wistful. "This time the circumstances are different."

His father's eyes narrowed. "Her ring doesnae glow when you look upon it, aye?"

"Nay, but you know as well as I do, it will shine only when both people see clearly their love." William frowned. "So, no doubt 'tis only a matter of time."

They walked through the heavy throng of clansfolk, and Hugh let the matter rest. William recognized that his father knew his thoughts, his concerns.

"What a grand day of celebration this has been!" Annie's face was flushed with excitement.

"Aye, lass." William appreciated the woman's beauty and spirit, her need for stimulation, and endless lust for life. She wore a deep green dress, and her chestnut tresses ignited in the firelight.

"I take it you've met my father." William grazed a finger over one of her lazy curls. Nothing. No bolt of desire. No urge to gather the length of her hair within his hands.

"Oh yes, I've tried to meet everyone today." Annie nodded and smiled at Hugh. "In fact, Hugh and I had a grand time shooting arrows earlier."

This caught William by surprise. "Arrows, really?"

"Aye." Hugh launched a wicked grin. "The lass has a bit o' a talent!"

"I'd have to agree." Arthur appeared, a wide grin plastered to his avid face. He put a possessive, albeit friendly, arm around Annie's slender shoulders. "Though we had to fashion a bow to suit her size."

Annie elbowed him, her lips half frowning, half smiling. "That didn't stop me from whipping your arse."

Arthur was in his glory. "Such language for a wee thing."

William watched his friend. He knew of the desire Arthur had had for Caitlin. Annie was a near replica, perhaps a fraction bolder, which would only suit Arthur's taste the more.

"Proper language has never been her strength." Coira's words were a soft, prim declaration against the night.

William contained a gasp. She looked lovely in a gown of deep, skin-caressing blue. The firelight shone off her long wavy hair like the moon over a black sea. It burned within the almond-shaped cobalt gaze she shot him. Aye, this lass was a problem. And such a mite of a thing she was. How could one woman fill his senses so quickly?

She was not the tall, robust type he usually favored. Her curves were there and full enough for a man's hands, yet her waist was tiny. His hands could easily span the circumference.

"William?"

His father's voice brought him to attention. He chuckled at himself. Had he been daydreaming? He had no idea what everyone was speaking of. "Aye?"

Hugh's tone turned gruff. "We've visitors. Did you not just see them arrive?"

William's eyes went to the wood line. Damned unattainable woman had his mind chasing ghosts. His clan had gone quiet at the new arrivals.

"Hello, my friend." Iain's bellow greeted the throng of men on horseback.

William couldn't help but glance in Coira's direction. Now this should be interesting.

~Sylvan Mist~

Chapter Five

Annie was shocked.

Not because of the arm suddenly around her shoulder but of the group of men unhorsing in the midst of the celebration.

"Who are they?" she whispered in Arthur's ear.

He smiled and pulled her closer. "Let me introduce you."

His nearness flustered her. How tempting this monster of a man was!

Annie's eyes were on her sister as they approached. For she was quite sure one of the men who had just arrived was as English as they came.

"Arthur, how are you, man?"

He released her and clasped arms with one of the tall Scotsmen. "How could you ask me such with this wee bonnie lass by my side?" He snickered.

"Lachlan Campbell, this is Annie O'Donnell."

Annie smiled and greeted him. Save for the long, jagged scar running down his cheek, he was a handsome man with long brown hair and dark blue eyes.

Arthur continued. "And this is Niall Kynton, baron of Durham."

"'Tis a pleasure, miss." Niall kissed the back of her hand and smiled. As she had guessed, he was English. He was striking with pale green eyes and shoulder-length sandy hair. Tall and broad, he wore chain mail

~Sylvan Mist~

but little armor. She couldn't imagine why he was here.

Of course, Annie was unsure why she was here as well. Was it truly because of William? She cast a curious glance at him as he walked forward with Coira. Her sister was staring at the Englishman intently.

Oh, this should be good.

A discernible spark lit William's eyes when he introduced Coira. Annie was not surprised when Lachlan and Niall openly gawked at her. She had never seen her sister look more beautiful. Something had changed about Coira since arriving here, and Annie was still trying to figure out what that was.

Did Scotland actually agree with her sister?

****

Coira sipped from her goblet of whisky and remained quiet as the men conversed. Should she turn and walk away? Annie and Arthur had. She didn't want to be rude. But then she could only stand being stared at for so long. Not by William, God forbid, but by the other two.

Her eyes met Niall's. My, he was attractive. Coira was still trying to recover from meeting an English baron. She had yet to discern how he could stand so safely within this highland clan. She knew well the state of affairs between Scotland and England in this time period. Or so she had thought.

"Coira, where do you hail from?" Niall's deep voice isolated her while the other men continued to talk.

Coira speculated on an easy answer, a nonspecific answer. "From far away."

"Ah." His green eyes grew merry and one eyebrow shot up. "Another magical tie to the MacLomains?"

This caught her off guard. How much did he know? "One way or another."

~Sylvan Mist~

Niall held out his arm to Coira mere moments before she sensed Lachlan was going to. "Come, walk with me."

Walk with him? Where? She had no desire to be rude and accepted his arm. "And where shall we walk, my lord?"

His eyes roved her face and then shifted to the fire. "No further than the confines of firelight."

She relaxed considerably. "As you wish."

Niall received a mug and sipped from it. "You strike me very much a lady, Coira."

"Do I?" Coira found herself in a flirtatious mood. She never flirted! But William did and with every lass present. "And what makes you say that having known me mere minutes?"

He laughed and studied her from beneath thick lashes. "A man can tell a lot about a woman in mere minutes."

"I see." Coira sat beside him on a crude bench. "And what could you tell about me?"

His answer came quickly. "That you're well spoken, courteous, and soft mannered. And you're the loveliest creature I've ever laid eyes on."

Coira blushed. "You're too kind. However, I'm not available."

"No, are you quite sure?"

"She is." William's confirmation unraveled through the firelight.

Niall contained a scowl. "And here I thought you desired the other woman, MacLomain." He leaned around and looked across the way. "You may want to remind Arthur of that."

"Aye, he knows the truth of it." William sat on Coira's other side. "What I refer to is Coira's state of betrothal."

~Sylvan Mist~

"Betrothal? You came to the MacLomains engaged, my lady?"

"Aye, she did." William nodded. "Have you ever heard of such a thing?"

"Nay, 'tis foolish that." Niall shook his head and shrugged.

Coira held up a hand before either dared speak again. "I'm unavailable; let's leave it at that, gentleman. What I would like to know is what the bloody hell an Englishman is doing here?"

She froze. Not only had her voice risen and a curse erupted, but it had the dangerous hint of a Scottish purr. Oh no. Damn them all to hell and back again. This land was quickly turning her, and she held no magic!

William was just about to answer when his head whipped around. He turned a deep frown back on Niall, and they both stood. "Were you followed?"

"You know I wasn't." Niall strode for his horse.

William, Iain, and the rest of the warriors sprang into action as the woodland turned into a silent mechanism of motions and soft whistles. Within moments the men had disappeared into the forest and the women and children were quickly heading back onto the field toward the castle.

"Lass, come with me." Coira jumped back when an old man with long white robes appeared from nowhere. His frail hand took her arm and urged her to follow.

"Where's Annie?" Coira looked around, panicked. Her sister had vanished. Again! "Who are you?"

The old man looked very unhappy. "I'm Adlin, shaman to this clan."

She stumbled along after him. For an old man, he could walk fast. "I've heard of you, Adlin. You're a wizard."

"Aye, lass, you must move quicker."

~Sylvan Mist~

"But why?" She'd just muttered the words when an explosion sounded somewhere in the far distance.

Adlin uttered a fierce sound and swung back.

She almost screamed when he transformed into a mammoth eagle and surrounded her with his wings. White light blinded and then released her into an abyss of darkness. It smelled of melting sugar and musk. A torch flared to life and she stumbled, her voice a strangled whisper. "Where am I?"

Adlin stood nearby, back turned, preoccupied by something. He ignored her question and asked one of his own. "'Twas the crown that brought you here, aye?"

"The crown?" She struggled to understand.

The wizard whipped around, his face oddly serene considering his actions. "The crown of gold, 'twas the king of Dalriada's. Your mother has acted boldly. She knows something I do not."

Coira continued to shake her head. What was the old man babbling about?

He rattled on, more to himself than to her. "Now there will be a war unlike any other. A cleansing of the Highlands. Such bold action! Why did she not warn me? What foolery is this?"

Coira sighed and went to sit down in what had to be the castle's dungeon. A loud crash resounded from somewhere and shook the heavy stone walls.

"Nay, lass, dinnae sit." Adlin grabbed her hand and pulled her close. She barely blinked before a heavy cloak was thrust over her, and everything turned white again.

She heard his whisper from far away.

"I cannae go with you. I will send two to meet you. Dinnae fear them. You will recognize her."

Then everything broke away, and gravity vanished. Thunder tore her apart until she was whole again. She lay still for a long while, and let reality seep in. Sleep must have claimed her, for when she finally opened her eyes, the sun splintered the tall trees overhead. She closed her eyes and inhaled deeply. When she opened them again, Coira shrieked and sat up.

"What on Ireland's green Earth are you doing here?" She rolled her eyes when her father's famous statement erupted from her mouth.

The black stallion tossed his head in the air before he continued grazing.

"So we're to be a team in this whole mess?" The horse ignored her. What a surprise. The darn beastie only spoke Scots.

She stood on shaky legs and surveyed her surroundings. She was in a small clearing, wedged between a sharp cliff and a swath of larches. A bed of purple heather speckled the overgrown grass and mixed the smell of sea salt with perfume. Water trickled nearby. She breathed in the cool air, grateful for the cloak Adlin had given her.

Her stomach growled and she made a face at the horse. "How does the grass taste?"

He raised his head slightly and munched his answer.

"Flavorless, I would imagine." She almost preferred flavorless to nothing. "Well, are you going to let me mount you so we can move on? To where, I've no idea. This whole situation is ridiculous. And you're here, why? Silly me for wishing Adlin sent a human along, one who spoke English."

The horse whinnied a grunt of agreement and resumed eating. She wasted no time but strode to the stallion, grabbed his mane and swung up. He looked back at her with nothing less than disgust.

"Oh, that didn't hurt. Not a big strong boy like you! Besides, there's nothing around here to step on, and

~Sylvan Mist~

I'm sick of coaxing you with a fake accent." She patted his neck and smiled.

The horse didn't appreciate her kindness and proceeded to do what he did best, run. The forest grew thicker and she leaned in close to his neck, praying she wouldn't be thrown.

A loud whistle echoed through the wood line and the blasted stallion banked a sharp left. She lost her hold and went flying to the ground, landing with a solid thump on her behind. Breathless and shockingly sore, she sat speechless watching the black horse vanish into the trees.

That had not gone well at all.

"Are you okay?" A woman ran in her direction. Annie? No. But very close in appearance.

The woman leaned down and touched her arm. "Coira?"

"Yes, and you are?"

"I'm Caitlin. Can you stand?"

"Of course." Coira rose to her feet and avoided rubbing her sore backside. "I've been thrown from a horse before."

Caitlin smiled. "That's no average horse, hon."

Hon? It was only then that she realized how differently Caitlin was dressed. No dress but strange blue leggings and a fitted top. Very risqué. "You must be Shane's sister."

Delight lit up Caitlin's face. "I am! You've seen him?"

She couldn't help but smile in return. "I have." She adjusted her dress and looked away. "He's very handsome."

Caitlin laughed with delight. "Yep, that's my Shane. And we're your descendants, isn't that so cool?"

Yep? Cool? Coira should be dumbfounded to meet another relative from the twenty-first century, but after everything she'd experienced thus far, she felt somewhat nonplussed.

"Damn stallion needs to be broken."

Coira's head jerked up at the deep voice. A tall man with blue-black hair and startling light blue eyes was leading her supercilious horse their way.

"Coira, this is my husband, Ferchar, former MacLomain chieftain," Caitlain said with pride.

"Pleased to meet you." She dipped a curtsy. "I can see clearly the resemblance between you and William."

Ferchar issued a breathtaking smile, as was the way with these MacLomains. "Nice to meet you as well, Coira, and I'll take that as a compliment."

Her eyes dropped to his clothing. He wore no kilt but the same strange blue leggings and a black sweater. "I take it you two aren't staying in Scotland long."

"Good guess." Caitlin evaluated the highland wood line. "I'm afraid you're taking a little detour."

"Detour?" She didn't like the sound of this. Hadn't she detoured enough already?

A flash of light burst between two sturdy pines and William lurched through. "Aye, detour, now!"

Ferchar spun back and threw his hands in the air. Fire spun up into a massive tornado and encased her in dry flames. Not again! Energy rushed past Coira as William's arms came around her and pulled her close. Then there was simply the feel of soothing cool mist. More welcoming than she was willing to admit.

"Dinnae worry, lass. I've got you." His whisper caressed her ear, and she nuzzled closer to him.

"Where are we?" She spoke to him though unable to hear her own voice.

His hand cupped the back of her neck. "In between."

"In between?"

"Aye. Within Ferchar's fire is my mist. And mist doesnae have to move fast." His voice turned husky. "And my mist doesnae burn off with heat."

She couldn't stop the words if she tried. "Perhaps you've not come across a strong enough heat."

He chuckled, a low and tempting rumble from deep within his chest. "Mayhap you're right."

Unafraid, she lifted her head, eager to see his mist, his magic. Instead she saw his face, so close, eager. William's eyes shone silver, the beautiful planes of his face stark. "I've a need to kiss you again, Coira."

She had no answer for that and didn't turn away when his lips met hers. They weren't gentle. Had she wanted them to be? Lord, no. Passion uncoiled and she yearned for an unnamed savagery. His kiss deepened with violence, and foreign, thrilling energy seized her limbs, ripped her mind from her body, and bled all reason from her soul.

His arms encircled her waist and lifted her. He moaned when she wrapped her legs around him. She could no longer tell if they swirled or if the mist encasing them did. Coira didn't care. She wanted more.

So much more.

Laughter came from somewhere, everywhere.

"That old oak tree has seen a lot, huh?" Caitlin's words filtered clearly through the mist. A mist that was completely gone.

Mortified, Coira slid down William and pushed away only to bump into the rope swing directly behind her. "Oh, my goodness."

"Easy, Coira." William cocked an eyebrow and smiled. "You've made it to the twenty-first century."

Coira looked around. She was home! Or was she? The house was no longer gray but white. The barn was repainted. Then she saw the carriages parked in the drive. If that's what one could call them.

"This is an awful lot to take in. Please, come inside." Caitlin rushed to her side and steered Coira in the direction of the house. "Many things have changed in the past two hundred years, sweetie."

Bright lights overwhelmed her when she entered a completely restyled foyer. Gone were the candles and soft lace curtains. A green carpet lined the stairs and the walls were crème. So much was different that she simply couldn't assimilate it.

"Are you all right, Coira?" William took her elbow and led her into the kitchen.

She nodded and swallowed. Did she have any choice? Her family lived two hundred years in the past, and her sister eight hundred years. Eight hundred! Annie!

"Where's my sister? Is she well?" She refused to break down in tears.

"Aye, lass, she's safe." William's voice turned soft as he filled a small glass with clear liquid and pushed it her way. "Drink this. 'Twill calm your spirits."

She didn't hesitate but drank the whole of it in one gulp. The liquid burned her throat and stung her eyes. She coughed and looked at the three of them.

"What is this?"

Caitlin took her glass and refilled it. "My personal favorite when dealing with all things historical and Scottish." She handed the glass back to Coira. "Tequila!"

Coira's belly instantly warmed and she sat back. The kitchen looked foreign indeed. The fireplace was gone. In its place sat a big, square, odd-looking mechanism. Actually, the whole kitchen was full of strange pieces.

Caitlin sat across from her, and both Ferchar and William leaned against the countertop indulging in their own glasses of tequila. What an odd name for a drink. Not that she was so inclined to call the foul stuff a beverage. Yet it did relax her and quickly.

Coira went straight to the point. "What is going on?"

Both Caitlin and Ferchar's eyes traveled to William.

"We're wondering the same thing." Caitlin grabbed a bottle from inside another strange metal box, removed the cap, and drank. "I must say you've grown a bit, William."

He laughed. "Have I? 'Tis always bloody amazing to me how time passes differently for us all. When you last saw me, I was a boy, nearly fourteen years ago? Yet you both have aged, what, six months?"

Ferchar smiled. "It does work in our favor, aye? 'Tis good to see you again, cousin."

"Or is it still Gordon?" Caitlin teased. Coira looked to William, confused.

He answered her unspoken question. "I lived here for almost three years, love. 'Twas my vision to bring Caitlin and Ferchar together. The only way for that to happen was for me to come here and become a legitimate American, a foster child."

Coira lifted the glass and drank down her tequila. She held her glass out to Caitlin for a refill.

Caitlin frowned slightly. "Are you sure?"

"Yes, very." Coira took pride in the steady tenor of her voice. She turned her attention to William. "I noticed that my previous question was not answered."

Ferchar refilled his glass as well as William's, a smirk on his face. "The lass has patience."

Caitlin shot him an unspoken challenge, obviously touching on something they shared privately.

~Sylvan Mist~

William sighed and pulled himself into a sitting position on the counter. "Well, first off, I'm glad you received my message, Ferchar; 'twas a bloody close thing back there. Where's your babe? How were you able to leave him on such short notice?"

Ferchar rolled his eyes. "You came in a vision to me yesterday. The babe's with his great grandmother."

Coira received her third glass of tequila. So Caitlin and Ferchar had a baby? She sipped the liquid and worked hard not to stare at William's plaid. She was very close to discovering what Annie had been so curious about and for the life of her she had trouble looking away. If he just spread his legs a bit further apart. Oh, shame on her, she was engaged!

And feeling less engaged by the moment. Well, two hundred years' worth of moments.

"'Tis a war on the horizon unlike any we Highlanders have seen before," William said, grave.

"Magic?" Ferchar set his glass aside.

William nodded. "Aye, to rival our own."

Coira snorted and covered her mouth, eyes round.

"You're a lightweight, my lass." William jumped down from the counter, leaned over, and scooped her up.

The room tilted uncomfortably, and she grabbed hold of him. His muscles flexed beneath her fingertips. "No. I just find magic funny and useless."

"Useless?" He cast a pointed look over his shoulder at Caitlin and made his way up the stairs.

"Aye." Irritation flooded her. "You all bloody well lather on about your magic as if a human is bereft without it!"

"Bereft?" William made his way into the room Caitlin designated and lowered Coira to the bed.

"Aye, bereft!" Was she slurring slightly? Such liquor on an empty stomach, she wouldn't be surprised. "There's nothing wrong with being a mere mortal."

"There's nothing mere about you, sprite." William said something to Caitlin she couldn't make out.

"Damn you, I'm not a sprite, you poor excuse for a Scotsman!" God, she was mad all of a sudden.

He laughed and brought his hand to her forehead. "Go to sleep, lass."

That damned brogue of his! How dare he try to coax her with it? She had no intention of going to sleep and was just about to tell him so when the room blurred.

Then vanished.

~Sylvan Mist~

Chapter Six

"So, tell me, why are you here?"

The men sat in the living room, both of the women long asleep. William contemplated his answer while staring at the fire. Why was he here? To protect Coira, of course, although he knew damned well he could have protected her from Scotland. His clan was under Adlin's care now until he heard word. Adlin was the only one who could lead the MacLomains at this juncture.

He sighed. "I've no solid answer for you, cousin."

Ferchar studied the liquid in his glass and did not speak for several minutes. When he did, it was without humor. "Hell, man, she doesnae wear the ring."

"Nay." He looked to Ferchar. "Perhaps I choose to follow my own path."

Ferchar's eyes flew to his. "I tried that. It didnae work."

"Didn't it, though?" He sighed, sat forward, and braced his elbows on his knees. "You've found what you longed for, aye?"

Ferchar was not to be baited. "You know well that my path—" He stopped mid speech and regarded William thoroughly. "'Tis your own battle, lad, but you play a dangerous game."

"Aye." William stared into the fire. He would give his cousin what he wanted to know. "I couldnae help myself, I had to come."

~Sylvan Mist~

"You didnae have to. You wanted to. There's a vast difference. I suppose in all honesty, I'm the last one who should be giving advice." A small smile crept across Ferchar's face, and his eyes narrowed on William. "But I am your elder even if we are the same age now."

William had little to say. He shouldn't have come. He knew. But he was here now, and he had no intention of returning until Adlin called him.

His mind switched pace, and he frowned at Ferchar. "You will come?"

His cousin's elbows rested loosely on the armrests. The only tension lay in his eyes. "Aye, we all will."

"Do you know the whole of what is happening?" He knew Ferchar did not but asked regardless.

"You know I dinnae." Ferchar sighed. "But both of us will soon enough."

A rumble tore through the living room and swallowed the fire in the hearth. Ferchar sat up. William remained relaxed.

"You've got to be kiddi—"

Before Ferchar finished his statement, Niall burst forth into the room. An array of sparks haloed his form before they disappeared.

Ferchar stood, shook his head, and restated his sentiment. "You've got to be kidding me."

Niall was armored, filthy, and quite pleased with himself. "I made it!"

William stood as well and clasped Niall on the shoulder. "Did you get it?"

"Get what?" Ferchar didn't bother leaving the room but flicked his wrist. A bottle of whiskey materialized on the table alongside three glasses.

Niall ignored William's question and focused on Ferchar while he began to remove his armor. "Not even a hello for an old friend?"

Ferchar's features fought between a scowl and a grin. "'Tis been too long, cousin, and I see you're all grown up as well."

The two men embraced and Niall laughed.

"'Twas bound to happen. So nice that we can all be of a similar age. I must say, time travel suits me that way!"

"Aye, it has its benefits." Ferchar shook his head and redirected his attention to William. "What are you two up to now? Out with it."

William shrugged and filled the three glasses with whiskey. "Och, such accusation in your tone. Niall and I have stayed out of trouble for some time."

Niall received his glass and gulped down half its contents. "True enough. If anything, the trouble found us this time."

"Aye, 'tis trouble, sure enough." William grew serious.

Ferchar sat down and frowned at both men. "I'm not talking about the obvious. I'm quite aware of the potential war."

"Then what of it, cousin? 'Tis all we speak of, the war, that is." Niall tossed back the remaining whiskey and poured himself some more.

"Aye, war." William nodded once and set his glass aside. "Unlike any other."

"Aye, quite so." Niall met William's glare. "Such as it is."

"You won't win." William challenged.

"As it stands, I should have no fight on my hands." Niall sidestepped William's venomous glance and sat. "Aye?"

"Enough." Though his voice remained calm, Ferchar's interception was heated. "'Tis quite obvious, neither of you are speaking of the war that should be

~Sylvan Mist~

concerning you. Why are you here, Niall? And what did you bring?"

Niall reached into his pocket, pulled out an object, and tossed it to Ferchar.

"How interesting and not surprising in the least. What the hell are you both thinking?" Ferchar fingered the diamond-centered ring and shook his head.

"We were thinking about Annie's safety, and you well know that," William said. He held out his hand, palm up. "May I?"

Ferchar nodded and dropped the ring into William's palm. Involuntarily, his hand closed, and he shut his eyes.

A long black tunnel rose in his vision, and he was yanked forward. Though he knew Ferchar and Niall still sat nearby, reality swirled around him until no longer his cousins were on either side of him, but tall standing stones.

Then his last awareness of the twenty-first century ceased and he stood alone.

****

Coira knew she slept. Or did she? The forest was so beautiful, enchanting. Wisps of amethyst mist curled up the towering tree trunks and swam within the canopy of leaves overhead. As though wraiths surrounded her, she was urged forward down a winding path bordered by ice-covered red roses. Steam billowed from her mouth, but the chill of the air didn't touch her skin.

The world was crystalline, glimmering into shards of diamonds caught in moonlight. The same verdant mist which had circled her when she first traveled back to Scotland again encircled her legs, caressed them as a clearing came into view. She breathed deeply, sea salt? A wind brushed the woodland and caused the frozen rose petals to clatter and sing.

"Coira?"

She entered the clearing, the masculine voice tantalizing her. William? Coira blinked at the sight before her. He stood alone within a circle of tall stones surrounded halfway by the open roots of a towering oak tree. Nine rocks, perfectly spaced, circled the tree.

"Where are we?" She walked forward, felt a strange tingle when she passed the rocks, and entered the circle. William stood tall, plaid-wrapped, and utterly beautiful.

He spoke in Gaelic. "In a place of great magic. Very old magic, lass."

She accepted the hand he offered and shivered at the electrical charge that swamped her senses. "I'm scared."

"Dinnae be." He spoke softly, intimately. "It appears we've been given a gift."

"A gif—"

He pulled her forward and broke her inquisition with a searing kiss. His lips were soft and giving yet hard and merciless. Coira felt free from her body. She felt only him within her soul, powerful and captivating. William's hands cupped her face and deepened pure sensation. They stroked her jaw, neck, shoulders, until they traveled down her bare back.

Bare back! Instead of responding with anger at their sudden nudity, Coira moaned into his mouth and buried her hands in his hair. She felt the long, thick shaft of his arousal prodding her stomach. Instead of apprehension about exactly what he intended to do with it, she felt sharp, needy anticipation. Then she felt his large, calloused hands cup her buttocks. When he lifted her she instinctually wrapped her legs around his waist.

Eager to assuage the blistering heat and desire below, she rubbed her center against him. William sucked air in through clenched teeth and squeezed her against him.

Mist gathered close, then retreated, leaving his eyes to their silver regard. Slowly, inch by inch, he lowered her onto his impatient shaft. Coira dug her nails into his shoulders and gasped. She tried to wiggle away but he held tight.

"Shhh, love. 'Tis only temporary pain," he whispered, muscles and facial expression strained.

Unconvinced she wiggled again. This time he didn't wait, but pulled her down sharply onto his erection. She dug her nails deeper and whimpered. How could he have? This was simply too much!

Before she could say as much, he shifted slightly and a deep prod of sweeping pleasure washed through her lower half. Oh my Lord! Pure sensation rippled through her. Moonlight consumed, pulsed around them, and gave them to one another.

"Coira." His whisper turned urgent and forceful when he brought her to the ground and covered her.

She took him deeper, welcomed his magic, his gift. Relished the need he offered. Ice and fire and blissful pain so acute she screamed, or whispered. She didn't know the language erupting from her mouth as she urged him further. As he moved in and out and in and out. She allowed him to explore the deepest parts of her.

This was perfection, Heaven, everything.

Sweat coated their skin. Their breathing became harsh and fast. His pace increased. A strange mixture of both agony and pleasure began to tighten her belly muscles. A slow, twisting tension started to build. She panted and struggled for breath, urging him to move faster and deeper.

A foreign Gaelic poured from her lips against his neck while she trailed her mouth and tasted his salt.

"Bloody hell." William groaned deeply and thrust one last time, his member throbbing endlessly within her.

Suddenly, white light filled her vision and her body erupted violently. Ripple after ripple of shuddering pleasure fanned out through her body. She tried to hold on to him but couldn't. She could only stare up at his handsome face as it contorted in ecstasy. Then everything vanished, the moon, stones, and ground, leaving only pure feeling. Coira cried again and again until there was no more William.

Then she fell back into darkness.

****

"Bloody hell!" William's eyes snapped open, momentarily blinded by the low fire on the hearth. He tried to even his breathing and sooth his sated desire.

Ferchar and Niall sat silently beside him waiting. He opened his fist and gazed down at the ring. Cracks of blood curled from the wounds where he had squeezed the ring too tightly. He blew on the cuts and they vanished.

"Are you going to share?" Ferchar sipped from his whiskey, his shrewd gaze locked on William.

"Doubtful." Niall's expression remained grim.

William sighed and waited. At the moment, standing wasn't an option due to arousal. What the hell had just happened? Had he made love to Coira? Aye, indeed he had. Of that he was fairly certain. But how? Where? He'd never experienced such intense magic, such old magic.

What a lovely thing she was, pure no longer. So glorious she appeared in the moonlight, delicate and alive and with tremendous passion for such a sprite. Plowing into her tight little body had been the most intense thing he'd ever felt. His thoughts weren't helping his arousal and he sat forward, summoned his magic, took care of the uncomfortable problem, and stood.

"Interesting bit of magic you just used." Niall's eyes narrowed and he shook his head.

William ignored him and walked to the fire. When he turned back he grew very serious. "So lads, what do we know about our Irish ancestors?"

****

Bright sunlight ran along the floorboards until it covered her eyes in warmth. Coira breathed deeply and snuggled down deeper beneath the covers. It felt so good to sleep in. Sundays were wonderful that way. Church wasn't for a bit, and there were no schoolchildren to teach.

A strange sound accosted her. She couldn't place the peculiar rumble. Thunder? No. A loud slam echoed outside the window. She sat up and froze when the room brought her back to reality, twenty-first century reality. Coira jumped from the bed and ran to the window. Caitlin was walking away from the strange wagon toward the front door. Oh Lord, she was still caught in this nightmare. She eyed the oak tree beyond the window. It was much thicker than it had been two hundred years ago but it was still there. Unbelievable.

Feet clamored up the stairs. Someone knocked on her door. *Tap. Tap. Tap.* Caitlin's voice followed the last tap. "Coira?"

She frowned, walked over to the door, and opened it. Caitlin stood with a wide smile on her face and an armful of bags.

"Good morning! Rumor had it you had awoken," Caitlin said.

"Really?" She wasn't the least bit shocked with two wizards floating about somewhere below.

"Can I come in?" Caitlin held the bags up. "I bought you some clothes."

"Of course, it is your house." She stepped back and let the other woman enter.

"And yours." Caitlin dumped the bags on the bed. "Technically."

Coira shrugged. "I must admit, I feel rather homeless at the moment. No offense."

"None taken." Caitlin offered a sympathetic smile. "You've been through a lot, but no matter what century you're in, you're my relative, and this is your home."

Coira couldn't help but smile in return. "Thank you." She eyed the bags. "You actually purchased me clothes?"

"Yep." Caitlin busied herself pulling out garments. "I don't expect you'll be here long, but I figured something a bit more modern might be in order."

"This was very sweet of you, Caitlin, thank you." Coira grimaced at the odd garments, men's clothing really!

"I tried to choose as conservatively as I could for you." Caitlin eyed Coira up and down. "In the petite section, naturally."

"Naturally." She had no idea what Caitlin was talking about.

"Put these on. We'll all be downstairs in the kitchen." Caitlin waved at the clothes and headed for the door, then stopped. "Oh shoot, I'll bet you'd love a shower."

"A shower?" Coira was tugged, armful of clothes and all, out of the room and into the bathroom.

"A shower." Caitlin leaned over, turned a nozzle and started a stream of water from overhead. She briefly described the layout of the bathroom and the clothing to Coira before she left, closing the door behind her. Well, she'd best put herself under that stream of water. And she did. It felt incredible on her sore muscles. She wondered if the time travel had caused such soreness in her legs, or perhaps the fall from the horse?

Steam rose up as she slathered the soap. Like mist, it dimmed her view. Mist. Pain. Pleasure. She gasped in alarm when memories bombarded her. Erotic images caught in a dream. Moonlight and lust. William!

She placed her hands over her womb. Felt the soreness anew. Oh God, it had to have been a dream. Yet worry and distrust nagged at her. She was in the throes of more magic and wizardry than she had ever thought possible. Could they have? Was she still a virgin?

"No."

William's response clearly filled her mind.

Startled, Coira shook her head, shut off the water, and dressed. She must have imagined his voice in her head.

"You didnae imagine my voice, sprite. Must you really put those clothes on?" William's humor echoed in her inner ear.

He was speaking within her mind. But of course, he was a wizard and a MacLomain. She kept her thoughts silent, quite sure that without magic she'd have no ability to scold him. Why bother? The man was intolerable.

She wiped the condensation off the mirror with a towel, shocked by her reflection. Gone was the stern, haughty expression she'd perfected over the years. Instead, she glowed. Her prim lips were rosy and lush. Her eyes soft and skin flushed. An odd sensation rolled through her; indeed, she looked... sated? Oh dear.

She turned away and slipped on the white rubber shoes Caitlin had given her. Had she called them sneakers? She should've been mortified by the fitted outfit she had on, yet she wasn't. It suited her mood just fine. Frisky as it was. Coira laughed aloud. She didn't have a frisky bone in her body. That was Annie's device.

She headed downstairs and stopped short at the kitchen door. Speechless, she stared at everyone. Niall? Oh yes, there he sat across from William at the kitchen table. Both men had undergone a massive transformation. It was William who held her attention though.

His auburn-tinted black hair was brushed and he wore a fitted gray, short-sleeved shirt. His legs, long and muscled, were clothed in jeans. Thanks to Caitlin, she now knew what jeans were.

Coira was convinced she'd never seen a more handsome man. When his eyes found hers, she nearly crumbled to the floor. Luckily, the countertop was close and held her up.

"Good morn to you, love. I trust you had a satisfying rest." William's soft greeting burned a path to her core.

She swallowed hard and looked away. Too satisfying and well he knew it. Why would he have done such a thing to her? She was to be married to another man!

Ferchar was leaning against the counter, his eyes narrowed at the two men seated at the table. Caitlin handed Coira a mug of steaming tea.

"Thank you." She wrapped her numb hands around it.

"You're welcome." Caitlin smiled.

~Sylvan Mist~

"Yes, my lady. 'Tis good to see you this fine morn." Niall sauntered over to her, offered a half bow and a wry grin.

She smiled at him, another handsome devil. Who would ever have thought she'd be talking to a medieval English baron dressed in twenty-first century clothing? Never mind a Scotsman.

"Dare I ask what brings you here?" She sipped her tea, grateful her hands weren't shaking.

He leaned back against the counter next to her and smiled. "Well, I could not let you get away, could I?"

William snorted and crossed his long legs out in front of him. "Presumptuous fool."

Niall's smile widened, yet he kept his eyes on Coira. His conspiratorial whisper was loud enough for all to hear. "He's just jealous."

Coira's eyes narrowed on William, and she lightly touched Niall's arm. "He should be."

William only offered a devastating smile, deepening those delicious dimples. Damn infuriating Scot. Why bother with his antics? She had a perfectly presentable Englishman available. That train of thought brought her back to her fiancé, James, and she sighed.

He seemed so far away, too far away. Yet she was hard pressed to miss him, and that thought bothered her. She met William's eye. It was his fault, of that she was sure. He'd had her before her own fiancé! As though a cannonball struck her, fury ignited, and she straightened.

She would wipe that smug grin right off his face. "William, may I have a moment alone with you?"

He shot Niall a triumphant grin and stood. "But of course, love."

"I'm not your love. I'm your enemy."

With that, she turned and left the kitchen.

~Sylvan Mist~

****

William gave Niall a mock punch on the shoulder as he followed Coira out of the house. She was in a snit. Never had a woman mesmerized him like she did, one moment nervous around him, the next trying to make him jealous, now this, pure fury. He knew what was coming and relished the battle.

She was striding for the barn. What a view. He was tempted to forget the whole of Scotland and keep her here just so he could see her dressed this way every day, so bloody petite with curves in all the right places. When she first walked into the kitchen, he'd been dumbstruck by her beauty. Dressed in a form-fitting powder blue tank top and jeans she was every inch the modern-day woman.

Even her prim attitude was giving way to something else, something untamed and unrecognizable, sensual and gripping. He watched her behind sway with her strides. Did Coira even realize she was no longer walking as though she balanced a book on her head?

He entered the barn behind her and waited patiently while she surveyed her surroundings. It didn't take long for her to swing around and attack.

Hands on hips, she snarled. "What happened last night?"

He closed the barn door and leaned back against it casually. "You have to ask, lass?"

A becoming pink started to creep up her neck, and her eyes narrowed. "How could you! You had no right!"

"I didnae force you, Coira. You came to me willingly."

She shook her head furiously, tone level and low. "I possess no magic. You do. Everything that happened was obviously your doing. Please don't patronize me."

~Sylvan Mist~

He measured his response. "'Twas not my magic that brought you there. 'Twas someone else's."

The pink flush overtook her face now. "Why bother lying to me? I know the truth of it."

"Do you? When even I don't?" William chuckled. "What makes you think I'd use magic to seduce you, lass? I've no need for that. If I had wanted you, I would have taken you."

The pink turned to red, the hands came off her hips, and she strode closer. "You did take me, a coward's way, no less!"

This aggravated him. "Careful, Coira, I did nothing you didnae want me to."

"Didn't you? I would have never done that with you otherwise." She was within feet of him now. "You used me. Annie's out of your reach, so you took what you could get."

He reached out, grabbed, and spun her around until he had her back against the barn door. A horse whinnied in concern further down in the barn as he slammed his hands down on either side of her head, palms flat against the door.

He leaned close and made sure she understood how serious he was. "I didnae use you. I wanted you. I took you. I would do it again."

Her lips quivered, and she breathed deeply. "I have no way to trust you. No need to, I'm engaged. You know I am not the woman meant for you. What of my sister now? You've done so much damage with your actions."

William inhaled. She smelled of lavender and springtime. "What's done is done. I cannae undo it. I dinnae regret it. I dinnae know why we have this attraction to each other and you not wearing the ring. But we do. 'Tis strange, I've no real explanation for you. I dinnae desire your sister."

~Sylvan Mist~

Her hand rose to his chest when he moved closer. "But the legend tells that the Broun who wears the ring is the one predestined for a MacLomain wizard." Her hand pulled back, her brow furrowed, and her voice fell to a whisper. "And you are a wizard."

"Aye." William took her hand and lifted it, opened her fist, and dropped an object into her palm. "The legend also says that the ring's gem glows when the woman is with her one true love."

Coira stared at the ring in her palm, Annie's ring. "My Lord, what's happened to my sister?"

"Nothing, lass." He kept his hand on hers. "It was necessary that we remove it, so that no harm would come to her."

"Why would harm come to her?" Coira's voice trembled.

He lightly caressed her fingers, one at a time, noticing how the trembling that had been in her voice appeared to be traveling down her body. How he longed to cease talking and take her here. Taste the sugar of her lips again. See her surprisingly full breasts thrust proudly in his direction.

"Harm will not come to Annie, now that we have the ring. She is with Adlin. He will keep her safe."

Her eyes rose from the ring to meet his. "I don't understand why I've been brought here and not Annie. This makes no sense. Why leave the magical sister behind and bring me and the ring here?"

Och, he was having trouble concentrating with her big blue eyes so intent on him. The lass already had more power over him than she knew. "'Tis complicated. All I can tell you is that we had to separate you two. 'Twas Adlin who wanted you here. I know not the reason for it."

Coira's eyes warred between confusion and something else. "Why are you and Niall here? Aren't you the chieftain? Shouldn't you be there?"

His fingers stilled on hers, and he used his other hand to brush a lock of hair back from her face. A caress he had not intended. His voice deepened. "I couldnae stay away."

He took the ring and turned her hand in his. "My clan doesnae need me right now. 'Tis Adlin's clan at the moment."

"What are you doing?" She tried to pull her hand away, but he held tight.

"I'm keeping the ring safe until it's returned to Annie." He slid the ring onto Coira's slender finger.

He held his breath and against his better judgment stared at the diamond nestled within the heart. The diamond that signified his eye color caught within magic. He felt Coira's heartbeat increase, heard her breathing turn shallow.

Her whisper squeezed his chest. "It doesn't glow, William."

Coira yanked her hand away and shook her head. Her eyes turned moist for a moment, but she quickly blinked the mist away. She turned to flee, but he caught her hand again.

"It doesnae always happen right away, lass."

"I couldn't care less if it had. This is Annie's ring, given to her because she carries magic, not I. What happened last night was unforgivable. All of this is preposterous."

William moved swiftly and pulled her small form up against his. He ignored her gasp, wrapped one arm around her waist, and cupped the back of her head with his hand.

"Don't."

~Sylvan Mist~

He covered her word with his mouth, pulled her tighter against him, and kissed her more thoroughly than he had any other woman in his life.

~Sylvan Mist~

Chapter Seven

Caught in a blaze of spontaneous lust, Coira felt him lift her off the ground with one arm and drag her up his body to give his lips easier access. She buried her hands in his hair and then cupped his cheeks.

Deny him. Pull away. Run.

She did none of that but felt her back pushed against the barn door. His enticing, erotic words echoed within her mind, wrapped her in warmth and want. Fluid pooled down below and her own quick arousal startled her.

Before she could comprehend what was happening, a shudder raked her. His murmured taunts had brought her to amazingly quick release. She had to stop this. Fully clothed, sated, and so eager for more she was unable to control her body's response.

"William, Coira?"

William was obviously ignoring Niall's voice from the other side of the door. His hand slid beneath her shirt, rode her side until it cupped her breast.

"Adlin's made contact."

He groaned and released her. Befuddled, Coira's mind snapped back to attention. Her anger, hurt, resentment, all unleashed vivid streaks of emotion within her.

Their conversation returned with full force. He had come here because of her? Yes, obviously to slake his lust. And knowing Annie was meant for him! Yet she had not turned him away. Not within the circle of stones, nor now. Shame burned through her. What she had done was unforgivable.

The way she had felt when he slid the ring on her finger. Such trepidation and unexpected hope had arisen. At that moment when she gazed at the tiny diamond, all else had faded away, became meaningless. James, Annie, every noble aspect of her nature. None of it had existed.

When nothing happened, her chest had tightened so painfully she couldn't breathe. The ring blurred in her vision. He was not her true love. Now he knew. Now she knew. There was no turning back time, undoing what they'd done. Would she really want to? No.

That thought both petrified and sobered her. This had to stop. She fought the tears, fought him. Only to have him pull her into his arms once again. It was hopeless. The man had torn her reality to shreds within two days. She barely knew herself.

Niall pounded on the barn door. "Open up. We've got to talk."

She stepped aside and William opened the doors. He didn't look pleased.

"You've only to give us a minute." William took her hand and pulled her out after him.

Niall looked from William to Coira. He didn't look pleased either. Who would have thought she'd find herself between the Englishman and the Scotsman, only to crave the Scot. She pulled her hand free from William's as a large white beast of a contraption pulled into the drive.

"That's called a car, sprite. They're fueled by gasoline and more mechanisms then I've time to explain."

~Sylvan Mist~

Her eyes shot to William. His eyebrows simply rose and his lips curled into a sly grin. He really was talking to her through her mind! How bizarre and oddly intimate, his burr remained in her mind yet took on the essence of the man himself. His personality was wrapped within his words.

As the car came to a halt, Caitlin exited the house and made her way to the elderly woman getting out. The woman's hair was snow white and though she must have been somewhere in her eighties, her beauty was unmistakable.

"Hi, Gram!" Caitlin smiled and took the woman's elbow.

Caitlin saw them coming and stopped. "Gram, meet the newest group of time travelers."

"Coira and Niall, this is my grandmother, Mildred. William, I'm sure you remember my gram," Caitlin said.

Mildred walked forward, a wide grin on her face. "Why, look at you, haven't you grown up, William! I see you've gained quite a bit of height and bear that same striking resemblance to Adlin that all you MacLomain boys do."

William chuckled. "Aye, Mildred, 'tis good to see you again. I see you haven't aged a day."

She laughed openly at this, her merry blue eyes twinkling. Her attention turned to Niall and Coira. Niall wasted no time but stepped forward, bowed low and kissed the back of her hand. "Hello, Mildred, 'tis a pleasure to make your acquaintance."

"My my my, we've an Englishman? Now, this is unexpected!" Mildred's eyes raked over his tall stature with appreciation. "Welcome, Niall. I can't wait to hear what brought you to the twenty-first century."

Another car pulled into the drive as Mildred turned her attention to Coira. Her astute gaze went right to the ring, then back to Coira's face. "Hello, Coira, you must be a Broun, a distant relative perhaps?"

Coira smiled, guiltily aware that she wore a ring marking her as someone she was not. It struck her that, if Mildred knew Adlin and William, then she had likely heard of Arianna. "Yes, I'm from the nineteenth century. I'm Arianna's cousin."

Mildred nodded. "Yes, I've read all about Arianna and Iain. And you! You were but a child."

Coira hid her shock. "You read about me?"

"Yes, dear. You were responsible for Arianna fleeing the party that night, running into the woods, and traveling back in time. Well done, just look at what good came of that small moment in time!"

"But how did you read about me?"

Mildred's eyebrows rose and she grinned. Obviously, she was enjoying herself immensely. "You do know Beth Luken, right?"

Coira nodded.

"Well, she wrote a book titled *Fate's Monolith* in the year 1802, I believe, about Arianna and Iain's love story. Clearly you've never heard of Ms. Luken's novel, how peculiar."

"Indeed," Coira said. As far as she knew, Beth's first novel was published in 1804 and had nothing to do with any of this. "Yet I was told much of their tale. I've been informed most thoroughly about the MacLomain clan for some time now."

Mildred appeared intrigued. "How very interesting. And what of Beth's novel titled *Destiny's Denial?* Surely you must have read that one in that you're here now?"

Coira shook her head, confused. "I have no idea what you're talking about."

Ferchar removed a baby from the elongated tan car beyond. Its design was different from the other cars.

"That's called a van. 'Tis a more compatible family vehicle."

Coira's eyes fell on William briefly. His grin didn't amuse her. Did he follow her every thought?

Mildred continued. "Hmmm, it's a wonderful novel, *Destiny's Denial.* I'm in that one! It's Ferchar and Caitlin's love story. I was only given it recently, actually."

This brought her attention promptly back to Mildred. "How is that possible?"

Mildred turned back toward the house and urged Coira to walk with her. "My guess is magic, dear. It appears Beth knows some very informative... people."

She kept pace with Mildred, who walked with a cane. She'd never felt more clueless, and slightly bitter. How much did Annie know? Witch that she was, likely a lot. "And in what year was *Destiny's Denial* published?"

They were nearly to the front door when Mildred paused. "1805, I believe? Yes, 1805, but never released to the public, of course."

Coira was shocked. "Can I see these novels?"

Mildred continued to the door that Caitlin held open. "Of course, though I'm not so sure you'll be here long enough to do so."

She entered the house behind Mildred. Ferchar and the baby were already inside. William and Niall entered behind her. She looked to William. "Are we going back?"

"Aye, lass, soon."

How could he know that? She looked from Niall to William, and it dawned on her. They had been talking telepathically the whole time! Based on Ferchar's stern look and the private hushed words he and Caitlin were having in the other room now, Ferchar had been in on the little chat. How convenient it must be to possess such magical talent.

"If you but speak to me in your mind, I'll hear you, sprite. No need to get in a tither."

Damn you to hell! She nearly said it but refrained.

"There you go, lass. And such language for one who desires to be a proper English lady."

"You heard that?" She rounded on William.

"Heard what?" Mildred said.

"Aye, my feisty one, dinnae make a spectacle." William smirked and led them into the foyer.

"Nothing." This reply she gave to Mildred as they sat side by side on a crude settee.

"That would be a sofa, or couch." William sat in a chair across the way.

"Get out of my head!" Oh, she could do this. If she just concentrated on her impression of him, she could speak within the mind! She had no doubt it had to do with his magic.

"Now, why should I get out of your head, when I cannae get you out of my head?"

Coira felt the blush rise and couldn't fight it. Then she felt something much more personal, his warm hand cupping her waistline and the feel of his mouth on her lips, on her neck. Heat and arousal gathered low in her body and she gasped.

"Are you okay, sweetie?" Mildred frowned at her.

She went to speak but nothing came out. He was ruthless. What was he trying to do to her? "Stop whatever you're doing this instant!"

"I would have to agree." Niall cut into a nonexistent conversation.

"Agree with what?" Mildred asked.

Coira glared at Niall, then at William. What a messy, awkward situation dealing with two men such as these. Niall knew exactly what was passing between her and William.

"I would have to agree it's very interesting that we're all here. That the Brouns and MacLomains are once more reunited." Niall smiled at Mildred.

The woman was no fool. "I know well that you boys can speak within your minds. And as handsome as I may think you are, I won't abide such rudeness in either my or Coira's presence. Do we understand one another?"

Uncontrollable laughter bubbled forth from Coira. Oh, she liked this woman! Though a tad guilty that she had also been speaking within her mind, how wonderful that Mildred shut these pompous fools right down.

Niall and William were staring at her with a mixture of amazement and amusement. This only made her laugh harder.

"What's so funny?" Caitlin had just come into the room with Ferchar.

Coira wiped a tear from her eye. How free she felt. Then it struck her anew that she was acting just like Annie, and she burst into another fit of giggles.

"It appears I've tickled her funny bone." Mildred was giggling now herself. Then, as if it were contagious, William and Niall chuckled a bit.

"Dare I ask?" Ferchar leaned against the wall.

"No." Mildred smiled at Coira. "She just enjoyed the tongue-lashing I gave William and Niall."

"Oh. Good for you, Gram." Caitlin winked at Mildred. "It's always a good thing to keep these men in line."

Mildred sat back and sighed with contentment. "I do what I can."

"Would anyone like anything to drink or eat?" Caitlin looked around at her guests.

Everyone shook their heads.

"I take it you put Logan down for a nap?" Mildred gave Caitlin a knowing look.

"You bet. He always comes home a tired little critter when you watch him, Gram."

Mildred smiled with satisfaction. "I'm just amazed sometimes that I can manage him."

"I know you can walk without that cane, or you'd be sorely deprived of time alone with your great grandson." Caitlin sat down in the chair next to her grandmother.

"Who, me?" Mildred looked mortified, yet quite pleased.

Niall sat forward and directed his attention at Coira, his eyes drifting to her hand. "I see that you wear Annie's ring."

Ferchar muttered something under his breath.

William met her eyes. Why she looked to him when Niall had addressed her she chose not to analyze. She turned her gaze to Niall. "Yes, it appears I'm its keeper until I see my sister again."

"Hmmm." Niall stood, walked over, and sat down next to her. His close presence was as intimidating as William's. They were both such large men, intense in their demeanors.

"May I?" He nodded to her ring.

He wanted to see it. "Of course." She made to remove it, but he shook his head and merely took her ringed hand instead.

"It really is lovely," he said as he lifted her hand. They both froze.

Coira nearly choked as she gazed at the ring.

~Sylvan Mist~

The diamond throbbed with light, beautiful, soft, and mesmerizing. Niall tightened his grip on her hand. His eyes left the ring and met hers. He saw it too.

Her mind went completely blank.

Had she lost her wits? She looked back at the ring. It still glowed. She knew that William would be out of his chair before he even made a move. When he did stride forward, she felt as though a tidal wave came crashing over her.

Niall kept her hand within his grasp and raised the other in the air in a motion to stop William. Niall tossed his threat in the air with his hand. "Stop."

Ferchar went to grab William's arm but was too late.

William wouldn't be stopped.

****

He gave no thoughts to his actions. A chieftain, a warrior, a wizard, and still he acted impulsively. One hand fell to Coira's shoulder, and his other hand removed hers from Niall's grasp.

"This ring doesnae belong to Coira; 'tis not possible either of you see anything." He stood over her, far too protective. More feeling thrummed through his blood than he had ever felt before.

He was not one to bow to emotion, save for humor and perhaps duty, the passion that went with war. William loathed what he was feeling now, 'twas more vile than anything he'd felt before. Jealousy?

Aye, and severe it was. Niall was Coira's one true love?

As his thoughts gathered and his actions truly struck him, he released both her shoulder and hand. 'Twas not his place to intervene with what the gods deemed. And he would not.

Yet when Coira's eyes rose to his, they nearly broke him in two. Their sky blue depths held a

~Sylvan Mist~

mixture of confusion, anger, and hurt. Far worse than when she'd accused him of being magically sworn to Annie yet taking her. Caught up in the same whirlwind, that they desired one another was obvious.

Now everything had changed. The stone glowed for Niall and Coira. He had felt the magical stir instantly. When he saw the shocked looks on their faces, he'd acted rashly. He would not do so again.

"You have my apologies, Coira." He looked to Niall. "Niall."

He breathed deeply and salvaged his dignity. "It appears at times even the most avid interest in a lass can be...misleading."

He stepped away and sat in a chair.

The room remained quiet for many moments before Mildred finally broke the tense silence. "And so, the plot thickens."

"Gram!" Caitlin scowled and shook her head.

Mildred's eyes rounded, though she didn't look abashed in the least. "Well, it was a dreadful moment of silence, and there's no need."

She looked to Coira and Niall. "So, we've a love match then?"

Coira's face flooded with color. William clenched his teeth and remained silent as Niall responded.

"You're observant, Mildred." Niall did not take Coira's hand, but his eyes raked her face possessively. "It seems there may be a bit of magic at work."

Coira's gaze skittered between Mildred and Niall until it settled on the fire.

William spoke within her mind. He relished her essence, crisp, soft, giving, sensuous. He would miss it. "You have no need to be embarrassed or skittish, lass."

Her eyes darted to his and held. He gave her credit for that, most women would look away.

~Sylvan Mist~

"I'm not skittish nor embarrassed. I'm horrified. I've no desire to be connected to either Niall or you!"

Something he had no interest in analyzing eased within his chest. He couldn't contain a grin, though all was lost. *"You wanted it to be me, say 'tis not true?"*

The gasp that emitted from Coira and the mad scowl on her face gave him his answer. "Go to hell."

William tempered his smirk at her very outspoken attack.

"Get out of her mind, cousin." Niall's remark was low and marked mildly with threat.

"Cousin?" Coira's eyes whipped to Niall. "William's your cousin?"

Before Niall could speak, Coira stood and rambled on. "He would have to be, wouldn't he?" She stopped before the hearth and spun back. "William and you."

Her gaze was focused on Niall with this last statement. Then it tossed between him and Niall as she unraveled the truth. "You would have to be! The tale tells of only a MacLomain and a Broun. Niall, you're a MacLomain, you must be?"

"Yes, Coira, I'm Iosbail's great grandson." Niall remained seated and watched her steadily.

"Who's Iosbail?" Coira twisted the ring on her finger.

"Adlin's sister."

William longed to go to Coira and ease her agitation.

When Niall did, he nearly blocked his path.

Niall stood before her, cupped her chin in one hand, and grew very serious. "I am Scottish and English. And I am a wizard, one who travels, keeps some accord between the two warring countries. My magic is not as strong as the others, regrettably. But it is strong enough."

105

~Sylvan Mist~

Coira's eyes softened, and her chin trembled slightly. William knew what she was thinking. She was affiliating her lack of magic with Niall's weaker power rather than with the four wizards of Cowal: himself, Adlin, Iain, and Ferchar. He wanted to close his eyes to the heartfelt moment betwixt the two but could not.

"So fate deems that I'm with a man of English blood regardless." She stepped back slightly, and Niall's hand fell away. "But I am vowed to another. I'm so sorry."

William ignored the elation her useless words caused within him and said what needed saying. Pushed the words past bitter lips and made them sound matter-of-fact. "It doesnae work that way, lass. If the jewel glows, you've met the man the gods intended for you."

"No, it can't be." Those were the only words Coira was able to speak before the room was swallowed in white light.

****

Adlin stood in the center of the wide field. Autumn had arrived. The pines mingled green with a rainbow of foliage across the lower horizon, beautiful to behold. He lowered his head and closed his eyes.

The salt off the loch filled his memories, yet he pushed them aside. 'Twould not suit the moment. The rustle of his robes skirted the dry grass underfoot and whipped around his legs. Ah, there was naught like a highland wind, so true and direct, as blatant as any could ask of nature.

"What of it, Mother, Father?" He inquired of Mother Earth below, the gods above, and the ancients.

He spoke in the old tongue. "I am tired."

~Sylvan Mist~

They replied, separate but one. "You've done well thus far, son." The wind intensified. "Now you must face what is to be."

The white wizard, Adlin, kept his head bowed, his eyes closed, and responded. "Aye, as I always have. 'Twill be as Brigit wanted, as Fionn wanted."

A sigh rode the wind and caressed his conscience, his will, gave him strength, power. Nearly more than he was capable of controlling. The MacLomain wizard opened his eyes, looked upon his land. Scotland. And knew what his next move must be.

~Sylvan Mist~

~Sylvan Mist~

Chapter Eight

"And what is my next move, Arthur?" Annie couldn't keep the fire from climbing her neck and swallowing her face.

Arthur's hands spanned her waist, her back to his front, lifted and turned her a quarter circle from where she'd stood before. He didn't release her but lowered his head so that his cheek brushed hers. "For a lass your size, always quick movements."

She didn't move away, longed to press closer to him. Instead, she raised the sword and gave it a quick swoop in the air. "You make it sound as if there's nothing to me."

"Well." His wider reach plucked the sword from her hand. "There isnae."

"No?" She went to grab the sword back from him, but he easily held it out of reach.

His now infamous barrel-deep laughter broke free and he sidestepped her lunge. "No, you're half my size, lass. Take it as the truth, and stop making a spectacle of yourself."

She jumped high and made another attempt to take back the evasive sword. "Damn you, Arthur, why must our lessons always end this way?"

She fibbed, of course, and he knew it. Annie had come to love spending time alone with Arthur, while he taught her how to use nearly every weapon in the armory. It was late November now. She'd been here nigh on five months without Coira. William and Niall had vanished as well. She had little doubt where they were, though no one spoke of it. Arianna merely told Annie that her sister was safe.

Her time here had proven to be, by far, the most interesting months in her life. The night Coira vanished was unique, disturbing, and exhilarating. Arthur had protected her. Lifted and brought her to a small chamber in one of the castle towers. He had stayed with her all night as she paced, fretted, and continually eyeballed the flecks of light pulsating on the dark horizon.

The battles fought in the forest were minor, and the Cochrans were pushed back easily. Annie refused to ask Arthur how they had made it so far onto the MacLomain's land. She had read *Fate's Monolith*, the tale of Arianna and Iain, and understood when magic was at hand, anything was possible. And of course, Arthur offered no information. Merely that the enemy had been removed.

"You're fretting again, aye, lass?" Arthur leaned the sword against a tree and watched her.

Annie sighed. Was she that obvious? Or was it just that she and Arthur were becoming so close? She spoke always in the Gaelic tongue now. "Will I ever see Coira again? Truly, it has been a long time."

He closed the distance and held her hands. His hazel eyes grew serious. "You will, lass, I promise." His thumb lifted her chin to angle her head up. "Would I lie to you, Annie?"

Oh, how she had grown to relish his face. All this time and he had not tried to kiss her. She knew he wanted to. Knew why he did not. He believed her to be William's. William, who, no doubt, was with Coira. She was no fool. But how she wanted Arthur to kiss her, just once.

He must've seen the shift in her expression for he pulled away. She sighed and leaned back against another tree. These Scotsmen were too loyal. Yet she wondered how loyal William was, if in fact he was her one true love, which she highly doubted. A woman tended to know when a man wanted her. And she knew that William had not felt such sparks with her any more than she had with him.

This brought her gaze back to Arthur. Tall, wild, loyal, merry Arthur. She'd had enough of this.

"What's going to happen, Arthur?"

He leaned against the opposite tree and looked to the north. "There will be war."

Annie narrowed her eyes; she wasn't speaking of the impending war, and he knew it. They had befriended to such an extent they nearly ended one another's statements.

The war was all anyone talked about, this great magical beast of a thing which had men training in the fields until the wee hours. This vast future endeavor that had couples more amorous than ever, and many lasses declaring that they were pregnant. Oh yes, war was coming.

"You know what I speak of, Arthur. You and I." She had had quite enough of this and pushed away from the tree. She was walking his way, set on getting to the bottom of things, when a strong wind roared through the woods.

Both Annie and Arthur froze.

She closed her eyes against the heavy downpour of pine needles and heard only one thing over the screech of the wind, the bellow of Arthur's laughter.

****

Coira felt Niall's arms wrap around her. Shelter her. It was a vastly different sensation from William's

~Sylvan Mist~

embrace. Niall's body molded to hers, and she felt his warmth and safety. It could not compare to William's.

So, in the throes of magic, with three wizards around her, Coira felt the full impact of what it meant when the jewel had glowed for Niall and her.

And the pain was mind-blowing, humbling. What had happened to her in such a short period of time? Her virginity was gone, her personality transforming, and alas, she was completely taken with William. It was not love, couldn't be, so said the ring. Regardless, Coira had changed irrevocably. And she wondered, was it all the magic around her, the time travel?

Or was it the man?

Did it really matter at this point? As the white light of magic receded and the thunder tore her eardrums apart, Coira eased into the sudden surroundings of Scotland's medieval forest.

"Coira!" Her sister's exuberant voice hit her before she had a chance to breath. "Oh, Coira, they said I'd see you again, but how could I be sure?"

Niall stepped back as Annie crashed into her, holding her as though she hadn't seen her in years. She squeaked a response past her crushed lungs.

"It's been but a few days! I'm back, all is well."

Though reluctant, Annie pulled back. "A few days? Are you mad? It's been five months!"

She lost her breath for a moment. "Five months?"

Annie nodded avidly. "Aye, it's been a long time!"

"It has?" Coira felt the cold wind blow and noticed that the trees intermingling with the pines were barren. "My God."

"Aye." Annie's Gaelic was insistent. "Where have you been?"

"New Hampshire," Coira whispered and pulled away.

"So you went home?"

She shook her head and backed away slightly into the solid wall of Niall's chest. His hands fell onto her shoulders. "Yes, New Hampshire."

Annie's eyes followed. First they registered surprise, then understanding. Her gaze returned to Coira's. "And?"

Coira searched for words. She looked down at her hand, the ring, Annie's ring. Annie's gaze followed hers, paused a moment, then snapped back to her.

When Annie spoke, her voice was tender. "The ring was never mine, was it?"

Coira shook her head. She felt the tears well and could do nothing to stop them. So much anguish. Unexpected and perplexed, she did the only thing that made sense under the influence of so many new emotions. She made to remove the ring.

Annie lurched forward and grabbed her hand.

"No." Her sister slid the ring back into position, closed Coira's hand into a fist, and covered it with her other hand. "It's yours."

Annie's eyes stayed steady on hers. The witch, wisewoman, filled her sister's eyes. "If the stone glows, then you have found your true love. And the ring is yours."

Coira knew the level of Annie's magic, knew that her sister felt the burning confusion and pain within her. Annie's frown lasted a split second, then vanished. Coira found her voice steady and spoke. "It appears it may be."

She turned her attention from Annie and the ring to survey the others. Arthur stood silently behind Annie. Caitlin and Ferchar were nearby.

William leaned against a nearby tree, legs crossed and eyes to the south. She looked in the given direction and realized that they were just beyond the wide field, and he looked to his castle. Not to her but to the duties which lay ahead, as it should be. What had she expected? That he would be gazing at her with doe eyes? Wishing that they had seen the diamond glow?

Her mind did something unusual at that moment. It latched onto what she'd heard about the stone at the center of the heart. In the case of Iain and Arianna, the stone at the center had been an emerald. Her memory flashed back to the green of Iain's eyes, the emerald brilliance of them.

Wasn't it said that the stone was supposed to match the wizard's eyes? Had she seen Caitlin's ring? Coira couldn't stop her feet. She walked over to Caitlin and lifted her hand. Caitlin said nothing, nor did any of them. Why would they? They knew magic and most likely already understood what she was curious about.

She stared at the sapphire center of the heart. Her gaze narrowed quickly on Ferchar's eyes. Oh yes, they were brilliantly light blue. She knew well that the ring on her hand had a diamond center.

So impulsive it sickened her, Coira turned to William, thrust the single ringed finger in the air and spoke. "Explain this."

He had the nerve to smirk just before his face turned stoic. "Explain what, lass?"

She felt Niall move up behind her once again, but she cared naught. Passion ruled her thoughts. "Don't play a bloody ignorant blackguard with me, MacLomain. I'll not repeat myself."

William's gaze fell to the ring briefly, then rose ruthlessly to her eyes. "Why question the color of the stone when the ring was not given to you to begin with? 'Tis obvious to all that a bit o' the folklore is astray. The ring was not initially given to you and the stone is not the color of Niall's eyes. Not one person here will dispute that. And not one person here will question the glow of the stone."

Fury pulled her shoulders tight and she did something completely unnecessary and out of character. She shoved the ring within mere feet of his eyes and scolded in Gaelic. "Nay, the diamond is the color of your eyes!"

Niall moved forward when William's hand suddenly snatched her wrist. The MacLomain chieftain pulled up to his full height, the wizard apparent in his posture, in his intense, powerful gaze. Niall froze.

When William spoke, his eyes ripped into her soul, and the forest quieted. "Heed my words well, lass. The glow is where the power lies. A power far greater than any of us could possibly imagine. You will not question it, nor will anyone present. To do so will be the end of you, of Niall."

His eyes turned lethal, cutting. "I am not your one true love. Annie is not mine. Arianna is Iain's. Caitlin, Ferchar's." He tightened his grip on her wrist while he bit out more words through clenched teeth. "Niall is yours."

She would not pull her eyes away from his. He could take his black magic, for that's what it seemed, and shove it right up his arse. She breathed deeply and didn't struggle against his hold. Gone was the proper, prim woman she had been. Now she gave him what really lay in her heart.

Coira cared naught for anything but her sister, period. She ripped her wrist from his grasp. When she spoke, it was with a level of conviction that baffled even her. "I belong to no one. I will not bow to any god save my own. If it is a Christian god behind all of this then he will understand that he gave me free will and it is that, my free will, which I will implement."

She ignored the shock she saw not only in William's eyes but that which she felt from the others.

~Sylvan Mist~

She removed the ring. "I hold no magic. I am tied in no way, save by this blasted superstitious ring, to anybody. How dare you." She pointed to William.

Then she pointed to Niall. "Or you, presume such. I am not a piece on a chessboard. I do not follow your pagan ways, nor will I ever." She handed the ring to Niall. "I'm sorry."

Niall frowned and closed his fist around the ring. William, however, took more immediate action. His words were a sharp command, a tone she had not heard before. "Come with me, lass. Now."

He again seized her wrist and pulled her further into the forest. Coira fought him but it did little good; his strength was substantial. She stumbled to keep up and almost dropped to the ground beneath to hinder his progress. No, she would not do that. She may have become more verbal of late. Maybe a bit less strict in her presentation, but she was still a lady and as such would not behave like a child.

But curse his long legs!

"William, stop this instant!" Her words fell on deaf ears while he pulled her free from the forest into a small clearing. A waist-high rock sat overlooking a small stream. The fluid flowed swiftly enough to allow the sound of water running over sticks and pebbles.

He stopped at last, threw his hand in the air, and plunked her down on the rock. "I've created a sound barrier." He glared down at her. "Now you can shoot off your blasphemous, hateful, sharp tongue to your heart's content without offending the whole of Scotland. Damn you, lass!"

Shoot off her blasphemous tongue? How dare he! She almost made to stand but remained seated in light of the furious picture he presented. She chose not to yell but gave him a condescending tone laced with sarcasm. "You've a lot of nerve, my *laird*, my *chieftain*, *wizard*, or would you prefer *Great One*? I'll not repeat what I said back there, there's no need. Every word was the truth and will remain such. I've had enough of all of this."

For a flicker of a moment something indefinable flashed in his eyes—compassion?—then vanished, leaving them impenetrable diamond chips. "And how, pray tell, will you remove yourself from all of this?"

She was about to reply but he continued on. "Has it occurred to you at all that we MacLomains have not intentionally victimized you? If anything we've done nothing but protect you since you arrived. Neither I nor Niall summoned you, lass, that I can assure you. 'Tis old magic at work, which my cousin and I are not responsible for, yet you blame us. You are letting your emotions rule you, and you're hurting others. What you just did to Niall was deplorable."

Coira winced at the truth behind his words. She was acting on emotions, a truly harmful thing. Her straight back slumped a bit in defeat. Lord, what had become of her? Who did she have to vent on save an ancient magic she couldn't begin to understand, and what of Niall? She sighed and met William's eyes. "I don't love him."

William softened. "You don't know that. You've had no time to spend with him because of..."

His words died off but she finished his sentence. "Because of you."

"Aye, lass." William sat down beside her. "I should never have gone near you, 'twas indecent of me. Impulsive, considering the ring."

She tried to ignore the thrill his arm brushing hers invoked. "It was. I'm glad you can admit that now."

His lips curled up a fraction, nearly allowing his dimples to appear. "I am truly sorry, lass."

"I know." She whispered and tore her gaze from his handsome face. "Me, too."

William's hand rose to touch her face, but he pulled back. "You are here now. Things have been set in motion. Perhaps in the end you will not end up with Niall. 'Tis between you and fate what comes of it."

She looked back to him, admired the way the sun stroked forth bits of copper from his ebony hair. "I do have to stay here for now, though, don't I? I cannot go home."

"Nay, lass." William searched her face. "'Twas your own mother who set things in motion with this war. And it was because of a MacLomain that you were pulled back. Now you and your sister must be protected, kept safe. Many things at work here even I dinnae ken—Annie wearing the ring initially, the jewel matching my eyes, and the ring glowing for one who is not one of the four MacLomain wizards."

She felt a sudden burst of compassion for him and placed her hand on his arm, felt the muscles tighten beneath her touch. "So you're denied your one true love, denied the infamous Broun connection?"

It was both a question and a statement, and she honestly didn't expect an answer.

William's gaze lingered on her hand before it returned to her eyes. His voice hit a soft, serious, baritone pitch. "So it appears. But I will tell you this, my sprite. I shall always wish it were otherwise."

Her body reacted to his words, fire spreading everywhere. She pulled her hand away and nodded. She could not deny that she agreed with him. There was no use for falsehood anymore. She couldn't change anything. It was time to accept her circumstances until they played out and she could return home. "So, it would seem, for now, I've another MacLomain to become better acquainted with."

~Sylvan Mist~

A muscle jumped in his jaw as he stood and offered her his hand. "Aye, so it would seem."

~Sylvan Mist~

Chapter Nine

William sat alone before the fire in the main hall, lost in thought. Sparks spit and hissed within the huge pile of logs on the hearth. He'd never had to conceal misery such as this, a gut-wrenching feeling that soaked his heart.

Coira's words still burned within his mind. "So you're denied your one true love, denied the infamous Broun connection?" She had no idea how truthful her words were. Damn the trials and tribulations of his position. There was no hope for it.

His eyes drifted to the many faces carved into stone above the fireplace, ancient relatives long gone. He smiled when Adlin's wizened face poked through. "Have you a moment, lad?"

William summoned a servant hidden within the shadows and she brought over another mug of whisky. "For you, always."

Adlin appeared in the chair beside him, his white robes skirting the floor. The old wizard was the only one who consistently wore his wizard's garb, made Scottish with the clan's plaid wrapped over his frail shoulder.

"You're a good lad, William." He took a sip from his mug, his face showing the strain of mourning the loss of his sister. "So you've found yourself in an odd situation, aye?"

William drank too deeply from his whisky. "Nay, not odd, merely uncomfortable."

"'Tis truly a bizarre thing." Adlin kept his gaze on the fire.

William was no fool. "And I imagine you'll not tell me what you know."

The white wizard's eyes met his, their light blue hue sharp and regretful. "I know many things. And, as is the way of things, they are not mine to tell. Fate is not mine to control."

"Aye." William watched Adlin. "So we are both doomed in love."

Adlin sipped from his mug once again. "Aye."

William felt the sting of Adlin's word touch his soul. As it stood, the wizard would not lie about this, having loved and lost twice, which brought his thoughts to Mildred, Caitlin's grandmother. She had been Adlin's true love, and he'd had to sacrifice her to ensure her safety. He had cut the bond betwixt them and connected her with another man with whom she'd fallen in love.

The similarity of their circumstances struck William. Though he'd been given no such option, the plight of coming so close and losing everything was torturous.

William shifted directions. "The Cochran wizards have been in this castle."

He was not surprised when Iain and Ferchar suddenly appeared. They had been summoned by Adlin. Ferchar was wrapped in his plaid again and leaned against the opposite wall. Iain sat in another chair and received a mug of ale from a servant.

Ferchar spoke first, one eyebrow quirked. "You summoned the Cochrans?"

Adlin looked to the faces carved above the hearth. "Aye, 'twas a necessary thing."

"Regrettably," Iain said.

"And were they disappointed they didnae find what they were looking for?" William crossed his legs and snickered. "Fools."

Ferchar looked to William. "So you knew they'd been here? I'd have thought the meeting would be elsewhere, considering."

William nodded and looked to Adlin. "I had little doubt they'd be brought within these walls."

Adlin smiled, his blue eyes twinkling for the first time in days. "I couldn't help myself."

Iain cut in. "And I had little choice in the matter, would have never allowed it."

"And that is why you are the youth, and I'm the elder." Adlin chuckled. "I've gleaned much from the enemy's wizards by allowing them entrance. I'm actually quite surprised they came."

Ferchar received a mug of whisky and cocked his head. "And you learned what?"

"That they're nearly as strong as us." Adlin met Ferchar's gaze.

"Nearly?" Ferchar nodded. "Aye, nearly is good news indeed."

William understood that the Cochran wizards stepping foot into this castle gave Adlin full evaluation of their power. Not through warfare, nor words, but simply their presence when they stood in the heart of the MacLomain clan's magic.

"And why do you suppose they agreed to come here, Adlin?" William sat forward. "The Cochrans may be daft, but certainly not that much so?"

"Nay." Adlin nodded and grinned. "Not so daft, just arrogant. 'Tis my belief they thought they would find what they had sought here, and betwixt the three of them, with you and Ferchar gone, would be able to penetrate and learn more about us. What we're capable of."

Iain laughed. "'Twas really a grand time."

William looked first to Iain and then to Adlin. "I know they did not find what they sought. And I know it took them many months to make an appearance. So, pray tell, what do we know now?"

Iain sat forward and rubbed his hands together. "We know they've amassed a massive following, which we had gathered previously. We also know they're bloody eager to fight. It's a festering disease within them, and they intend to attack with not only their magic but others', and there are quite a few clans with wizards."

Ferchar grinned. "And how many is quite a few? How much magic are we dealing with?"

Adlin frowned and eyed the men. "More than we're capable of taking on, mark my words. While we'll outnumber them with men once the clans come together, they've more magic. We will need wits and strategy if we're to win, and still, we'll lose many."

The aura of battle lust drained from the room at Adlin's declaration. William set his mug aside and asked the one question they'd all been eager to know. "So where shall this war take place?"

Adlin's voice strengthened, deepened, held a touch of magic within it. "East Lothian."

William, Ferchar, and Iain froze in shock.

Then they heard Adlin's voice within their minds.
And Ireland.

****

Coira shoved her sister away and pulled the wool blanket over her head. She tossed her muffled words into the makeshift mattress. "Leave me be!"

Her sister lifted the blanket and peered at her, bright and sunny and incredibly awake. "You can't sleep all day!"

With that statement, Annie pulled away the covers and plunked down on the cot.

"I certainly can. Do you realize how much time traveling I've done? I'm exhausted." She turned her head in the opposite direction.

Annie crawled over Coira and plunked down so that she was eye to eye. Her golden eyes sparkled with mischief. "You didn't tell me nearly enough about the twenty-first century yesterday. I want to hear more about the cars, and the interior of the house, and the—"

"Stop!" Coira sat up and yawned.

"If you insist." Annie shuffled off the bed and smiled down at her. "Let's talk about how much you've changed!"

She put a hand to her forehead and shook her head. "No."

"Well, how about William and Niall, now that's some—"

"No, Annie. No!" Her sister flinched at her harsh tone. Coira sighed and stood. "I just don't want to talk about any of it right now." She put a reassuring hand on Annie's arm. "All right?"

Annie bit her lip and nodded. She offered Coira a bowl of porridge and pointed to a tub of steaming water. "They brought this up for you." She pursed her lips. "Because I told them I was going to wake you up."

"Ah, it looks good, thank you." She declined the porridge, removed her clothing, and slipped into the water. "What time is it?"

"Late afternoon." Annie sat on the edge of the tub.

Shocked, she looked to the arrow slit window. Indeed, a dull light came through. It was a nice enough chamber with a few animal skin rugs, two torches in pewter brackets, a tapestry of a forest, and two chairs, but chilly. She looked to the floor where the extra blankets she'd been given lay in heaps.

She remembered little about what she'd dreamt, only that it was not the same recurring dream that had plagued her for so long. In fact, she'd not had the dream since traveling back in time.

She dunked beneath the surface of the water and then broke free. "It was a grand family reunion last night, don't you think?"

Annie laughed. "Oh, it was. So wonderful! I believe Caitlin and Shane cried all night, and then when Caitlin met his daughter, it was just too much. Simply fabulous!"

Coira washed quickly, dried off, and slipped into a dress, a beautiful gown of light blue with a bodice cut somewhat low. She peered down at her cleavage and frowned. "Yes, it was wonderful watching everyone come back together." She looked to Annie, curiosity piqued. "So tell me, what's this I heard about Beth's novels?"

Stark innocence enwrapped Annie's features. "Novels?

"Don't play innocent with me, Annie. Why did I not know that Beth published two novels, *Fate's Monolith and Destiny's Denial*, in the years 1802 and 1805?"

"Oh, those." Annie suddenly became busy readjusting her crème-colored skirts. "I just heard about them myself."

Coira pulled a crude comb through her long hair and glared. "You did not! You lie to me. I've always known when you lied."

"How?" Annie's quick response gave her away.

"Because you chew the corner of your lip." She set the comb aside. "Now tell me."

Annie sat on the side of the bed. "Honestly, I didn't learn about the novels until a few years ago.

Remember, I was only nine years old when the first was published. Why would mother have told me then?"

Coira believed her but was hurt anyway. "Why was I never told? I may not possess your gift, but I was told well about the MacLomains and such."

A frown etched Annie's mouth, and she shook her head. "I wish I knew, Coira. I was told to say nothing by both Beth and Mama. Please believe me."

She peered intently at Annie. Her sister was telling the truth. Coira may not have inherited the magic, but she had inherited her father's keen intuition. "Have you any idea why this would have been kept from me?"

Annie shook her head. "I don't. And trust me, I've wondered. They wouldn't tell me."

"Well, then, I guess we'll find out eventually, won't we?" Coira smiled and headed for the door. "Shall we join the MacLomains?"

Her sister leapt from the bed and followed. "I thought you'd never ask."

Coira laughed softly as they made their way down to the great hall. A few clansfolk sat randomly along the ten long trestle tables. Her eyes roamed to the massive, thirty-foot Viking tapestry that dwarfed the others. Unlike the scenes of women and men intertwined and ocean waves, this one claimed dominance and defeat. The man at the Viking's feet pleaded for his life. It was apparent the Viking was not likely to give it.

The day proved unseasonably warm for this time of year and a simple plaid over their shoulders was sufficient. The community thrived and enjoyed the weather. Coira discovered she was surprisingly content to be here again.

Just as they reached the bottom step, something indistinguishable, perhaps an egg, went sailing by and

~Sylvan Mist~

hit a young boy squarely on the back of his head. The child screeched and ran through the crowd, disappearing just as a heavy-set woman erupted from the kitchen, her face red with fury.

Caitlin was right behind her laughing helplessly. She spoke through giggles to the irate woman. "Really, Euphemia, you'll never curb that temper of yours, will you?"

Euphemia planted her hands on ample hips, growled, and eyeballed Caitlin. "Ye've no idea what a beastie that laddie's been. I've a mind ta feed him to the Sassenachs."

Annie chuckled as they approached. "He's but a wee thing, Euphemia."

The woman clucked, muttering a few choice obscenities before she said something halfway civil. "He's as bad as these blasted goats, he is!"

Caitlin smiled and put her hand on the woman's shoulder. "Euphemia, have you met Coira? She is sister to Annie, cousin to Arianna, and my distant relative from the past."

Euphemia trained her brown eyes on Coira. "Nay, 'twas brief, it was, when you were here before, lass." Her scowl turned to a smile. "Welcome, Coira, I be the head cook around here."

Coira said her greetings and remained silent as the three women conversed. Eventually, Caitlin, Annie, and Coira left Euphemia to her ranting and made their way through the crowd, over the drawbridge, and out onto the field.

The low sun vanished behind a large white cloud and turned the dry grass into a sea of shadows. The mountains held the sun's glow at their peaks, and the loch swam somewhere between deep aquamarine and slate blue. Warriors were practicing at arms in separate clusters. Some pursued archery, while others were sword fighting. Young boys played mock combat with sticks, and little girls watched with admiration.

Coira smiled. "I can't get over such a quick change in seasons."

Annie shook her head. "Aye, it must be strange for you. You've been all over the place in a very short time."

Coira eyed both women as they walked. How similar they appeared. "And have either of you been able to ascertain why I'm the one that need be flung throughout the centuries?"

Annie and Caitlin shook their head. Caitlin spoke. "Trust me, when these MacLomain clansmen wish to keep secrets, they're impregnable."

Annie nodded and scuffed her foot. "It was aggravating being here all these months and told so little. Especially when they took my ring—"

Annie stopped speaking when Coira shot her a look. It appeared her sister realized she'd stumbled onto a somewhat unstable subject.

"Ah, there they are." Caitlin broke the sudden tension and looped one arm though Annie's and the other through Coira's, leading them toward the western side of the field. "Isn't it something having all three chieftains together again? And all so tall and strapping now."

Coira's eyes drifted over the three men who bore such striking similarities. They stood among a small circle of men surrounding a dueling Arthur and Niall. The two men in the middle wielded five-foot claymores and, based on their heavy breathing, had been battling for some time.

"Hey, there." Caitlin's words were husky with passion as she came up beside Ferchar and wrapped an arm around him. He returned the gesture and smiled down at her with such adoration Coira's throat closed with emotion. How she envied them, what they'd found together. She wished she had found that depth of emotion with her fiancé, James, but knew better now having watched these couples who were so totally in love.

Iain continued to watch the men fight, and William turned his attention her way. The sun again ignited auburn highlights in his midnight hair and those startling light gray eyes settled on her attire.

"'Tis a lovely dress, lass. It suits you."

She kept her tone as civil as his and made light of the feelings crashing in on her. "I think I might prefer a plaid. You men look far more comfortable."

What had she just said? Had she just joked with him? Her mind seemed to still be at a loss around William, which would surely change with time.

He threw back his head and laughed, displaying straight, white teeth. "Och, that would surely be a sight."

She regarded his plaid with speculation and again spoke before she thought. "Can you deny that you're comfortable beneath that?"

Her face blazed to life with her question. It would behoove her to move away from him this instant. She entered dangerous territory with this line of conversation.

Thankfully, William's retort was one of amusement and not the flirtatious return her question deserved. "Aye, lass, comfortable enough."

As she met his eyes again, her thoughts returned to the tapestry, and she suddenly remembered something she'd completely forgotten, seemingly the moment it happened. How odd, because it had happened at dusk while she and Annie walked across the field on *Fheill-Eoinm* before she traveled to the twenty-first century.

She frowned. "Can I ask you a question?"

"Aye, of course." He offered one of his charming dimpled smiles.

"Who was the woman on the hill at dusk early eve on *Fheill-Eoinm*?"

"I dinnae ken? What woman do you speak of?" He cocked his head.

"There was a fire, and a woman with long white robes upon the hill that night." She felt as though she were retelling a dream. "She was casting a bouquet into the fire."

William's silver regard darkened to molten gray. "If I were to guess, I would have to say 'twas your imagination."

She shook her head adamantly. "No, she was there, I know it."

William merely shrugged. "I dinnae ken, lass, I'm sorry."

Niall's voice rose above the others. He stepped back and lowered his sword. "Enough, Arthur, we'll not best each other this day."

Arthur grunted a response and grinned. "Leave it to an Englishman to back away from the battle first."

Niall's eyes swung to Coira. "We English aren't cowardly. We're simply intelligent and realize that battles such as this can't compare with a beautiful woman."

Arthur snickered when he looked Annie's way. "Mayhap you've a point, my friend."

Two others stepped forward to practice as Arthur and Niall made their way over to Coira and Annie. Where Arthur secured his claymore to his back, Niall sheathed his at his side. Where Arthur wore a plaid, Niall chose leggings.

"And I thought you defeated all men?" Annie chided and smiled up at Arthur.

~Sylvan Mist~

Coira almost shook her head in amazement. Though she'd not spoken to her sister about the situation, clearly Annie was smitten with Arthur. And in the way their eyes met in mutual understanding, Coira could tell Arthur felt the same. Something Coira had never felt. What had transpired while she was gone?

"You look lovely, Coira."

Niall's praise brought her to attention. "Thank you."

She felt guilty for her near flirtation with William mere moments before. Could she not heed his words? The ring was for her and Niall, and as such she should devote undivided attention his way. He wore a dark tunic which set off his sandy hair nicely, and his light green eyes shimmered in the late sun.

"Shall we take a walk, my lady?" Niall held out his arm to her.

She smiled and accepted it. "I would like that." Though it was likely her imagination, she felt eyes boring into her back as they walked toward the forest leading to the loch. William's? No, it couldn't be. He'd made very clear what must be. And he was right.

"I've thought long and hard upon what I should say to you, Coira." Niall led her into the forest where dry grass gave way to a carpet of golden needles.

Slightly uncomfortable in his presence now, Coira reverted to her old self. Her prim self, which was easier than expected with this Englishman, or perhaps not? She should feel grateful to recapture a bit of who she was a mere week before, yet somehow she felt like an imposter within her own body. "And what have you decided to say, my lord?"

Niall leaned his head slightly in her direction, his eyes intent on hers. "That I do not wish to rush you. I am no fool and saw well what existed between you and William."

"But of course." As Coira murmured this, the trees thinned, and the loch's shore rose before them. She had expected this courtesy from Niall. "And I appreciate that."

They left the trees behind and walked along the cobbled ground until they met sand. Niall's shoulder-length hair blew back in the wind and gave her his full profile.

He took her hand, and they walked along the shore. When at last he spoke, his words were solemn. "'Tis a strange situation you've been thrust into, Coira. I have often thought since we met such a short time ago that the oddities of fate and magic will always surprise and intrigue me."

He squeezed her hand and continued. "You have surprised me."

"Why is that, my lord?"

"Please, call me Niall, 'tis more appropriate, I think." He offered a small smile when she nodded agreement.

He continued. "When I first met you, I knew you to be a lady, one born to such demeanor naturally, and one who would be such in any century."

"Thank you," she said, truly flattered.

Niall sat, nodded his head, urging her to sit on a log facing the shore and the setting sun. "Yet you have proven yourself not only a lady, but a survivor of sorts."

She sat next to him and eyed the loch bathed in gold and copper. "A survivor? I hardly see myself as that."

"Then you do not see yourself clearly." Niall continued to hold her hand. "You have been through so much in such a short period of time and have obviously

~Sylvan Mist~

enthralled both William and I with your easy adaptability. I know you have already been through more time traveling than any Broun thus far."

"Yes, I have adapted, because I have had to." She would not allow herself to become bitter about such a thing. What good would it do? "But I can tell you I'm no survivor in the common sense of the word but merely going through the motions. Tell me, sir, is that what you consider surviving?"

Niall's eyes met hers, his tone serious. "You do not give yourself enough credit. Is it not true that you hold no magic and were a history teacher before all of this?"

She gave a low laugh. "Aye, I suppose such a woman going through this would be considered a bit of a survivor."

Had she said aye? Oh, but she had. Scotland was seeping into her, second by second, filling her veins with something new and foreign.

Niall leaned down, took a bit of sand in his hand, and let it run through his fingertips. "You must wonder what will come of all this, Coira. What do you see between us? Could you imagine ending up in England, medieval England, with me, or do you envision returning to your time?"

Coira had not expected him to be so blunt but couldn't fault him for it. So she was honest. "I envision returning to my time, and I had not given much thought to being with anyone save my fiancé."

"Come now, Coira." Niall's thumb swept over the back of her hand. "Please do not tell me that William has not given you pause for thought? I know he has. And I also know you wonder about you and I and the glow of the ring. Tell me I'm wrong?"

She turned her eyes to the sun, which sat so low now that crimson streaks ran from the horizon, glazed the windswept loch, and fell at their feet. "I will not lie. William was not someone I expected to enter into my life. Hoped would not."

She turned her attention back to Niall. "But it does not change things. I'm still engaged, and you and I have been deemed by the fates to be together." She covered his hand with hers. "Please forgive me about William, I didn't know that—"

His eyes turned a smoky green in the trailing light, and he brought his finger to her lips to silence her. "You've no need to ask my forgiveness."

Niall removed his finger and cupped her chin. "May I kiss you, Coira?"

His fingers on her skin were warm and dry. Should she deny him? No. Yet somehow she felt unfaithful, to James or William. She would not over think her indecision. All in all, if the ring held true, was it not to Niall she had been unfaithful all along? No. Because she held no magic, and all of this was not of her doing. Still, she would allow Niall to kiss her, for surely there was something here.

She nodded and accepted his lips on hers, soft, gentle, patient lips. They did not pressure her to open to them but guided her slowly. He moved closer and his other hand slid to the back of her neck, angled her head, yet the kiss stayed gentle. She waited for the telling heat to rush throughout her body and seize her limbs in fire.

He moaned and pulled her closer, whispered her name. At last the kiss deepened, and his tongue swept into her mouth. She met his movements, searched for something, anything.

There was nothing.

She bowed her head away from the kiss and pulled back. "Perhaps we should return to the castle. It will be dark soon."

Niall's eyes swept her face, his expression unreadable. "Aye, it will be." He stood and offered his arm again. "Shall we?"

Coira accepted, and they walked back to the castle making idle conversation. She wondered what he had felt when he kissed her. He carried magic and surely would have sensed her lack of response?

When they were nearly back to the first portcullis, Coira finally broached the subject she'd put off, and he'd been tactful enough not to bring up. "I am sorry I gave the ring back to you, Niall. I did not mean to be cruel. I'm just not ready for such a thing. Will you hold it for me?"

They stopped directly beneath the portcullis prongs. His gaze was sincere and held no animosity. "Of course, Coira, you know I will."

She smiled and they continued walking. As they did, she wondered when, in fact, she would ever be ready to put that ring on again.

Chapter Ten

The clan was in a merry mood this eve. As was the way with Highlanders, the reunification of family was cause to celebrate for days. They had brought in ten extra-long trestle tables, and Euphemia ensured a feast fit for a king.

There were platters of salmon, mussels, scallops, and shrimp, as well as goose, capons, pheasant, partridge, and wood pigeon. The harvest was a good one, and the MacLomain clan had plenty of supplies stowed away for the colder months.

William walked over to one of the tables, grabbed an elderberry, and popped it in his mouth. Smoke drifted from the fire and made a light haze overhead. The pipes were lively, and many people had started dancing.

"And how are you this eve, son?" His parents joined him at the table.

"Good." He put his arm around Muriel's shoulders. She was still a lovely woman, her long dark hair flecked lightly with silver.

Hugh squeezed his shoulder and nodded. "We missed you, son. 'Tis a grand thing to have you amongst us again."

"Aye, 'tis an interesting journey thus far." William smiled and received a mug of whisky from a passing servant.

"Have you had any new visions?" A frown joined Muriel's question.

"Nay." He wouldn't tell them if he had, and they knew that. He couldn't help wondering when the visions would come. It had been some time. His mind still pondered Coira's declaration at the beginning about him pulling her back. Each time he was compelled to ask her, something stopped him, something born of magic.

It was an odd sensation, one he'd been unwilling to discuss even with Adlin. So many unusual forces were at work, he suddenly felt a novice at magic, which made no sense at all.

Not to mention Coira's comments about the woman on the hill during Fheill-Eoinm. She had had a vision of the ancient past. Of that he was sure but would not tell her such a thing.

He had little doubt that she'd witnessed a Celtic ritual and had seen a priestess or druidess. In the Druidic ceremony for the longest day of summer, *Alban Heruin*, the druidess cast her bouquet into the fire to add power to the sun and to pay tribute. How Coira could possibly have witnessed such a thing both bothered and intrigued him since the lass carried no magic.

He pulled his mind from Coira and looked down at his mother. "Would you care to dance?"

Muriel's face lit up. They joined a lively jig, and when they finished, Muriel pleaded a moment alone with him before the fire. "Is it true then? That the ring is for Coira and Niall?"

William couldn't get away from this line of questioning, and his eyes sought Coira and Niall sitting together across the room. Her gown was a fetching shade of silver, hugging her slim figure and accentuating her cleavage.

"Aye, 'tis true enough." His eyes returned to Muriel's. He did not miss the flicker of compassion that crossed her face.

She spoke softly. "You love her."

He kept hidden the sudden swell of irritation the simple declaration brought him. "No, I dinnae love her. I haven't known her long enough for that."

Muriel sighed. "I do believe that Iain once said something similar in regard to Arianna."

Because he spoke to his mother, he was honest with himself. "And, alas, the ring was meant for them where 'tis not meant for Coira and me. If it were love I felt for Coira,'twould matter naught. The feeling would have to be a false one."

"Would it? I seem to remember that Chieftain Alan Stewart fell in love with Caitlin."

"And that was his demise in the end." His voice came across curter than intended. "Above and beyond that, I have no desire to intrude upon either Coira or Niall's happiness."

Muriel touched his arm, heart in her eyes. "I've seen the way she looks at you." Her voice grew wise. "And I've seen the way she looks at Niall. 'Tis different."

William remembered her words on the field earlier, the obvious flirtation he knew she had not intended. How hard it had been at that moment, with her eyes matching the blue sky behind her, not to pick her up, carry her into the castle, and discover exactly how she would look in a plaid and nothing else.

He closed his eyes and swallowed. "I dinnae love her, I cannae."

When he opened his eyes, his mother had left, filtering back into the crowd, letting her last statement hang in the air. He again looked to Coira and Niall. Niall had just popped a hazelnut into her mouth, and she was laughing around her chewing. Her laughter was infectious, he knew, and Niall soon chuckled alongside her. Damn lucky Englishman.

"Would ye care to dance, my laird?"

He looked down at the lass who had approached him, Sarah, a comely girl with white blond hair and big brown eyes. She would be forever known for causing the clan to go into a state of panic when she was a wee bairn, and Ferchar was the laird. Her pet goat had gone astray, managed to dislodge a dagger from the armory, nicked a lass crossing the drawbridge, and caused a scream that had the guards lowering the portcullises.

The clan flew into a state of mayhem that people still snickered about today. William and Sarah had become friendlier with one another before Coira and Annie arrived. She struck him as a suitable way to move on. "'Twould be a pleasure, lass."

The celebration ensued. He focused on Sarah and enjoyed the spirits. She was a happy one and a practiced flirt. He wondered, though, if she had an argumentative bone in her body. He also wondered if she would be capable of articulate speech and a dose of haughtiness, or propriety, just enough to engage him on occasion, a defiant shell he could break down only to have her build it up again.

And he wondered if she would ever want to wear a plaid in the fashion Coira intended.

Bloody hell, he was a fool and knew it. On impulse, to prove to himself his thoughts were foolish, he pulled her close at the outer edge of the dancing crowd and kissed her deeply. Her response was quick, and her arms encircled his neck.

"You see, my lady, these Scots are randy bucks, not nearly as civilized as we English."

~Sylvan Mist~

Though he was tempted to push Sarah away quickly, William slowly eased away from the kiss and kept an arm around her waist. Of course Niall and Coira would happen upon them now. "Thank the gods for that, when you've a bonnie lass on your arm, hmm?"

Coira looked even more striking at close proximity, the silver of her dress mingling the clear blue of her eyes with misty pewter.

She didn't quite meet his eyes when she spoke. "There's naught wrong with letting the pleasure build and saving such things as...such displays of...well, attraction for a more discreet location."

Ah ha. There was his proper little sprite. Not his...Niall's. Nonetheless, he could still have a little fun and break her down so he directed his statement at Niall. "Oh, the torture of that, my friend, such a prudish outlook for you, I'm afraid."

Before Niall had a chance to respond, Coira intercepted. Fire lit her eyes. When she spoke, it was not what he had expected her to say. "I'm no prude!" She looked to Niall. "I would like a kiss, sir, now, to prove this swine wrong."

Niall wasted no time but pulled her into his arms and kissed her as thoroughly as William had just kissed Sarah. Multiple thoughts floated through his mind at the brazen display. Why had she not battled him with words as she was supposed to? This was very unlike Coira. He would have never taunted her had he seen this coming. And how completely pleased she seemed with Niall's ministrations. He banked the aggravation he felt building when Coira pulled away.

Her lips might be rosy from Niall's kiss, but her eyes were not glazed with passion when they met his. "Mayhap you have the right of it, my laird, especially in light of my surroundings, that such behavior does have its benefits."

Sarah giggled at this. "Och, the Broun lassies do end up fitting in with this clan just fine, they do!"

William pulled forth his usual humor with great effort and fueled his churlish mood with an unwise offer directed at Coira. "I see I've the wrong of it, lass. Pray forgive me. Would you care for a dance?"

Coira had not expected him to ask; it was apparent on her face. A brief moment of silence passed before she responded. "Yes, my laird."

Niall and Sarah engaged in conversation while William led her into the crowd. As was the way with such things, the pipes played a slower tune, allowing the couples more intimacy. Because it would have looked awkward not to do so, he pulled her into his arms. As he knew she would, Coira felt good against him.

Beyond good.

Bloody fantastic actually.

He breathed deeply, her hair smelled like a mixture of lilac and lavender, fresh, flowery, and incredibly womanly. The urge to run his hands through its thick length nearly overwhelmed. Her small frame felt soft and giving against his. Fool. He should've never asked her to dance. Damn.

Her voice was whisper soft when she engaged him, so quiet that he barely heard her. "Why must you always goad me into such foolish behavior?"

He brought his mouth close enough to her ear that she would hear him yet the action would not appear too intimate to others. "'Tis truly not my fault that you're so easily goaded."

She pulled back and looked up at him, her head quite tilted at this proximity. "You've a way about you,

~Sylvan Mist~

William MacLomain, and it's not nearly civil half the time."

"Have we returned to that, lass? You just proved that civil, proper behavior is not something you wish to adhere to amongst my clan, and there's naught wrong with that. 'Tis better to be who you are. We Highlanders are a lusty lot and dinnae tend to hide it behind closed doors."

"I can see that." She licked her lips, and his arms instinctively tightened around her waist.

Her eyes held his, and her pupils dilated within the thick curtain of her black lashes.

He had to pull away from a dangerous direction. "And are you and Niall becoming better acquainted?"

Her eyes dropped. "You know we are. He's a very interesting man, quite pleasant actually."

"He's a good man. I wouldnae have let him have you otherwise." Curse his impulsive tongue around her.

Again, Coira's eyes rose to meet his. "As you said before, my laird, I'm to give him a chance because of the ring. Do you now change your sentiment otherwise? If so, it is too late."

He arched an eyebrow. "I only say that if he were truly a bad man at heart, neither I nor Adlin would allow this union."

Now her eyebrows rose. "How interesting to hear from one such as you, a wizard, that you've the ability to disengage Niall and I though the ring glows. Pray tell, how does one go about doing such a thing?"

She was bewitching him again without holding an ounce of magic. "There are ways, lass, but we would not do such a thing, for you know Niall is a good man, and he is your one true love. One does not interfere with fate."

~Sylvan Mist~

"Well, one should." She visibly flinched, then blushed. "I didn't mean to say that. I'm sorry. Niall has proven to be a pleasure."

It was time to step away. "Let us return to our partners then, shall we?"

She nodded and allowed him to lead her back to Niall and Sarah. He wondered to himself as they all began idle conversation, what sort of hell had he truly been thrust into?

****

This was the worst kind of torture, being near him and trying to pretend she didn't care about him. She'd become a wanton in light of such feelings. Why had William bothered to ask her to dance? It did nothing to help her current distress. But then again, was her distress ever likely to ease when she was around him? To have openly kissed Niall like that!

She knew well why she'd done it—jealousy—and it disgusted her. Watching William kiss Sarah had churned her stomach to rock. She'd had no desire to approach them to begin with, but Niall had insisted. Perhaps to show her that William had moved on? Likely, and she could not fault Niall when it was becoming more and more clear she was having trouble moving on herself.

And then to dance with him! As always, his beauty daunted her even more at close range. Being so near to him brought her thoughts back to the dream. The stones and what they'd done together. Heat rose to her face as images flashed within her mind. A wave of dizziness seized her.

"Are you well, Coira?"

Niall's inquiry and hand on her elbow distracted her wayward thoughts, and she nodded.

William spoke then, as both he and Sarah were still present. Worry etched his features. "I've not seen you eat but a few nuts since you initially arrived within the MacLomain clan."

"He's right. When, besides those nuts, have you eaten?" Niall said, concerned.

She sighed. Those nuts had not stayed down. In fact, she'd experienced no hunger—save that brief moment with the horse—since initially traveling back in time and had eaten nothing. Fluids, yes, but no food. It had been just under a week and Coira tried to disregard the oddity. She had no weight on her before, therefore had no idea how she was still standing at this moment.

Though she hated to do it she lied. "Yes, I've eaten."

Their eyes narrowed on her. She'd never been much good at fibbing. William spoke first. "You lie, lass! You've not eaten beyond those nuts, have you?"

She swallowed hard, shook her head, and refused to meet his eyes.

William was quick, and his curt tone cut through any remaining deception. "And the nuts are no longer in your belly, aye?"

"Come. Now." He grabbed her arm and briskly led her through the crowd toward the food, Niall and Sarah right behind them. At the nearest trestle table he seized a bit of bannock, tore off a small piece, and handed it to her. "Eat this."

She shook her head. The sight of it rolled her stomach. "Please, no."

He took her hand and continued to pull her out the door into the cool air. Niall and Sarah remained with them appearing both confused and alarmed.

"Eat this, Coira. You must force yourself to. I'll not take no for an answer." William brought the morsel to her mouth.

She grimaced and took the bannock from his hand. "Why is this necessary?"

"Dinnae make me wait. Eat it."

She'd never heard such urgency and fear in his voice, so under the avid scrutiny of the three of them, she put the piece in her mouth, chewed thoroughly, and swallowed. "Are you happy now?"

"Maybe." William continued to watch her closely.

Unbelievable! How dare he? She was just about to tell him what she thought of his rude actions when nausea rolled through her. This time much faster than when she'd eaten the nuts. He must have clearly seen her expression for he whipped her around and leaned her over the far stair. To her horror, she lost the piece of bannock as well.

Mortified, she held still for several moments until the nausea receded. When she stood and turned back, they all were watching her intently. Fury and embarrassment made speech extremely difficult. "Please, leave me be. I'm fine."

William and Niall stepped forward at once and voiced their opinion simultaneously. "You are not fine!"

She raised her hands in the air to ward them off. "I am, please. Besides not being able to hold food down, do I strike you as ill?"

"Nay, lass, I'll not have it." Again William took her arm and led her back into the hall. "'Tis not normal, this, something is wrong. Perhaps we'll try some soup."

As they cleared the entrance and the cheerful crowd loomed ahead, a peculiar sensation overtook her. A sense of calm she'd never felt before. Though the throng of boisterous, celebrating clansmen and women danced and chatted before her, she could no longer hear them.

She had no fear.

Instead, she felt exhilarated as the sound of crashing waves filled her inner ear. The distant cry of a seagull caught in the wind.

Without thought, she turned her head and looked up at the massive tapestry of the Viking. How she wished she could touch that tapestry, but it hung too high.

Then, as if someone had leaned over and pulled her feet from beneath, she fell until the black of the tapestry consumed her.

And all else was lost.

****

Her blurred vision sharpened as she soared toward the Viking. The man at his feet remained frozen and immovable. Tall and heavily armored, the Viking bowed at her approach, turned to the rough sea behind him, and pointed at the distant horizon.

She had no control over her body and switched directions, flying over the sea. It was an odd sensation, as though she had no arms or legs, just vision. The ocean waves swelled and rolled in the moonlight. The air was scentless, saltless. Coira felt no heat or chill, nor wind on her face as she sped above the sea.

Then, high above the ocean, a cliff rose before her. On it stood a lone figure. As she drew closer, the form became that of a man. He stood tall and striking, his blond hair moved by a phantom wind. She raced forward until she hovered mere feet before him. His eyes were of the land, pure and direct.

His voice whispered in her mind, its essence of the forest. "I am Fionn Mac Cumhail. Do not be afraid."

She was not afraid. This man meant her no harm. Her inquiry rolled from her mind. "Where am I?"

"You are in Eire."

A flicker of green light poured forth from him and she was suddenly whole, her skirts whipping in the

~Sylvan Mist~

wind. She breathed deeply of the cool salty air and heard the crashing of waves against the cliff hundreds of feet below.

Coira spoke aloud. "Ireland?"

Fionn nodded and his gaze fell to her hand. "You must put the ring back on."

Startled, she looked to her bare finger, then back at him. "It is not my ring."

He took her hand in his, and she felt warmth fill her, loving warmth, as though from a caring parent.

"But it is your ring. You know that, my child."

She shook her head, an odd dread filling her. She did not want the ring to be hers. Her heart could not accept that. "Please, no. It is my sister's. It has to be, for it was given to her."

Fionn's appearance shifted to that of an old woman. Her motherly eyes encompassed Coira. "The ring is yours, so says the land of Eire." The woman's hand released hers and rose to Coira's heart. "In you is the land of Eire. You must wear the ring."

They spoke a form of Gaelic she was not familiar with, yet the words came easily, as though this language had always been on her tongue, unused. A familiar panic arose. "I don't love whom the stone glows for, nor will I ever."

Fionn's lips curved into a small smile that made her heart sore. She'd never felt such love. When the elderly woman spoke, her palm flattened against Coira's chest. "You will love whom the stone glows for, have no fear."

Coira felt a jolt release from Fionn's hand into her chest. A flood of energy, power, fire, and peace threaded through every vein in her body. Her bones, joints, tendons liquefied, until she was once again a hovering presence without form, her body gone.

~Sylvan Mist~

Fionn's form turned from an elderly woman back to that of a man in a blur of green mist. His eyes glowed brightly with moonlight, and his muscled body appeared to heighten as she felt herself being pulled away. Then he was far off, a fleck on the distant cliff. Still his words reached her. "I am one with the land, one with the forest, my Sylvan Mist, formed from all which is Ireland, will stay with you always." Then his whisper followed. "But that is our secret."

The sea rushed away in front of her until it faded into darkness, an abyss of foreign whispers. So many tongues speaking she couldn't discern what they said. Just that she was privileged to hear them. Then a horrible thunder ripped through her.

And the voices were no more.

~Sylvan Mist~

Chapter Eleven

"Coira?"

She heard the voice from far off. Recognized yet could not identify it.

"Coira? Open your eyes."

That was the last thing she wanted to do. She wished to return to the cliff. Return to Fionn.

"Coira, you must."

Adlin was speaking. She knew now. Yet the compulsion to return to Ireland, return to such peace and warmth remained overwhelming. She desired it as she'd desired nothing else before.

"Coira, do as he says, open your eyes."

She halted at the sound of that voice, not Adlin's. Her need for Ireland began to recede as he continued to urge her back, made her need Scotland again. Crave it. She opened her eyes and found William's face close to hers, his silver eyes concerned and urgent.

She traced the planes of his face with her eyes, so beautiful, masculine, and alive. Gone were the dimples of humor, in their place the shadowed alcove between his high cheekbones and strong jaw. Without hesitation, she reached up and touched his face, traced the angled slope.

She spoke softly. "I had such a wonderful dream."

He appeared speechless for a moment. Then he moved his face away. "I know."

"You do?" Coira realized that she was lying in a canopied bed. She blinked and looked around. Before she could evaluate her surroundings, two things struck with force.

The first was that not only was William there, but Adlin, Ferchar, and Iain. The second and by far the more daunting was that they wore robes. Adlin wore his usual white, as did Iain. Ferchar and William's were black. Oh dear God!

She tried to sit up, but William wouldn't allow it. "Nay, lass, stay where you are, dinnae move. You'll lose your bearings if you do."

She remained still. Her body felt so weak, brutalized. Therefore it was not a hard order to follow. "Where am I?"

"In my chamber." William remained sitting on the bed. "You've been here for a month, lass."

Instant nausea and fear swept over. She tried to speak but couldn't. Instead she closed her eyes and willed her stomach to settle. After several moments, she opened them again and swallowed.

When she tried to speak again, her vocal cords were agreeable. "So I am sick?"

"Nay." Adlin spoke and moved closer. "You are not sick."

Adlin continued as he sat on the other side of her. His kind, blue eyes were warm. "You have never been healthier, this I promise you."

She held his gaze. "I don't understand. A moment ago I was admiring the Viking tapestry, then... She left the rest of her statement unspoken and private.

Now Adlin's veined hand came to her cheek in a light caress. His eyes struck her as knowing, compassionate. "I ken, 'tis a lovely tapestry, that one."

She relaxed beneath his hand. "It is. I wanted to touch it desperately. It really is hung too high."

William chuckled and her gaze swung back to him. She had to admit he looked ravishing in black. And her newly impulsive tongue told him so. "Black suits you, my laird."

Interestingly, she was not shocked by her own words. She felt a new and unfamiliar sense of freedom and returned to talk of the tapestry. "It really is hung too high. Such a lovely bit of work, and one can't even touch its bottom skirts."

William's startling pewter gaze lost its concern and grew merry. "Most can, sprite. You're just a wee thing. That cannot be helped."

She smirked. "And you're all too bloody tall. Lower the tapestry."

As though everyone present in the room had vanished, he leaned forward a small fraction. "Mayhap if Niall approves, I'll lift you so that you can touch it."

This statement struck her an icy reminder of things she had forgotten. Had he done that intentionally? As she gazed into his eyes, she realized he had, not because he wanted to but because he had to, because of the others present. Something felt different within her. She suddenly saw William's emotions, saw his heart clearly, and it startled her. But now was neither the time nor the place to evaluate such newborn perception.

She was positive her observation was correct. How was that? Coira refocused on Adlin. "What's happened to me, then? Why are you all here dressed in robes?"

Adlin's pale blue eyes darkened. For a flicker of a breath, she felt the intensity of the magic he carried. "We're here because a great change has taken place within you, Coira. Can you tell me what you dreamt of all these long days?"

A shiver rippled down her spine causing nerve endings to sizzle. Though she longed to keep her

~Sylvan Mist~

dream journey secret, Coira knew she must share with them. As if they were truly her kin now, and to deny them the truth would be to shun her family. "I traveled to Ireland."

All four wizards came to rapt attention.

"I flew past the Viking in that tapestry, over the sea until I came to stand upon a high cliff." She paused, unwilling to share more.

Adlin's soft voice urged her on. "And who did you meet there, child?"

She looked from man to man until her gaze settled on her hands. "A man, no, a woman, well, a bit of both, named Fionn Mac Cumhail."

Though no one spoke right away, she felt the mixture of interest, apprehension, and tension that saturated each of them.

"You know of him then?" Coira looked to Adlin.

"Aye, lass, we do. He is considered a mythical creature now but was in fact a man of magic who lived for hundreds of years. He was of the forest, one with the animals." Adlin's eyes returned to their normal brilliant blue.

"Why would I see him? I don't understand."

"He wanted to give you a gift." He looked to William though continued to speak to her. "A gift of magic."

William appeared as startled as her. Adlin's gaze returned to Coira. "Do you ken, lass?"

Speechless, she shook her head. Blood pounded through her body, overtaking senses. Magic? She had magic? No, her brother, sister, and mother had magic. William, Ferchar, Iain, Adlin, and Niall, they had magic, but her? What foolishness.

Adlin took her hand and squeezed it. "Ireland gave you magic. Fionn gave you magic."

At last, Coira found her voice, wobbly as it was. "That's impossible."

"Anything is possible." Adlin smiled. "And you've the touch now, just as strong as any of us here."

Her eyes widened and an unmistakable fear filled her. "How could I be as strong as you? Aren't you four the most powerful in…"

Her voice trailed off. Adlin must be mistaken.

"'Tis not for me to question why you have been given such power, Coira." The elderly wizard again squeezed her hand in reassurance. "Just accept that you have, and you've much to learn."

She refused to meet William's eyes or for that matter anyone's but Adlin's. Her feelings crossed between mortification and unworthiness. After all these years, her entire life, she now had what she'd always sought, magic, and enough so that these great wizards would all be present when she awoke. It was staggering information and difficult to swallow. But she knew Adlin would not lie to her, had no reason to.

She gathered what little confidence she felt and asked the next logical question. "And who will teach me to use this magic?"

"Iain. He will be your mentor." Adlin looked to his fellow wizard.

She tried to mask her timid internal response when she met Iain's eyes. "Why you?"

Adlin answered her. "His magic is more kindred to yours than either Ferchar's or William's."

She didn't know what to say to this, had no real understanding of what separated the wizards from one another.

"You will learn quickly, lass. He will teach you well." Adlin stood. "Are you hungry?"

Her stomach rumbled in response, and fire flooded her face with embarrassment. "Yes."

~Sylvan Mist~

Adlin smiled, nodded to Iain and Ferchar and headed for the door urging them to follow. "I'll have food sent right up."

Fionn's request slammed in to her. "Oh!"

"Aye?" Adlin stopped at the door.

"I'm to put the ring back on." She shrugged slightly. "That's what Fionn said."

Adlin's eyes shifted color once again as he stared at her then nodded. "I will have Niall bring the ring to you, Coira."

The three wizards departed and left her alone with William. At last, because she had little choice, she met his eyes. He wore a speculative look. Then he surprised her by taking her hand. "Dinnae be afraid, lass."

She held his gaze, entranced by what she saw there. "What makes you think I am?"

He brought his hand to her chest, over her heart. "I can feel it, here."

"What else can you feel, William?" She felt emboldened, free with her words. Afraid to learn she held magic, yes, but unafraid of how she felt toward him regardless of her destiny with Niall.

Though his gaze turned stern, his eyes could not hide what she sought. His voice deepened, grew husky. "I feel lo—"

"And she awakens at last!" Niall's voice broke through William's statement as efficiently as a knife through a grass blade.

William released her hand and stood, facing his friend. "I'll leave you two." He looked back to Coira, his eyes now devoid of emotion. "You will be up and about soon, lass. 'Tis nearly Hogmanay, and the celebrations shall be grand, especially now that you are with us again."

She dropped her eyes from his and nodded. How she hated Niall's arrival just now. Hated her desire to understand more clearly these feelings between herself and William.

William closed the door and left her and Niall alone. She looked to him and patted the side of the bed. "Come sit, my lord."

Niall sat down and offered a smile, his green eyes raking her face with concern. "How do you feel, Coira?"

"Good. Hungry."

He laughed. "I would imagine. You've been without food for a long time."

She sat up a bit. "You mean no one has administered any sort of... well, have I been without food for over a month?"

He nodded. "You have."

"How is that possible? I should be dead by now."

He sighed. "It seems you were put through a fast. Though it amazes me, you're alive and well."

"A fast?" She grimaced. "I don't understand, not at all."

Niall appeared uncomfortable for a moment. "'Tis what happens before one takes on magic. The novice must fast, free the body of food. In your case, it was done for you against your will."

She snorted. "I have had very little free will since I've been with the MacLomains. An imposed fast does not surprise me in the least."

"The MacLomains had nothing to do with your fast."

"No?" She chuckled.

"No. As I've been told, 'twas someone else."

Another shiver ran through her. Fionn. Ireland. It was him for sure. That must be the reason neither William nor any of the other wizards had sensed her fast. It was not of their making.

A tap resounded on the door, and Niall gave permission to enter. A servant girl brought a tray over and set it on the table next to Coira, bowed slightly and then left the room. Her mouth watered at the array of meats and hard cheeses.

She ate ravenously while they chatted. She'd never been this hungry in her life. After she popped the last bit of cheese in her mouth, Niall handed her a glass of wine, and she drank deeply. Sated, comfortable, and somewhat drowsy, she leaned back. "So what have I missed around here?"

"Christmastide." He gave her a lopsided grin.

"Oh no! Really? Such a shame, I believe I would have liked to have been part of Christmastide here." Her thoughts drifted momentarily to home. Had such a long period of time passed there? She hoped not, her poor mother and father. And James!

"Yes, Christmastide was lovely, if a bit subdued, I'm afraid." Niall finally took her hand in his.

"Subdued?" Coira sunk down and relaxed. She wasn't alerted by his statement knowing full well William would have told her if something was amiss with Annie.

"But of course, Coira, you've been lost to all of us for a long while. Not even Adlin could assure us you would awaken."

She gazed into his eyes, sad now. He truly cared about her. He was in love with her. Window after window was being opened, and the emotions of those around her became exceptionally clear. Gone was the speculation. And as such dawning struck her, she realized how exhausted Niall looked, how drained William had looked.

"Oh my, I'm so sorry. How is Annie? I should see her immediately."

~Sylvan Mist~

She went to sit forward, but Niall gently pushed her back. "Your sister is fine. She knows that you're awake now, and all is well. She will wait until you've rested some more."

"Wait? Annie? Never. My sister has no patience." She relaxed again and smiled.

Niall offered a wry grin. "Honestly, we all had to hold her back from running to you, but Arthur is a big man, not much can get by him."

"I believe you might be right about that!" She grinned and her eyelids grew heavier.

"I will leave you now to slumber, my lady." Niall stood.

Her eyes regained their balance, and she held tight to his hand. "Wait, Niall. I must have the ring back."

"Oh, yes." He fished it out of an errant pocket. "Here it is."

He lifted her hand and slid the ring back onto her finger. As he did, an amazing feeling of peace surrounded her, and she felt the presence of Fionn somewhere within her. Ireland, waves crashing against a cliff, moonlight on water. She knew that she would never again remove this ring.

It was hers.

She nearly told Niall how strongly she felt about the ring but stopped when she saw the look on his face. "What is it, Niall?"

His eyes rose from the ring and met hers. "Look at it."

She dropped her gaze to the ring and gasped. The diamond center no longer glowed.

~Sylvan Mist~

~Sylvan Mist~

Chapter Twelve

William rode his steed at a leisurely pace through the silent, dark forest. Days before, there had been another skirmish with the Cochrans along the northern border. Their wizards were able to get past the MacLomain allied clans to the north and south using magic. It had not been a major battle by any means; the Cochrans had numbered thirty and whisked away through magic when it became obvious they would lose the fight.

Their wizards would no longer leave valuable mortal men behind, which told William they'd grown more cautious since the fight in the woods when Coira and Annie had first arrived. They saved their fighters merely for added manpower in the war to come, not out of value for human life.

He had left the castle the morning after seeing Coira. Of that he was grateful. It had been difficult to see her and not speak of the torture her strange slumber had put him through. The living hell he had endured, waking day after day to see her small frame motionless in his bed. He'd given Niall the chamber next to his and moved to the one Coira had originally been in.

Night after night, he'd smelled her scent on the small cot, dreamt of her eyes, face, and soul. He wished that he could take her place so she would again be full of life and spirit.

When Adlin summoned them to her chamber that day and requested they come robed, he knew a powerful force was at work. When Coira awoke, his relief was so intense it pained him. When he learned that she now carried magic as potent as his, he had been both shocked and mysteriously elated.

The outer portcullis opened as he flew across the field. The salty wind died when he crossed the drawbridge and entered the inner compound. The hour was late and all quiet. He swung down from his horse, turned away the stable boy who ran out to meet him, and walked his mount into the stables. He enjoyed the ritual of brushing down his horse and ensuring its feed.

Before he left the stalls, he stopped before the great black stallion Coira had ridden. "You've a wild spirit, lad. We'll not be able to break you, will we? Only her."

The horse scuffed his hoof, whinnied, and threw back his head in answer.

William laughed. "So I'm right."

He left the stables and entered the hall. Not a soul stirred. 'Twas the eve of Hogmanay and the preparations had already ended. He climbed the stairs, entered Coira's previous chamber, removed his clothing, and lay down. Her scent engulfed and lulled him quickly to sleep.

The dream arose, white and blinding. Snow covered the mountain slope, hid her from him, but not his enemy. The archwizard knelt in the snow, obscuring Coira. He sat back and looked across the way at William.

Horror and rage filled William. "Release her." His scream of fury was a whisper on the wind.

~Sylvan Mist~

The Cochran wizard cast a sidelong glance his way. "Interesting that you chose words over action. Do you ken the difference? The result of such foolishness?"

The enemy snickered and pulled free his sword.

Overwhelming fear seized William, and he surged forward only to find himself standing on the field before his castle. Coira was high astride her stallion. Springtime bloomed all around. The grass was a brilliant green, the loch sparkling blue beneath the warm sun. A wide array of animals peppered the field behind her, red deer, arctic foxes, birds, raccoons, wild boars.

As he'd seen it when they raced toward the castle together at the beginning, wildflowers covered the field and spread before her. Now there were many more, every color of the rainbow and every shade in between. Her hair was alive in flight, the ebony tresses trailing and mixing with the horse's tail in the wind.

He'd never seen anything so mesmerizing, enchanting. As Coira neared, she swung down from her horse and ran the remaining distance to him. He lifted and swung her around. How long had it been since he last felt her in his arms? As he lowered her to the ground, her arms locked around his neck and brought his lips to hers.

So soft, sweet, giving, he held her tight, crushing her body against his. He murmured her name, relished the taste of it on his tongue. "Coira, my sprite, how I've missed you."

"Coira!"

The single word slammed shut one reality and opened another. Took away one woman and gave him another. He pried open his eyes. Early twilight filled his chamber, and Sarah filled his arms.

****

~Sylvan Mist~

Coira was glad to be up and about. Just yesterday, she'd left William's chamber for the first time in nearly five weeks. And how wonderful it was to be here at such a time, for this marked the last day of 1225. And, as was becoming quite apparent, the Scottish celebrated the New Year, Hogmanay, with more relish then she'd ever witnessed in America.

"Isn't this so exciting?" Annie was jumping out of her skin.

"It is, actually." Coira laughed, spirits high. Perhaps her good mood was a remnant of the mug of spiced ale she was served first thing when she awoke and throughout the day, as was tradition on Hogmanay. Or perhaps it was for another reason altogether, which instantly made her feel guilty.

As though her sister read her mind, Annie shook her head and bit her lip. "I still can't believe the stone no longer glows for you and Niall."

Coira sat down at a trestle table in the great hall. "I know. I'm as shocked as you."

Annie sat next to her, both of them facing away from the table. "Poor Niall, he's taken with you, that one is."

"It's strange it would suddenly stop glowing." Coira kept a schooled expression. Though it had been painful to see Niall's reaction, or lack thereof, she could not dispute her acute relief. She was fond of Niall, but knew she could never love him.

"I wonder if it has anything to do with you having magic now, which I still find unbelievable. I can't wait for you to learn how to use it. Better yet, wait until Mother hears about this." Annie grew quiet at this last statement, and Coira knew that they were both wondering if and when they would see their parents again.

The setting sun cast a long orange glow onto the animal furs lining the hall. She'd slept away most of her day and felt glorious and refreshed.

She wore a lavish velvet gown of such a dark shade of blue it appeared almost black. Little beads dyed pale blue ran around her waist and formed a V near her lower stomach. The same beads were sewn into the low neckline and along the outer rims of the long, sweeping sleeves. She felt like a princess.

Though both she and Annie did not, some women wore barbettes and filets. Not one wore a face veil however. Coira had never been fond of any sort of hat so she was glad it was not customary within this clan.

Annie sipped from her goblet of wine and eyed her curiously. "Did you know that William has returned?"

"Really?" She cursed her quick response but couldn't help it.

Her sister giggled. "Aye, he's been outside helping to light multiple bonfires on the field for some time. Poor Sarah was in a bit of a snit this morn, I'm afraid. It seems William ended their little affair last night."

"Has he now?" Coira drank from her goblet, enjoying the warmth of it in her limbs. She couldn't deny the news pleased her.

Annie nodded. "I'm sure it has to do with the ring and you! Anyway, this eve should be an incredible celebration. The snow has held off, and the air is unseasonably mild, or so says the clan. They believe it's because the gods are in favor of them in this upcoming war."

"I see." She was half listening. So William had returned. She wondered what he would make of the ring not glowing. Did he already know? Had Niall told him?

"There's something I would like to share with you, Coira," Annie said softly.

~Sylvan Mist~

Detecting the slight urgency in her sister's voice, she gave Annie her undivided attention. "What is it?"

"Well." Annie fiddled with the rim of her goblet and blushed furiously. "Something's happened, changed."

She became alarmed. "Annie, are you all right?"

"There ye are, lasses." Arthur's booming voice filled the hall when he entered from outside. He had ridden with William, so she'd not seen him since she awoke.

Annie leapt off the bench and ran into his arms. He gave her a good swing before issuing a thorough kiss. Coira knew her mouth hung open in astonishment but was unable to shut it. Then, as the couple turned her way, it dawned on her exactly what her sister had been about to tell her. It seemed the two had been intimate.

Arthur held Annie's hand and looked to Coira. "How are you feeling, lass?"

She smiled, her gaze traveling from her sister to him. "Good, thank you. It's nice to be amongst the living again."

"I can well imagine." He beamed down at Annie. "Have you told her the good news?"

Annie blushed profusely and shook her head. "I was just about to when you strode in."

"Good news?" Coira barely managed to push the words out of her mouth. It couldn't be.

"Aye." Annie looked shyly up at Arthur. "There's to be a wedding tonight."

Annie looked her way. "Arthur and I are getting married."

"Married!" Coira stood.

Annie released Arthur's hand and came to stand directly before Coira. Her heart was in her eyes. "I know it seems sudden to you, but it really isn't all that sudden for us. We've spent a lot of time together over the last months, nearly every day actually. Will you give us your blessing, Coira?"

Still stunned, she remained motionless. "What of our parents, Annie? You can't marry without them present. And what do you intend to do, stay here?"

Now Annie became the reasonable, logical sister. "Our parents are not here. You are. And I can marry without them present; neither of us knows if and when we'll go back. You know that."

Annie was right. They didn't know what fate intended for them. Arianna and Caitlin had both returned to their times, but circumstances had already varied considerably for Coira and Annie. And if her sister found the right man and was eager to marry, who was she to stop her?

Coira's gaze drifted to Arthur. He stood silently, watching her, eyes direct. She saw no deception there, only compassion. Hope. "Do you love my sister, sir?"

"With all my heart." His response came instantly and genuinely.

She took Annie's hands and looked deep into her golden eyes. "And are you in love with Arthur?"

A sheen of moisture glistened over the gold and turned Annie's eyes bronze. "Aye, more than you can possibly imagine."

Coira's emotions bubbled up and a tear slipped free. "Then I suppose you have my blessing."

The two sisters embraced one another tightly. Now she understood why Annie had traveled back in time. Not for William but for Arthur MacLomain, her one true love. A strange sensation rushed through her at that realization. Relief? Though she knew the ring had glowed for her and Niall, that fact had not entirely wiped clean the possibility of Annie and William ending up together.

She pulled back from her sister and eyed her beautiful crème-colored dress. She touched Annie's chestnut hair. "We really should adorn your hair with something."

"Now that I can help with!" Arianna had just walked down the stairs. In her hand, she carried a ring of white and pink flowers. She walked up to Annie, placed it on her head, and secured it.

"Oh, they're lovely." Coira admired Annie and lightly ran her finger over one of the petals. "How are these flowers possible in December?"

Arianna giggled and wiggled her fingers. "It must be magic!"

"What's this about magic?" Iain came up behind Arianna, wrapped his arms around her waist, and nuzzled her neck.

She leaned against him and smiled, her head turning and tilting back to look up at him. "Annie looks beautiful in your mother's wedding gown, aye?"

His eyes dragged from Arianna to look at Annie. "She looks wonderful. Almost as lovely as you did, the day you wore it."

Arianna elbowed him playfully and pulled away. "Should we all go down to the bonfires then?"

Everyone agreed and the five of them left the castle. They walked through the boisterous community overflowing both the inner compound and beyond the outer wall where the fires blazed brightly in the dusky shadow of twilight.

Many men still carried their weapons, wary of their persistent enemy. Women gossiped while others danced, spinning in circles, their skirts colorful bells in the night. Children ran and played, causing mischief wherever they could.

~Sylvan Mist~

As they drew closer to the fire, the lively music stopped and the crowd grew silent. She nudged Annie. "What's going on?"

Annie shook her head. "I have no idea."

Just then a lone bagpipe began to play. Hauntingly beautiful, the sound rose into the sky and wrapped itself around the MacLomain clan. Coira closed her eyes as the music seeped into her. She felt its message swell within her soul.

There was sadness and loss within the melody. But love as well, an ending and a new beginning, freedom at last. She understood that it was the magic inside of her translating the song of the pipe, the mourning of its player. Her eyes snapped open, and she pushed through the cluster of people until she stood along the inner wall of clansfolk.

Her heart thudded heavily inside her chest at the sight. Five bonfires were clearly visible and at least thirty feet apart from each other forming a wide circle around William.

He stood alone in the center playing the pipe, radiant in his masculine beauty. He wore calf-high black boots and his plaid, which wrapped over one wide shoulder. A large battle-axe was strapped to his back, and his hair was free save for one small braid on either side. The firelight carved every fine-honed muscle in his stomach, torso, chest, and arms.

A burning sensation thrummed through her veins and filled her body with such seizing fire she felt winded. Though his eyes didn't look her way and remained focused on something distant, she heard his words clearly within her mind.

Look to the distant hill, lass.

Reluctantly she did, oddly compelled to obey, and her eyes went to the slope in the distance overlooking the dark, faceless loch.

~Sylvan Mist~

A young woman stood alone. Her dark hair thick, lush, and blowing twisted around her lithe frame. As her new magic came to life, Coira could easily make out the woman's far off features in the night. She was lovely, surreal, at peace. Coira looked around. It was obvious no one else saw her standing there. Who was she?

Then Adlin's white robes became apparent when he appeared on the hill and stood beside the woman. She turned his way, smiled, and embraced him. And as the enchanting pipe music finally trailed to an end and its last singularly devastating note rose into the highland sky, the woman faded leaving the wizard standing alone. Coira suddenly felt Adlin's sadness and that of William, Ferchar, Iain, Arianna, and Muriel.

The crowd remained silent for many moments while William lowered the pipe and set it aside. Then he flung his arms in the air and cried to his clan, his commanding voice carried wide and far. "'Tis the last day of this year, my fine folk, let us now be merry and celebrate!"

With that the crowd burst to life, pouring forth into the area between the fires as others took up the pipe and another round of spirited music began. She stood unmoving, wondering what had just happened. There was such a thick throng of people around she couldn't see two feet in front of her.

Out of nowhere, William appeared and loomed tall before her. Her breath caught at his nearness, his upper nudity. *Thump. Thump. Thump.* Her heart raced. It was one thing seeing him unclothed in a dream, quite another seeing him in reality, a tangible blood and flesh man. The persistent movement of people around them pushed him closer. For a man of his height and stature, he gave very little if any resistance to the tidal wave of kinsmen.

They were in their own small room where the walls were made of human flesh and heat. Where for just this moment in time nothing really existed but them. He smelled of the forest and spice. Her eyes inevitably traveled from his kilted waistline up his torso, over his shoulder to the heavy blades of the axe. From there they traveled slowly to his face. A staggering swell of desire poured a blaze of need over her skin, into her pores, until it liquefied her bones. Lord help her, this was maddening!

With his forefinger and thumb, he gently cupped her chin and tilted back her head. His eyes glowed, their diamond intensity crawling inside and exploring. When he spoke, his words were within her mind, erotically hypnotic and magical. "You are the most beautiful lass I've ever seen, Coira."

A bolt of feminine lust intertwined with her very proper, respectable response. "Thank you. You look handsome as well."

His eyes flared, primal and intense. He was aroused, eager. A low masculine growl filled her mind, ,heart, and lower body, as though the very air around them vibrated.

"There you are!"

Annie's timing had never been good, and Coira almost cursed aloud but bit her tongue. After all, it was an important day for her sister. She flexed her taut cheek muscles and offered Annie a wide, dazzling smile. Or at least that's how she hoped it appeared. "Yes, here I am!"

Annie was followed by Arthur, Ferchar, and Caitlin. Arianna, Iain, and Muriel were nowhere to be seen. Her sister turned caring eyes on William. "You play the pipe with expertise, my laird. It was an exquisite tribute."

Coira remained silent, remembering the way the bagpipe music had made her feel. Tact held her tongue. For whom was that music played?

"William has always had a talent with the pipe," Ferchar said, nodding. "Iosbail is pleased. It was a lovely reminder of her life."

Iosbail! Adlin's sister, William's mentor. A shiver ran through her as she realized that was why William had urged her to look at the hill. She'd just seen Iosbail's ghost!

"She's pleased with you, lass."

She met William's eyes, now their normal light gray. His assurance proved comforting somehow. She spoke aloud. "It was the most mesmerizing thing I've ever heard."

A smile touched his eyes, not his lips. "Thank you."

William turned his regard to Arthur. "I believe we've a wedding to attend, aye?"

Arthur pulled Annie close and appeared the happiest man alive. "I believe we do!"

~Sylvan Mist~

Chapter Thirteen

William watched Coira as Annie took her last vows and became Arthur's wife. They stood inside the small chapel located in the inner compound. Muriel and Arianna had provided a magically enhanced outpouring of climbing roses which covered nearly every available beam, column, and spindle in the dwelling.

In the midst of the perfumed air and the backdrop of deep crimson roses and leaves, he found himself mesmerized and enthralled by Coira.

Her dark velvet dress wrapped her tiny waist and amplified the slight flare of her hips and the swell of her cleavage. As they stood witness to the ceremony, she presented an angled profile. Her long, black hair curled more than usual and her big blue eyes turned luminescent framed by thick, tear- soaked eyelashes.

A roar of approval rose up from the people crowded within the building, breaking his reverie. Arthur dipped down and scooped up Annie. He faced his clan and winked. "Enjoy the festivities, my friends. You'll not see me or my lass again for many days!"

Everyone laughed as Arthur made his way through the crowd, his wife nestled snugly in his arms. Coira squeezed Annie's hand just before the lass was carried away.

William stood silently, waiting while everyone filtered out. Coira knelt before the crucifix hung above.

Her head was bent in prayer as this was her place of worship. He looked to the flowers again, nature and Mother Earth swirling within them, and he offered his own prayer for the couple newly married.

At last Coira rose and turned, cheeks wet and rosy. "Thank you for staying behind, William."

He reached up and wiped away the moisture from both cheeks. "Where else would I be?"

Her startling eyes rose to his. "You are a good friend, perhaps one of the best I've ever had."

He reached over and picked a rose. With a swipe of his finger over the stem, he removed its thorns and magically ensured its life without its vine. It would not die. Carefully, he tucked it behind her ear. "I will always be your friend, Coira."

William pulled her close and held her. He pillowed her head on his chest and helped calm her heart. She'd been through so much, more than any mortal or gifted woman should have to endure.

And now she was one of them.

Iain would teach her everything he knew. Help her understand the unique magic she carried and how it tied with the Christian God she worshiped, just as Iain's did. He still wondered at the purpose behind her newfound magic but knew Adlin would share when he was ready, for he was fairly certain that Adlin understood everything.

When she was ready, Coira pulled back and smiled up at him. "Shall we rejoin the festivities?"

"Aye." He took her hand and led her down the aisle until they emerged again into the crowd. Now out of the chapel, his thoughts turned instantly back to desire, and the ring.

Oh yes, the ring!

He'd already spoken with Niall and knew it no longer glowed for them. Shamefully, William had almost declared a holiday when he was given the news. He felt horrible for his friend but elated at the same time.

Though the stone still did not glow for his eyes, he didn't care. Nor did he think Coira did. As long as it glowed for no one else, she was his to pursue. And he would until his dying breath. He did not release her hand as they walked back over the drawbridge. Her small, delicate hand, softly cupped in his.

William drew in a ragged breath. He had no desire to return to the festivities. "Come with me, lass. I want to show you something."

He didn't miss the relief on her face when he detoured around the bulk of dancing party-goers. Following the rim of the outer curtain wall, they made their way over the dark field closest to the forest line until they reached the far side and entered the dense woodland opposite the castle.

Because of her magic, he knew that her night vision was vastly improved. With no moon overhead, the enveloping darkness would've blinded a mortal. He was vividly aware of her scent and texture as they traveled deeper into the woods. The air cooled, and a wind shuffled the bare branches far overhead.

"Where are we going?" Her whisper made obvious her eagerness and tempered desire.

He stirred at her words, her longing, and decided this method of travel was not sufficient. Turning back, he pulled her close. "Dinnae be afraid."

She nestled close. "I'm not."

With that, he summoned his magic and transported them.

****

Coira breathed in the scent of his skin, closed her eyes, and rubbed her cheek against his chest. She loved the feel of his magic, how it engulfed and made her feel whole.

He had been so wonderful tonight. She hadn't thought that seeing Annie marry would be so difficult. How she wished her parents could've been there to see her sister glowing with love for Arthur. As they took their vows, Coira envisioned herself and Annie as children, young adults, and then adults, and all that they'd shared together.

She could still see Annie at seven running ahead of the family on Christmas Eve eager to pick out the tree, so full of energy and zest. Then she remembered Annie at seventeen in love for the first time. Or so she had thought. She recalled the boy who broke her heart when he went to work at another gristmill down in Methuen and met the daughter of its owner. He had ceased ties with Annie and left her to lick her wounds.

But her sister had bounced back as was her way and started to pen stories. Though exceptionally talented, she was not yet published. It mattered little to her though, because she had found what she loved. And now she had Arthur. Their wedding had been beautiful and stirred Coira.

"Coira?"

She pulled back at the deep rumble of William's voice against her ear. Lord, the man was handsome.

"Yes?"

"We're here."

Before she had a chance to respond, his hands encased her neck and cheeks, and his mouth covered hers. It was not a peaceful feeling she felt when his lips touched hers but a wild frenzy of passion. She whimpered into his mouth and gave as harshly as she received.

With the tortured expression of a chieftain denying his clan the right to live, he reluctantly pulled away, his words a broken, jagged sound. "Come."

She tried to catch her breath as he led them the few remaining steps into a clearing. It was stunning… unbelievable, ripped the last gasp of air from her lungs. "Oh my…"

They were in a grove of ancient, towering oak trees. A small stream cut through one side, running off from an unseen drop, just enough so that the sound of water falling could be heard. The remainder of the clearing was a bed of thick wildflowers—in December?

In starlight, everything was devoid of color.

"I came here often as a boy. Here, lying within the circle of these trees, I had my first vision." He took her hands and pulled her forward, while he walked backwards.

She gazed around again, met his eyes, and smiled as she pictured him as a young boy. She would've liked to have seen him then. "It's incredible, William."

Then she felt something stir in her, magic perhaps. Elation overcame his features, and he pulled her within inches of him. He brought his hand to her forehead, between and above her eyes, and ran his finger in a quick pattern before removing it. "Look again."

He pulled back and waited.

She blinked when the world changed, transformed. This can't be real! Though the physical objects remained, they were flooded with life and color. She stepped back and turned in a slow circle. The oak trees had turned to glowing silver. The thick trunks and every pinstripe branch shone with diamond veins, cocooning them in a sphere of throbbing brilliance.

The wildflowers beneath them were a mixture of yellow, red, and purple. Her eyes traveled to the stream. It shone a light, shimmering blue. Every pebble and stone was white, some partially covered with a rich, green moss.

As if the last thread of the woman she had become in New Hampshire was yanked free, Coira instantly felt the jubilance of childhood engulf. She thought back to her youth and how she'd decided at the tender age of six it would be best to act like a lady and not give into the throes that Annie was so famous for. Why had she ever decided such a thing? As her past rushed in, she shuddered.

She should have helped pick out the Christmastide tree! She should have never made a point to walk as though a book balanced on her head at eight! And why on Ireland's green earth had she wanted to be English?

The last thought staggered her. She stumbled to the stream, dropping to her knees. The flowers were warm through the fabric of her dress, as if touched recently by the sun. She plunged her hands into the crystalline water; it too was warm. Coira cupped the blue water in her palms, enchanted that it remained blue against the pale backdrop of her palm.

She flung back her head and laughed. Then she tossed the water into the air. Without a second thought, she moved into the water, scooped and splashed it over her. Kneeling in the stream, the water only came up to her upper thigh but how sumptuous it felt!

Then William was there too, kneeling with her, laughing with her. "'Tis wonderful, aye, lass?"

She continued laughing and splashed him with water. "Scotland is wonderful!"

"Och, sprite, I could've told you that!" He ran a large hand along the water's surface and flung a hearty amount of water her way.

She sputtered under the onslaught. "Not fair, your hands are bigger than mine!"

With that statement, she went wild, splashing him as quickly as she could and laughing with an abandon she'd thought lost to her. He retaliated and splashed back, soaking her thoroughly, while he laughed just as hard. She was so engaged in the haze of splashing she didn't see him coming until he was there, and her hand met with male flesh.

His laughing stopped and his voice thickened. "Coira."

She stopped, breathing hard, aware of the heat beneath her fingers and looked at him. "Aye?"

They'd shifted back to Gaelic. When, she had no idea. All she could see was William, soaked, his dark hair plastered against his head. Tiny droplets of water fell from his hair-roughened chin and trickled down his neck.

"I want you, Coira." His hand fell to her wrist and traveled up her arm until it encompassed half of her neck.

"I know, and I you," she whispered and brought her other hand to his cheek, caressed it, and then dropped a finger to his lips just as he was about to speak. "Don't talk anymore, William."

He moved so quickly she could only compare the movement to a seasoned warrior, one who saw opportunity and moved before the enemy knew he was upon them. But William was not her enemy. No. He lifted her out of the water and carried her mere feet before he laid her down in the bed of wildflowers. Even warmer air rushed in causing a snake of mist and fog to drift throughout the oak trunks until they were encased by blue color and mist.

Instead of using magic, William removed her sodden dress inch by inch, kissing the flesh left in its wake. It was incredibly arousing watching and feeling her breasts break free... then her stomach and legs. His sizzling hot tongue laved and worshiped and she almost felt like some sort of ancient goddess. A mythological creature who existed in pure sensuality, who teased and aroused her man almost as much if not more, than he did her.

Full and heavy, her breasts heaved beneath his attention. She groaned when he sucked, then bit, then licked her pebbled nipples. A small part of her wanted to cover herself, say this was wrong, but that small part meant nothing and the notion quickly vanished when his tongue began to move in slow, featherlike circles over her belly.

"You're so tiny. So perfect," he breathed against her eager skin. His hands encircled the whole of her waist as his teeth skimmed over the delicate inclines of her hipbones.

Coira's eyes drifted shut as sensation after sensation swamped her, left her limbless, without thought, structure, or coherence. His hands traveled the length of her, studying every curve as though he memorized her dimensions. As though he was willing to do so for the remainder of his days... as though the mere action was the only thing keeping him alive.

"Oh, my." Her words were a breathy moan.

He murmured a barely coherent sentiment against her inner thigh. "I thought you said not to speak."

She could give no response when he spread her legs wide, when his tongue began to explore the delicate folds of her private place. Strangely enough, she didn't feel shy. She didn't try to stop him. No, she wanted this. She wanted him tasting her this way, she wanted him to adore her this way. She was beautiful because he loved her like this. It almost felt as though she could see through his eyes. He'd never been so eager for a woman in his life.

Groaning, eager, feral, he roughly grabbed her thighs and dove. Swooping, determined, downright hungry, he feasted and took as he covered her core with undivided attention. With a strange sounding keen she didn't recognize as her own, Coira grabbed the back of his head and arched. She didn't care if she bucked. She didn't care if he thought her wanton as pleasure tore through her body. Crying out, she broke into uncontrollable tremors. Whimpering, she released his head and turned her face into the cool flowers.

My heart. My poor, poor heart.

The trees overhead seemed to lower, the flowers grew, and their perfume became richer. The trickling stream became a crashing roar, and the mist a dancing pulse of moisture in the corner of her eye.

William's body slowly rose up and covered hers. Carefully, as though he found her rare and delectable, his tongue snaked out and licked away her tears.

Slow, easy minutes past before he stopped and stared down. It was as if he allowed her heart to gain some balance... as though he himself needed to gain some balance.

When he at last stared down at her it was with a dominance she didn't recognize. But it was dominance. She belonged to him. Would always belong to him.

Pushing her legs wide, his strong hand slowly engulfed her inner thigh and pushed it up and up. In that one simple, almost gentle movement, with eyes staring into hers, he laid claim. He made her feel his masculine strength, made her fully aware that he was a powerful man and she but a small lass beneath him.

It didn't matter why he did it... she liked it, needed it, needed him. Coira whispered, "Please."

It might have been the breathy plea. It might have been pure need, but William's pupils flared and he thrust sharply. She cried out, the sensation so intense and perfect. He stretched and filled her, took up every little part of her. What they'd experienced in a dream couldn't nearly touch this. He thrust so hard and thorough it almost felt as though he tried to push away every other man that'd been in her life. It was as if he knew that with the pure pleasure of his body filling hers, she'd forget them all.

He was right.

The air thickened, became more humid, and his being was all she had in this vast world, this unknown place of such exquisite ecstasy and pleasure. When his lips took hers, she became someone else. Left completely and finally all that she had been to become the person she would be.

She returned thrust for thrust, no longer afraid to meet him as an equal. As her newfound power rushed through, he met her with equal fervor. Fevered and profound, he moved deeper into her soul, knocked down every last defense she may have hidden, and plunged her into the blinding abyss of truly new beginnings. Gave her his view of her, how she looked to him.

Her mind and body was pushed over the edge, and they both cried out harshly when he thrust so hard his seed gushed into her. Her limbs went numb as her womb clenched with greed. She locked him within her potent release and they moaned, unable to stop the endless sweeps of mutual pleasure.

Blissful peace overwhelmed as he lay upon her, keeping his weight from crushing her. He moved slightly, and she shuddered yet again and held him close. She was still unable to speak, to move. She felt paralyzed, caught in a surreal place.

Then, as if her body ordered it, she abruptly fell asleep.

****

William knew the moment she slumbered. Felt her body relax beneath his, and saw her face smooth with sleep. Carefully, with the reluctance of a man turning away a loch full of gold, he moved off her.

She belonged here, in the forest, with nature at her feet. He leaned on his elbow and stared down at her. If he could live the rest of his life in this clearing with her, he gladly would, whether the damned ring ever glowed for them or not. Coira's lips curled up as though she had heard his thoughts.

How utterly beautiful she looked lying there, damp hair drying amongst the wildflowers, lips swollen and dark pink from his kisses.

He ran the back of his finger down her cheek. She had been reborn this eve. To watch her release the last of what she'd been before had been a humbling experience. Gone was his prim Englishwoman and in her place an enchanting lass who had accepted her heritage and was willing to embrace her new gift.

His eyes traced the contours of her body until they fell to her hand. Slowly, gently, he lifted her palm to his lips, kissed it tenderly and whispered his heart against her warm skin.

"I love you, Coira."

****

The great white eagle flew past the fires burning low on the field below and saw them clearly as the five points of the pentagram.

He flapped his wings and flew northbound along the loch's shore. Nor the mountains nor water beneath could be discerned save for the midnight definition caught within the keen eye of magic. The eagle caught the flow of wind newly born and swooped low, skimming the pointy tips of the pines.

With a sharp turn he banked left until he saw what he sought. By magic, light, and love, like a private beacon in the night, he knew that they had found one another.

And, as though the gods of old wished to make a mockery of him, the haven of light beneath turned to pitch. Blood clouded where there had once been magic and love. Devastation ravaged the heart and left it barren.

With a horrendous cry of pain, Adlin turned again toward the castle in the far, far distance and flapped his wings. Why? What purpose did this serve? As the wind worked against him and the air grew colder, he knew that he would be given no answer to his question.

Not yet.

Chapter Fourteen

Coira awoke slowly. The brilliant diamond elegance of the oak limbs overhead had turned a deep green. William slept soundly by her side, his body wrapped around hers protectively. She studied him in slumber, the thick half moons of his black lashes against his skin. His well-formed lips and straight nose, so utterly perfect.

How sated and peaceful she felt in his arms.

"Coira."

She didn't recognize the soft, lilting voice that entered her mind and without thought her eyes wandered to the river's edge. Somehow it had moved farther away from where they lay. And at its shore a woman knelt. She wore a long white robe cinched at the waistline with a gold rope and her ebony hair was full of small braids laced throughout with little beads.

Drawn, Coira carefully moved away from William, stood, and walked to the water's edge, somehow fully clothed again. She knelt before the woman and spoke aloud. "Who are you?"

The woman's light brown eyes found hers. "I am Chiomara Ruadh, Druidess of Eire."

"Druidess of Eire!" A sense of love and well-being suffused. "I saw you on the hill the eve of *Fheill-Eoinm*."

"Yes." Chiomara gave a small smile before her expression smoothed. "It is time for the *coelbreni*, omen sticks."

"Omen sticks?" Coira frowned and watched the Druidess pull forth a handful of small hazel sticks before tossing them to the ground between them.

A strange wind rushed through the forest, rippling the stream. Goose flesh arose on Coira's arms and a dark sense of foreboding overtook. She looked to William only to find him gone. Her eyes shot back to Chiomara.

The Druidess's eyes slowly rose from the sticks and met hers. A tear trickled down her cheek as the trees overhead turned a deep red and the stream black. In a somber tone, she said, "It will not save you. But it can save him."

Then a cloying darkness began to seep into the wildflowers, ripping them of color, life, and light. Even though the Druidess reached for Coira, she felt the darkness pulling her away, cornering her. Just as the last of the darkness found her and she crumbled to the ground, Coira heard the distant scream of an eagle.

****

"Are you awake?"

Coira's eyes popped open to find Annie sitting on the edge of the bed. What was Annie doing here? Both the Druidess and the darkness were gone. Instead, she was staring up at the rich blue velvet that hung over William's bed and Annie's flushed happy face.

She sat up abruptly. Had she simply been dreaming? Such relief swamped her that she started to tremble. Oh, thank heavens, what a horrible nightmare. Gathering her senses she frowned at her sister. "What are you doing here?"

Annie giggled. "I could ask you the same thing!"

Coira shrugged. "You know William has been gracious enough to allow me the use of his chamber while I've been recovering."

Her sister gave a mischievous smile. "And that's all very well and good, except now you're naked!"

She looked down and gasped before quickly schooling her expression. "So I decided to sleep in the buff."

"Never in our entire lives have you slept in the buff, Coira! In fact, I wouldn't be surprised if you found a way to bathe fully clothed. Of course, I learned you don't the other day when you disrobed and bathed in the smaller chamber when I was right there. I was shocked. You've never been that immodest. This place has really changed you."

She agreed with her sister on that count. Scotland had indeed changed her and continued to do so. "There you have it. I've changed. Now I sleep without clothes."

Annie winked, grinning ear to ear. "And I'd almost buy that story if the whole castle didn't already know William slept in here with you."

"What!" She swung out of bed, retrieved a chemise and dress, and slipped into them. "How do you know that?"

Coira wasn't even aware that he'd slept in the same bed. The last thing she remembered before the horrible dream was lying in an oak tree grove far off in the woods.

Annie lay back on the bed, her arms spread wide. "Really, Coira, this place is loaded with gossiping servants and clansfolk; you can't keep a secret around here. And he's the chieftain as well! What a declaration he's made about you, huh?"

Face burning, she moved aside the fur trappings over the window and breathed in the crisp air. The sky was a pale blue, and a fine wisp of cloud embankment covered the distant horizon. He certainly has made a declaration. She was his mistress! He could have spared her honor and left her in her old chamber. They weren't married, never mind she was engaged to another man!

Yet that hadn't stopped her from willingly making love to him. Oh no, she'd done that with her eyes wide open, had wanted it more than anything else. He was not at fault for that, but he was at fault for this, bringing her here. Presumptuous Scotsman!

She stepped away from the window. "Well, what's done is done." He'd still hear her opinion about it.

Annie was propped up on her elbows now, a silly grin on her face. "So we entered womanhood together."

No, they had not. She hadn't told Annie about her and William's previous encounter and had no intention of doing so. "It appears we have."

She walked back over to the bed and plunked down next to Annie. "It was a lovely wedding. Speaking of which, why are you here with me and not still in your husband's chamber?"

"Husband." Annie whispered the word with awe. "How wonderful that sounds." Annie bounded to her feet. "Actually, Arthur went in search of food and said he would be right back. Then I heard two servants chatting in the hallway about well...you and William, and I had to come see you!"

Coira stood up and shooed her sister toward the door. "Well, you better get back to your marital bed. No use making your husband mad on the first official day as man and wife."

Annie chuckled and scurried off. Coira stopped at the wall walk, where a few men at arms stood. They nodded to her as she took a moment to relish the chilly air and scenic view. Winter was coming quickly now, and the air held the tang of potential snow.

"Hello, Coira."

She turned and smiled. "Iain, so good to see you."

Arianna marveled yet again at how handsome these MacLomain men were. If Iain was any example of what she could expect of William's aging process, then☐☐☐☐She caught herself mid-thought. How could she allow herself to think about what William would look like fifteen years from now? How presumptuous of her! She would not be here, would she? Did she want to be? Yes. That realization struck her like a hammer blow to the skull.

Iain leaned against the low stone wall, his keen emerald eyes watching her closely. "You've been through a lot, lass. How do you fare?"

She was grateful he had the tact not to mention William, for no doubt he knew what everyone else knew. "Honestly, I feel a strange mixture of elation and dread."

Iain tilted his head slightly. "Elation because having magic has freed you, made you see yourself clearly, and dread because the future is extremely unpredictable."

How precise he was. "Yes, exactly."

Iain looked to her ring. "I know it might be difficult, but don't let your world revolve around that ring. It will glow when it's ready. Did you know that Arianna's ring did not initially have a stone in it?"

This startled her. "No, I didn't. How is that possible?"

"Damned if I know. Her aunt had it embedded in the ring and gave it to her as a Christmastide present before we returned to Scotland." He smiled wistfully. "So you see, Arianna and I did not depend on the ring at all to show us one another's love."

She nibbled the corner of her lip in contemplation, grateful for his insight. "I will keep that in mind, thank you."

"Consider it your first lesson in magic. One must not over think things, but let each moment come as it will. A calm mind will access magic more readily then a cluttered one."

"When will you start teaching me how to use my gift?" Though she didn't wish to be rude, the next question came of its own accord. "And why is it you that must teach me again?"

Iain studied her intently, as though he searched the answer. "We will start today, Coira, and I dinnae ken why it must be me to teach you, only that if Adlin wishes it, then so it will be. I have speculated 'tis because you and I worship the new Christian God, where William and Ferchar follow the old gods, pagan."

William wasn't Christian? It struck her anew how much she'd changed. The old Coira would've been mortified. Now, the fact didn't bother her in the least. He had his gods and she had hers.

And now she had magic.

"So I start learning magic today? So soon?" An undeniable rush of excitement swept through her.

"Aye, today." Iain grew very serious. "'Tis important that you understand you were given so powerful a gift for a reason."

Her eyebrows drew together. "I don't understand."

Iain sighed. "I would prefer to enter my position as your mentor with honesty. I believe one of the reasons you are here and have obtained magic is to participate somehow in the upcoming war."

She swallowed. Her throat turned to a dry abyss. She refused to panic openly. "Honestly, that thought terrifies me."

Iain took her hand and squeezed it in reassurance. His compassionate gaze held hers. "You have every right to be afraid. All of us fear what is to come, but know this, Coira, you are not alone. You have all of us. Not only us wizards but the whole of the clan. The moment you arrived you became kin. Do you understand?"

She felt the calming effect he sent into her, the magical essence of it. Relaxing, she offered a wobbly smile and nodded. "I do. Thank you."

He released her hand and offered a charming lopsided smile. "Good lass. Then let us travel down to the hall. 'Tis the best place to weather the smoke."

"The smoke?" She followed him back into the corridor and down the spiral stairs to the second level.

"Aye, 'tis the first day of the New Year."

They walked side by side down the wide stairs leading to the main hall. "Would you care to elaborate?"

"Elaborate on what?" Arianna asked as they approached. She stood before the mammoth fireplace.

Iain wrapped his arm around Arianna's waist and gave her a quick kiss on the cheek. "Elaborate on how bloody smoky 'tis bound to become in here soon."

Arianna wrinkled her nose slightly and looked at Coira with explanation. "Aye, 'tis the saining, the protecting, blessing of the castle." Arianna looked to Iain. "No disrespect, but 'tis a strange custom."

He smiled at her, love shining in his eyes. "None taken, lass. 'Tis the way of the Highlanders."

"You could only be referring to today's castle cleansing."

Every muscle in Coira's body liquefied at the sound of William's voice. How adept he was at sneaking up on her! She turned slightly to find him standing directly behind her, just where she figured he'd be.

She narrowed her eyes, ignoring the vivid thrill brought on by his proximity. "I'll not ask again what all of you mean."

William leaned close to her ear and spoke, his warm breath causing ripples of sensation to travel the length of her spine and lower. "'Tis a tradition on the first day of the New Year, the blessing of household and livestock. This morn a member of each household drinks a wee bit o' magic water from a dead and living ford, which is a river ford routinely crossed by both the living and the dead."

His lip touched her ear briefly sending another wave of heat through her. Then his words grew softer. "Those who drink the water then take it to their household and sprinkle it on every chamber, bed, and inhabitant. Then the burning juniper is carried throughout the dwelling, and all doors and windows are covered to let the juniper smoke thoroughly fumigate. At last, the windows and doors will be opened to give the cold, fresh air of the New Year entrance."

At that, the doors to the hall were firmly shut, and Muriel appeared carrying a torch which released a thick, heavy smoke into the air. Behind her came Adlin with a bucket of water, which he proceeded to sprinkle over all of the hall's inhabitants.

Only after Adlin had made his rounds and he and Muriel went up the stairs did William speak again, this time while standing beside her. "How did you sleep, lass?"

Embarrassment flooded her face, and her earlier aggravation resurfaced. She kept her tone devoid of venom, however. "Well, my laird, and you?"

A striking smile lit his face, and his dimples made an appearance. "I slept like a bairn."

She narrowed her eyes and gave a sharper retort than intended. "So I've heard."

William's silver eyes sparkled with mischief. "So you should have."

That was the last thing she expected him to say! So her honor meant nothing in light of what he wished to make obvious to his clan. Again she spoke with lethal intent, her own words shocking her. "Not without marriage between us, my laird."

She knew she contradicted herself somehow, was a hypocrite of sorts. Still, the man had nerve.

More than she was willing to accept at the moment. Arianna and Iain smiled and excused themselves, making their way toward the trestle tables to break their fast. Coira laughed internally. Even she was thinking in medieval terms now.

William sat in a chair before the fire and pulled her down onto his lap. She struggled to pull free, affronted that he would be so blatant.

He held tight, eyes merry. "And here I thought you had rediscovered yourself last night, lass. That you loved Scotland, but now you act as though you're still a proper Englishwoman!"

She stilled in his arms. He made a valid point. Yet, in all Coira had discovered about the woman she was, would be, it did not affect the way she felt right now, and she wondered at that. Not for long. "Regardless of what I may have learned last night, William, it does not change the fact that you have openly declared to your clan I'm your mistress!"

"And?" He pulled her closer, his muscled arms a cage against retreat. "Is that not what you are?"

A heartbreaking anger overwhelmed and she hated what dwelled at the root of it. "I am not!"

She struggled again, but he held tight, his whispered words fueled the heavy beating of her heart. "'Tis marriage you want betwixt us lass. I know."

Her eyes met his and drowned in the misery she saw in their pewter depths, sadness, want, regret, and such need. She simply repeated what she saw in his eyes. "You want it, too."

He cupped her cheek with his palm and held her eyes with his. Diamonds burst to life within, filling her with truth. "More than you can imagine."

She couldn't contain the sudden well of tears nor the overflow onto her cheeks. "It is not possible, though, is it?"

His thumb brushed across her lower lip. "Not yet."

His demeanor grew more serious. "I meant to offend neither your pride nor honor by leaving you in my bed, lass. I did it because I wanted you there, wanted to feel for just a moment that you belonged to me. I'm sorry."

She knew his words and heart were true and was humbled by his honesty. Without pause she brought her lips to his and felt their magic spring to life in an instant. How scrumptious he tasted as his tongue swung into her mouth heedless of the people that filtered around the great hall behind them.

When at last they pulled apart, she repeated what Iain had said to her. "Arianna and Iain married without the glow of the stone. In fact, it was not even in the ring when they married."

"I know." He pulled her head against his chest and stroked her hair. The fire flared and crackled before them. "But our circumstances are different, sprite, so put it from your mind."

She murmured against his chest. "How do you know that?"

"Because we are not them, because your ring has already glowed for another, and you've come into a level of power that surpasses both Arianna's and Caitlin's."

Lulled beneath the steady stroke of his caress, Coira closed her eyes, unwilling to debate or force an issue she had no true understanding of. "Then I shall be your mistress."

A low chuckle rolled through his chest. "No, you will be more than that, Coira."

~Sylvan Mist~

~Sylvan Mist~

Chapter Fifteen

"Duck, now!" Annie cried.

Snow blinded and ripped the claymore from her vision. Still, Coira listened to her sister and crouched to the ground, spun, and returned to a standing position. The wrapped hilt of her sword felt cold in her hands but gripped well, and the balance suited her. Laughing, she twisted, moving quickly and efficiently due to her size, and sliced the blade until it was mere inches from Niall's side.

"Well done, my lady. Well done!" He lowered his blade and wiped snow from his brow. "You are a quick learner."

She smiled and gave a slight bow. "I've a good teacher."

Annie laughed from the side lines. "You would never have done that had I not told you to duck!"

Arthur offered his opinion. "Nay, lass, she has the agility of William's father. That man can move with a speed unheard of."

Coira and Niall returned their weapons to the armory and joined Annie and Arthur as they went back to the castle. It'd been a busy two weeks since Hogmanay. The majority of her days were spent learning to wield magic from Iain and weaponry from Niall. She was surprised at first to learn William would not be teaching her the use of weapons. The

~Sylvan Mist~

laird's duties kept him preoccupied, therefore Niall had been designated by Adlin.

She welcomed the heat of the great chamber when they entered. Adlin had insisted she train in both arms and a good part of magic out in the elements, which were turning nastier by the day. The wizard's desire only confirmed Iain's belief that she would indeed be part of this war.

The hall was clear except for a few servants. Iain and Arianna sat alone before the fire. Coira was heading toward the lower step when Arianna's voice rang out. "Coira, Annie, come visit with us."

She smiled and walked over. Both beamed with joy. She sat down in a chair and enjoyed the warmth of the fire on her face.

"We have good news to share." Arianna sat close to her husband, features so animated Coira took pause.

She looked from one happy face to the other and knew. "Oh my, no?"

"What?" Annie said.

A tear fell from Arianna's eyes, and she nodded avidly at Coira. "We waited to tell everyone until the initial months passed, since we've lost others."

She flew out of her seat, ran to Arianna, and embraced her. Unbelievably and wonderfully, they were expecting a child. It mattered naught that her cousin was in her mid thirties now; she could safely bring a child into this world if she was careful. Coira had heard about the two previous miscarriages Arianna suffered and mourned for her loss.

Without pause, she turned and embraced Iain as well. "Congratulations! How wonderful for you!"

Annie stood close behind her, babbling a slew of congratulations. Coira sat back down, her hand resting lightly on her stomach. How lovely it would be to have a child. Could she be expecting? She and William had

~Sylvan Mist~

not been intimate since that night in the forest, per Adlin's request to William. Apparently, pregnancy would impede the process of learning magic. How, she couldn't imagine, and William could give her no understandable answer. Just that it was necessary she learn the craft quickly.

Yet they continued to share a chamber, which, though she loved their endless conversations, was becoming difficult. When they lay together at night in one another's arms, it was a slow torture for them both.

Shifting restlessly in her chair, she followed bits and pieces of the conversation. Her eyes drifted to the carved faces over the mantle. She stared into their strong features and recognized her magic stirring. Compelled, her eyes fell to the fire. The flames danced back and forth in a hypnotizing rhythm. At first, she wasn't alarmed.

Then a voice was screaming, pleading with her to turn away from the fire. William? She tried to pull her gaze from the flames but was unable. Paralyzed, she watched with horror as the flame shot tendrils of crimson edged with black toward her. What was happening? She'd learned much from Iain, but this magic felt far different from anything she'd experienced.

Dark and evil, exactly like her nightmare.

She started to scream through the inferno of flames which engulfed without burning or charring her skin. But the cave of heat muted the sound, made a mockery of her newborn whimpers.

As though it had never existed, the fire suddenly ceased as did all sound, and she dropped into oblivion.

****

William stared blankly at the chair, and a violent rush of rage unleashed within. She was gone! He'd felt the dark magic stir from the armory and transferred himself here, just in time to witness the horrified look on Coira's face when the fire and magic consumed her.

Iain, Ferchar, and Adlin were there instantly to aid in fighting the evil that engulfed her. Yet she was gone. They had failed.

He roared in defiance and turned on his fellow wizards. "Bloody hell! How is this possible?"

He nearly choked on his anger while Adlin calmly walked to the fire, his hands locked behind his back. "They must have locked onto her outside the castle."

Annie bit back a sob, and Arianna led her away. "Outside of the castle? No. Impossible." William began to pace, fighting his anxiety and fear.

Adlin gazed steadily at him. "Are you so sure, lad?"

He stopped short and narrowed his eyes at the wizard. "What do you speak of? Be blunt, I'm in no mood for riddles."

Iain and Ferchar sat and held their silence as the younger man faced the elder.

"Did you not take her into the woods on the eve of Hogmanay?" Adlin's eyes shifted to a darker blue.

"Damn, have you no mind to your own business, shaman?" He made no effort to disguise his sarcasm.

Adlin's eyes glowed, and William took an involuntary step back. "Take care how you speak to me, Chieftain."

Unable to bank his aggravation and worry, William did not apologize. "I was with her the whole time. 'Twas no different than her wandering the field beyond the castle wall."

"Wasn't it, though?" The white wizard's anger grew, a formidable thing. "The oak grove is a much different place from the bloody field, and well you know it!"

~Sylvan Mist~

William clenched and unclenched his fists and asked an ignorant question. "Had I no right to show the lass the spot?"

Adlin's eyes shone brightly, and wrath pulsed around his aura. "In that they want her, no, you didnae!"

The wizard spun to the fire, obviously cooling the temper all three had never witnessed. William said nothing but started to feel the guilt associated with Adlin's words. He had acted foolishly that eve taking her there. How eager he'd been to show her such magic, to see it reflect in her eyes, to offer her a piece of his childhood.

Instead, he'd brought harm to her. He lowered slowly into a chair as the full impact of the situation hit him. Coira was in the hands of the enemy, more specifically, in the hands of a Cochran wizard. Then something occurred to him and he looked to Adlin's back, perhaps understanding a bit more why the white wizard had responded so strongly. "You knew they locked onto Coira that night."

Adlin turned back, his eyes and composure again normal. "Aye, I did."

Why had the wizard not warned them? Surely, they would have been able to protect her had they known. William knew he was not going to like what he was about to hear.

Adlin looked at each man, his gaze sad, serious. "War has been declared. 'Twas Coira's fate to be the signal. Her abduction means it is time."

William lost his ability to breathe. Bloody hell. He could only stare at Adlin. Her fate? Her fate! He leaned forward, sickening fury clouding his vision. He struggled to keep his tone low and level. "How could you? That lass has no place in any of this."

Iain stood. "You know as well as the rest of us, William, that she is meant to be a part of this war. And thus far, she's been trained for such."

William closed his eyes, working to get his temper under control. His sprite meant for a war such as this. The thought made him sick.

He felt a hand on his shoulder and opened his eyes. Iain offered naught but compassion in his gaze. "She knows how to protect herself, and 'tis not their intention to kill her. Coira shows an adept facility with magic and she's levelheaded. She will be all right."

"I hope you're right, my friend." He stared into the fire, and then looked back to Adlin. "So, alas, we removed both her and the ring from Scotland because you knew she was its rightful owner, as we all quickly learned. And while she was in New Hampshire, the Cochrans were invited into the castle, of course not finding whom they sought, Coira."

Adlin nodded. "Aye, which you knew readily when you returned. 'Twas not my intention to deceive you about the ring being meant for her. Both you and Niall were obviously smitten with the lass, and it seemed just as well that the ring should be with her and all of you in the future. I could not have foreseen it glowing for Niall. 'Twas my belief it would do so for you."

The last of William's anger drained to be replaced with an acute sense of loss. "And now it glows for no man."

"No, and perhaps it never will." With that last declaration, Adlin vanished.

****

"Och, but she's a bonnie wee lass, she is."

Coira opened her eyes in darkness and panicked. Trying to touch her eyes, she found her hands and feet were tied together. She tried to speak but couldn't.

Another man's voice, deeper, responded to the first. "Aye, and she's mine."

"Of course, my laird."

So she was with a chieftain? She tried to move again to no avail.

The deep, raspy voice spoke, this time to her. "Do not bother struggling, lass. The blindness will wear off soon enough, and you'll understand why I say that; you're tied well, you are."

She tempered her fear and concentrated on what she could discern about her location without the benefit of voice and sight. A fire crackled. The faint smell of smoke combined with cooking meat. A horse whinnied off to her left. A small group of men spoke softly to her right.

A hand touched her face, and she shrank away. "You'll not always shy from me, lass. I promise you that."

She tried to speak again and was surprised her voice worked, though a weak croak. "You flatter yourself."

The slap came hard and swift, whipping her head to the side. His voice fell close to her ear.

"Watch your words. I'll not hesitate to kill you."

Blackness receded, and her vision turned to a blurry mess of orange and gray. She implemented what Iain had taught her days before and centered her being. Felt calm suffuse. She had no use for this man and told him so. "Then kill me, better that than being here with you."

A hand dug into her hair and yanked back her head. Her vision sharpened at last, and she saw clearly the man who held her. He was the same Scotsman who had tried to take her from William the moment she'd arrived in Scotland. His black eyes were a startling contrast to his platinum hair.

When his dark gaze met hers, she saw clearly the evil within. "You're brave lass, too brave."

A waspish smile curved his lips. His eyes roved her face, nostrils twitching. "'Twill be my pleasure to break you of your strength."

His other hand wrapped around her neck and a wide, devious grin raked his face. "I see MacLomain has already had you. 'Twill be just as pleasurable—"

He licked his lips. "To cleanse you of his stain."

Her inner calm was not holding up well, but she kept weakness from her eyes, and her words were foreign even to her own ears. It was the Druidess on her tongue. "You have only the power to command my body, never my spirit."

He leaned back slightly, his eyes narrowing to black slits. "What possesses you, I wonder?" He cocked his head. "'Tis the Irish to be sure, how unexpected."

She kept her gaze steady on his. Coira didn't care to think about what his next move would be. She blocked him from entering her mind but had little knowledge of what he was truly capable. Could he push past her walls?

Through her lessons with Iain, Coira knew his name was Brodick and the extent of his powers rivaled the MacLomains. He was chieftain of the Cochrans and had rebuilt the clan over the years to equal William's. The man now worked toward one goal: to make the MacLomains suffer for the death of his father. He wanted both Iain and William to die, Iain because he had led the clan then, and William because he led the clan now.

Brodick yanked her to her feet, quickly released the rope around her ankles, and pulled her through the slush. The icy fluid soaked the bottom of her dress and stuck to her ankles. One of many fires hosted the bulk of the Cochran warriors. They stood as a massive wall of plaids and filth from travel.

Her legs ceased moving when she spied the holy man standing at the forefront. What was this? No. Brodick wrapped an arm around her waist and lifted her, walking the remaining distance between them and the cleric. When he slammed her down to the ground, her knees nearly buckled. No!

"Be done with it, man." Brodick ground out his order and held her locked within one heavily muscled arm.

The holy man appeared calm, as though he performed such acts of blasphemy every day. "So it shall be."

Coira shook her head in denial and tried to fight the evil magic swamping her. She wondered if the man marrying them sensed it. If he did, he obviously didn't care and recited his words for the surrounding clansmen to hear. A horrible thunder crashed against her ears and filled her mind. Her magic could not nearly compare with Brodick's, and she started to shake as her mouth worked of its own provocation, controlled by another, binding her to this terror beside her.

When at last the thunder receded, the deed was finished, and she was married to Brodick Cochran. The ground vanished beneath, and only Brodick kept her standing. Men cheered and raised skins of whisky in the air. How could this be? Why her? Such sadness and horror overcame her that Coira, as hard as she tried not to, cried.

Where was William? Adlin? Iain? She called for them within her mind again and again. Nothing. Then she was lifted in the air and heard faintly Brodick's declaration even as it boomed in her ear. "And now I'll officially remove the MacLomain scum from this lass and make her one of us."

Another round of cheers erupted when Brodick carried her away from the crowd and entered a crude tent forty feet away. She tried to struggle but found her body unresponsive, dead.

Nothing lit the crude dwelling save for a dull red glow of Brodick's creation. It was the same shade the oak limbs had turned when she spoke with the Druidess in her nightmare. He laid her on a disheveled throw of plaids and leered. "I've looked forward to this since first I saw you."

She searched for words that could save her from this loathsome situation but found none. All she could do was whimper within her mind. Where was her defiance, anger? She closed her eyes while he removed his clothes and pleaded within her mind one last time for the one person who could make everything better.

"William!"

****

The MacLomain warriors, twelve hundred strong, had just crossed their northern border when a heavy sleet began to fall. The inclement weather didn't slow them, and they kept a steady pace heading northeast into the Highlands. They would travel by night and leave the peninsula behind by daybreak.

Clans Stewart and Campbell would be joining them midmorning, then by nightfall the MacLeod, MacLauchlin, and MacMillan clans. It was a massive undertaking, and many more smaller allied clans would be joining along the way.

The Cochran clan had decided to wage war in the northeast Highlands where their strongest allies resided. Brodick Cochran left the women and children of his clan almost defenseless, and if William didn't know the man better, he might have wondered at that.

~Sylvan Mist~

But the enemy chieftain thought only of revenge, not his kinswomen. He would place himself strategically and be ready for the war when it came.

William had just called camp and was lighting a small fire when he heard Coira's scream within his mind. His head snapped up, and he looked to the east. He nearly sprinted forward when Iain's hand gripped his upper arm.

"No, dinnae move, come now."

His heart stampeded through his blood. Ferchar and Adlin appeared and the four of them walked alone into the woodland. The elderly wizard worked quickly, his arms flinging up into the air. He began chanting while the others took their positions. They joined in, the ancient language rolling forth from their lips, rising into the air, and streaking over the whole of Scotland.

Fully robed now, the MacLomain wizards called on their ancestors. They called on the old gods and the new god. The sleet did not touch them, and fresh blades of grass grew beneath each man. Pine trees leaned closer, their needles bending and dropping to protect. A light sheen of fire released from Ferchar and encircled them, while William's mist shrouded them from onlookers.

William searched for her within his mind. Coaxed her spirit forth, whispered reassurances.

"Stop." Adlin spoke firmly and dropped his arms, his expression at peace. "We have help."

****

Her clothes were gone. William was not.

She heard him clearly within her mind, knew he would help her. Brodick lowered himself over her, his expression feral and eager. She turned her head just as William pulled away from her. No! "William!"

He was gone. His essence had deserted her. She gasped when Brodick's skin met hers. Lust rode his demand, and he seized her jaw, turned her face to his. "You'll look at me, lass." The demon snickered. "He has no power over me. Have you not figured that out yet?"

"But I do."

Brodick turned his head, startled, then scowled. "Leave me be. This is not your battle, soldier."

"It was seven hundred years ago, and it still is today."

She took advantage of Brodick's loosened fingers and turned her face to the sound of the familiar voice. Fionn, beautiful, bright, and masculine stood mere feet from them, his expression blank.

"Fionn," she whispered.

The Irish warrior didn't look at her but kept his eyes on Brodick. "No more."

White light poured from Fionn and overtook the small tent, blinding her from everything. She heard Brodick curse and move away. If fighting ensued, it was kept from her. The world faded from view, and she floated, alone, unafraid. No harm would come to her this eve.

She smiled and closed her eyes.

Then she walked, side by side with Fionn, again in the form of the old woman she had met on the cliff. The forest was quiet and protected from the harsh elements that surely must be afoot in the air. Only his sylvan mist swirled around them. She hadn't forgotten their secret.

The old woman spoke tenderly. "Are you well, lass? Did he hurt you?"

Coira breathed deeply. "No, but he would have. Thank you, Fionn."

She brushed aside the sentiment with a wave of an elderly hand. "You've naught to thank me for. Evil does not become nor own you."

Coira stopped walking. "Why do you come to me, Fionn? Why did you give me magic?"

The woman turned once again into the tall masculine warrior. His eyes took her into him. "I did not give you anything you did not already possess."

She had no response to that and continued walking with him through the wide, silent tree trunks of the Highland forest. His presence was comforting, and when a light mist arose, she barely noticed. As though awakening from a dream, the mist started to dissolve, and four robed figures materialized in the distance, two white and two black.

She blinked rapidly as they drew closer. William? It couldn't be, could it? Please, God, please. She started to run, unaware that the warm copper needles underfoot had turned back to snow. The air chilled, and a cool wind whipped up.

One of the black-robed figures broke free from the four and started running toward her. Then, in the blink of an eye, he was there pulling her close against him. She could barely catch her breath he held her so tightly. Coira wrapped her arms around his neck when he scooped her up into his arms. "Oh, William, thank God."

He strode swiftly away from the others. "Bloody hell, dinnae ever scare me like that again!"

"Scare you?" Coira buried her head against the fur he wore. She looked at her hands and realized they were bare. "He took my rings, they're gone."

"But you're not," William whispered.

He said nothing more but held her close until his strides slowed and he stopped. Again, she found herself in a crude tent. This one, however, was built against the side of a broad oak tree. Amazingly, a very small fire warmed the area and illuminated the glorious colors of the MacLomain plaid spread neatly over the ground.

He laid her gently on the plaid, covered her with another, and sat down. He said nothing, only studied her for several minutes, his tender gaze consuming. "Are you well, Coira?" His jaw clenched. "Did he hurt you?"

Coira lied. She simply refused to see the pain in his eyes if she was truthful. "Aye, I'm well. He did not hurt me."

"Dinnae lie to me." His eyes flared and he went to touch her cheek but stopped. "I see the bruise he left behind."

She sighed. The slap, it would naturally have left its mark. She took his hand and eased his concern. "He did not have the chance to rape me, William."

His strong body visibly relaxed. "I'm so sorry he even had the mere opportunity."

"I know." She stroked his palm. "And I'm sorry I couldn't stop him from taking me."

He brought a finger to her lips and shook his head. "You've no apology to offer in any of this. None. 'Tis my fault entirely that he found and took you, do you ken?"

Coira hated the pain she saw in his eyes. "I have learned many things about you, William MacLomain, and first and foremost, I know you would never willingly put another in danger."

His eyes clouded over. "But I did you, lass, as surely as thistle blooms in autumn."

She lifted an eyebrow in question knowing his explanation would be something born of magical repercussions.

"That night I brought you to the oak grove, I endangered you. 'Twas then that they locked on you."

He frowned and his brows lowered. "I should never have brought you there."

She sat up abruptly, the plaid falling to her waist. "Please don't say that, William. It was the most beautiful night of my life, and I'll not have you regretting it."

He cupped her cheek, running the pad of his thumb gently over her cheekbone. "I'll not regret it for that reason, sprite, but I'll not easily forgive myself for endangering you. I'm just grateful that in the end, no damage was done."

She grimaced, her eyes falling from his, regret and sadness rendering her speechless.

He put a finger beneath her chin and tipped back her head with renewed concern. "What is it, lass? What happened?"

She stared into his intense eyes and whispered, "I'm married."

William's eyes narrowed a fraction, unbelieving. "What do you mean?"

"I mean that Brodick Cochran and I were married." A pent-up sob broke from her.

He shook his head in denial and anger shot his words at her. "'Tis not possible!"

Coira's throat closed. *God, this is so hard. I don't want him to hurt like this.* "It is possible and he did. There was a holy man and witnesses. He used black magic on me and ensured my willingness."

William's lips thinned and his strong jaw clenched. "I will personally kill the man for this." He shook his head, contained fury evident in a throbbing vein in his neck. "It cannae be legal."

She slumped in defeat, having no response for him.

Suddenly possessive and concerned, William drew her into his arms, his hand lightly stroking her back. "But he did not consummate the union."

"No, Fionn came before he could." She pulled back at that, startled. "I didn't have a chance to thank him again! Dear me, I completely forgot he was there when you came."

"So that's who saved you." William cocked one eyebrow, his demeanor less intense. "You have made a powerful friend, lass."

"Did you not see him with me?"

He shook his head. "You appeared alone." His gaze roved over her with appreciation and fingered her gown. "Wearing this, you were lovely, like a fairy emerging from the mist. I've never seen a dress such as this."

Only then did it occur to her that she wore anything at all. If one could call it a garment. For the dress was a gossamer light fabric. Pure white and long, it molded to her skin to the waist, where it flowed like water. A telling heat rose to her face when she realized that she wore nothing beneath it, and her nude form could very nearly be seen.

Her eyes snapped to his and froze.

William held her gaze. "I do believe the majority of your magical lessons are over."

Understanding dawned in her wide blue eyes. "Do you?"

"Aye." He lifted his hand and grazed the side of her breast. Goose flesh rose and her nipples tightened into perfect little beads. Her body responded instantly, and he pulled her up against him into a kneeling position. He refused to think about her announcement of marriage and what Brodick had very nearly accomplished after that.

His body went into overdrive, no longer connecting with the mind. So many times he'd wanted to be inside her again. To touch her soft skin and hear the little sounds she made. To feel her tight, hot flesh gripping his eagerly. Two bloody weeks of torture! Not that he would trade their endless conversations and having her asleep by his side in the morn. Yet the building tension had been a constant trial to his self-control. His need was so intense, he'd very nearly left her alone and slept elsewhere, his desire at its breaking point.

His hands slid over her silky dress, cupping and molding every curve. He loved the way her breasts filled his hands, then her waist became so tiny, then her hips flared, so womanly and enticing. Everything about her brought out his need to dominate, brought out the baser need to conquer and defeat. Coira was bloody perfect.

She turned him into an animal.

Her hands moved over him, matching his urgency. With a flick of the wrist, he removed his clothing. He pulled her dress up to her waist, and his kisses became rougher, frenzied, as did hers. He knelt back, cupped her smooth, taut backside, lifted her until her legs wrapped around him, and brought her down onto him. Wet and eager, she accepted him.

Both groaned in relief.

The fire sputtered and died, leaving them in darkness untouched by cold. Grass and moss sprouted to life all around and a dusting of heather blossomed. Vines grew along the base of the oak sheltered by the tent and crawled along the edges. The scent of lavender overwhelmed him.

She overwhelmed him.

He thought she murmured his name but couldn't be sure. The roaring sound within his mind took over. Her magic mixed with his, trailing images within his mind, those which she put there, erotic, sensual, and wild. William wanted to plunge and plunge into her hot, wanting sheath until she screamed, until breathing became impossible, until she cried with pleasure.

Until he bloody well ripped her apart.

Slowly, he had to take this slowly. She'd been through too much. He held her hips, tried to set the pace, but she squirmed and fought and won. Moaning deeply, passion became a storm. She threw back her head and steam rose from her skin, sweat trickled down her neck. He followed the trickle with his tongue and growled against her cheek. Fire flung them forward, whipped them to frenzy.

"Coira." He cried her name into her hair, matching and molding his thoughts to hers.

Crying, her blazing heat clamped around his cock. His muscles locked, sweat poured off him. Nearly crippled, he cried out again and wrapped his arms so tightly around her she gasped. Slick with sweat, his orgasm made him delirious. His body shook as though the very earth quaked and he held onto her even tighter.

"Ohhhh," she wailed and held onto him just as tightly, her body trembling and shaking. He felt her tears on his cheek, down his neck.

William whispered his love into her mouth without voicing the words. Leaning her back, he laid her on his plaid. He wiped the tears from her cheeks and came down beside her, pulling her close. The fire flickered back to life, and sudden springtime pulled away.

Her blue eyes rose to his, their shade nearly black in this light. "I love you, William. I don't know exactly when it happened, but I do." Her eyes filled again. "And I'm engaged to one man, married to another, and before it was stolen, wore a infuriatingly undecided magical ring on my finger."

Still struggling for breath, he put a silencing finger to her mouth and shook his head. "There's naught we can do about any of that right now. But this love we share is ours for now, regardless."

Though obviously winded, she appeared apprehensive and nibbled her lower lip. "How can you be so calm? I know you love me as well, I can feel it. Aren't you frightened of losing this, us?"

He cursed and pulled her tighter against him. "With all my heart, lass, but worrying will not help."

She snuggled against his chest, a contented sigh erupted. "I suppose you're right."

At once, she became tense again and pulled back, her eyes rounded with fear. "What if Brodick Cochran magically takes me again?

He ran his hand along her hair and cupped the back of her neck. "He willnae. You are protected now by Fionn. Brodick cannae touch you."

She shivered. "Thank goodness."

His thumb skirted her collarbone, igniting another shiver, this time not from fear but from desire. Instantly aroused, he pulled her back to him, covered them with a fur blanket, and kissed her deeply.

They would worry about their future in the morning.

~Sylvan Mist~

Chapter Sixteen

Coira awoke with a contented smile. William loved her! Even if she'd sensed previously what lay in his heart, it was wonderful to hear him say it. Confirm it. Daylight remained muted by the animal skin overhead, and a small fire still crackled nearby. She snuggled deeper into the furs, inhaling his scent.

"Blasted horse!"

The declaration came from right outside of the tent. Coira scrambled up and realized she was already clothed in a wool dress. A pair of boots lay close by. She slid them on, wrapped the MacLomain plaid and a fur cloak around her, and exited the tent only to come nose to nose with a black stallion. His snow-dampened muzzle nuzzled her cheek.

"Och, lad, but that's a bit much first thing in the morn." She spoke with the Scottish tongue freely now. How could she not? She was in love with a Scotsman.

The horse whinnied and nuzzled her again as though he approved. She smiled and ran her hands along his muzzle. This pleased him immensely. So they were to be friends then, very good. To have this horse as an ally could only be a boon.

"Good morn to you, lass." Ferchar stood nearby, hands planted firmly on his hips. He glared at the horse and shook his head.

So he had been the one she'd heard. She laughed and walked around the side of the horse. "He's a wild one, aye?"

Ferchar's blue black hair was a startling contrast to the snow behind him. His sapphire eyes met hers and he chuckled. "Aye, it appears this beast will answer only to you."

Coira eyeballed the horse. She really should name him if they were to be buddies, and suddenly she knew, without a doubt, that he was hers. Running her hand along his smooth, shiny coat, it came to her. "I think I'll name him Gaiscioch."

Ferchar cocked an eyebrow. "Interesting name. Dare I ask?"

She shrugged, not sure why the Irish word seemed appropriate but quite convinced she had chosen wisely. "I'm not sure why, but it's the right name."

"Ah." He offered one of those famous MacLomain smiles. "Well, then, Gaiscioch it is."

She watched Ferchar from the corner of her eye. He was the wizard she was least familiar with. It was unbelievable to her that this man comfortably lived in the twenty-first century. At the moment, he looked every inch the medieval Scottish Highlander. But then, William had spent three years in New Hampshire as a child. She wondered at that, if he preferred it there instead of here? No, she sensed somehow he would be unable to leave this country behind.

"'Twas not so hard leaving my homeland to be with Caitlin. I love her more than Scotland, more than anything on Earth."

Startled, she looked up at Ferchar and bit the corner of her lip. "I'm not very good at hiding my thoughts yet, am I?"

He grinned and spoke within her mind. *"Nay, but you will be. 'Tis good to remember though and practice."*

She wasn't irritated in the least by his mental intrusion. In fact, feeling his essence gave her a better understanding of the man. He felt nothing like William, Iain, or Adlin. But she knew instantly he was kind and good.

"Out of my lass's mind, cousin."

She smiled at William's voice, as always so close behind her. His lass? The claim shot a thrill straight to her heart. His tempting brogue entered her mind.

"Well, you are."

She kept her hands on the horse but tossed a look over her shoulder. His silver regard leapt at her in the early dawn. "Good morn to you, my laird."

His arms came around her waist and pulled her back against him. "And to you, love."

She worked to steady her breath, her heartbeat. No such luck. Oh, how this man affected her. Without thought, she leaned her head back against him. "I've named my horse."

"Mmm, I know." He nuzzled the top of her head. "'Tis an unusual name for a Scottish horse. Gaiscioch, Irish warrior."

She rolled her eyes. "Are there no secrets in this clan? I only named him just now."

"Nay." She heard the smile in his voice. "Not when you dinnae block your thoughts from those of us with magic."

His mouth came next to her ear, his deliverance possessive. "And you'd best never block your thoughts from me."

She turned her head slightly, ignoring the romantic threat in his statement and focusing on the subdued order instead. "And you'd best not tell me what I can and cannot do."

He chuckled, the sound not completely genuine. "Easy, lass, we'll not bicker."

Ferchar interrupted, likely on purpose, easing the sudden tension. He had his arms crossed over his broad chest and was eying Gaiscioch with trepidation. "He'll need to be taught some commands, whistles and such."

She grimaced. "Have we time? Doesn't it take a while to teach a horse such things?"

"Nay, not with magic at our disposal, but only you can do it, lass," Ferchar said.

"Me?" She wasn't so sure. "I'm new to this. Shouldn't Gaiscioch be taught by someone who understands more?"

Ferchar shook his head and met the horse's eyes. "Nay, he'll listen to you and he's intelligent. Take a few hours and coach him."

She pulled away from William and reached up to stroke between the equine eyes. "I will."

William came up beside Ferchar, watching both Coira and the horse with undisguised humor. "I believe I'll watch you, lass."

She shrugged. "Do what you will." Then another thought occurred to her. "Isn't the clan moving north soon?"

"Aye." William confirmed. "The clans will leave soon."

His gaze grew serious when he looked at her. "But you and I will stay behind while you master this horse. The clans are safe for now. War is not here yet."

"But shouldn't you stay with your clan, William? Surely, someone else can stay behind?" Not that she wanted someone else to stay. She didn't. But she

~Sylvan Mist~

would not be responsible for the MacLomains being without their chieftain.

Ferchar glanced at William briefly before his steady sapphire gaze settled on Coira and he answered her question for his cousin. "The clan is safe. Remember, three of its former lairds lead the way."

She understood the logic in Ferchar's statement but wondered at the wisdom. Was it not the obligation of the clan's current chieftain to be present? This worried her. Was she clouding William's good judgment? As though Ferchar felt the shift in her thoughts, he walked away leaving them alone.

William did not play coy when he spoke. "Do you wish someone else to stay behind with you, Coira?"

She held his gaze, ignoring the heavy drops of snow falling between them. "No, you know I don't. Why ask a question you already know the answer to?"

He moved closer, his gaze shifting to that of a stranger. "Because it strikes me curious you would doubt that I know where my obligations lie. That you would think I've lost my heart to such a point my clan would suffer for it."

She swallowed hard but held his darkening gaze. William without a trace of humor, but blatant irritation, was something new. "You misinterpret me."

"No, I dinnae, God's truth." He positioned her back to the horse. His body became a wall enclosing her. "There is so much at work here, lass, and you've only just come into magic, into medieval Scotland. Just last week you despised us Scottish. Now you've the nerve to question my motives, my knowledge."

She felt the hurt radiating from him. Knew that she had touched on a fact which he denied, and well he knew it. Coira searched for tact, truth, and came up bereft. She looked up into his eyes and refused to shrink beneath his glare. "No, my laird, I do not question your motives, nor knowledge, but perhaps your heart."

He clenched his jaw, his hand rising not to strike her though it moved quickly, but to gently brush her cheek. "My heart will not rule prudent action. You have my word."

She turned her face into his palm and closed her eyes. "Aye. I'm sorry."

Coira opened her eyes to find him studying her.

As though he searched for a response he couldn't find. Without warning, he pulled her into his arms and kissed her soundly. His lips were cool and wet from the snowfall. She wrapped her arms around him, not wanting the moment to end. Wariness was growing inside her, a feeling that their time would soon end. She tried to ignore the nagging sensation, assumed it was the fear of war.

"I might've seen this coming!"

She pulled away from William at the greeting.

Lachlan Campbell approached with a wide smile on his face. She hadn't seen him since that first night when he'd arrived amongst the MacLomain clan with Niall.

William grinned. "I couldnae leave a Broun lass alone."

"Nay." Lachlan winked. "Just had to decide which one." He looked across the way to Arthur.

"Sounds like Arthur made out good as well."

"Better. He's married to his lass." William sighed.

Lachlan looked down at Coira. "'Tis good to see you again."

She nodded her head. "And you."

Coira looked beyond him, aware for the first time of the endless winter forest of Highland warriors. So many men, she couldn't begin to speculate on the numbers.

~Sylvan Mist~

"So far, well over three thousand."

She gasped at William's internal statement. So far? The magnitude of what lay on the horizon staggered her, so much imminent death and destruction. She wrapped the fur tighter around her shoulders, not to ward off cold but fear.

Adlin, Iain, and three other clansmen joined them. All were intimidating in their stances, dwarfing Coira. William offered brief introductions. They were the chieftains of the Stewart, MacLauchlin, and MacMillan clans. And all wore somber expressions.

The copper-haired laird, Jordon MacLauchlin, looked to the north, his already fierce features becoming more intense. "Will the MacLeods attack the enemy from the north, or have they decided to join us first?"

"They'll join us within the week," William said. "I'm afraid this war will be one less of stealth and more of massive confrontation."

She stood silently, listening intently to the men discuss strategy and warfare. How bizarre it was to be in the midst of this conversation, to be a part of such an incredible, albeit petrifying, moment in history.

Adlin looked at the sky. "The weather will worsen. We must make haste."

The men split off, each to their individual preparations. Campfires were doused, and warriors mounted their horses. The MacLomain clan departed first, a massive procession of plaid-wrapped warriors, horseflesh, and weaponry. She helped William untie the makeshift tent and store it.

"We'll ride a bit southeast, so you'll be able to work with your horse without hundreds of hooves moving past you." William helped her onto the stallion. Gone were the days of frustrating mounting.

~Sylvan Mist~

Grateful, she smiled down at him. "Thank you, 'tis too kind of you to finally assist me getting on a horse."

William swung onto his horse and winked. "You've proven yourself worthy, especially last eve."

She blushed. Scoundrel. "Shall we ride then?"

One corner of his lip shot up, and he chuckled. "But, lass, I just put the tent away."

She rolled her eyes. The man was impossible. "I'll give you no response to that."

He barked with laughter. "But you just did give me a response!"

"I'll not banter with you right now." She gave a wicked smile, held tight to her horse, and urged him forward knowing full well by now he'd break into a run. He didn't let her down.

Thankfully, Gaiscioch was sure-footed, or they certainly would have slammed into one of the many Highlanders trailing through the forest. As it was, many either grinned at her or laughed. Darn horse!

Eventually, the sporadic wall of men vanished and the woodland turned enchanting. Snowflakes the size of her thumbnail speckled the air and clung to tree trunks. An inch of newly fallen snow covered the ground, outlining the barren branches and stiff pine needles overhead.

William's mount came alongside. He leaned over to slow and then stop her horse. "I think the first thing you should work on is teaching this horse not to bolt. My heart was in my throat watching this beastie back there."

"Really?" She allowed him to help her down. "You didn't seem all that concerned the last time he bolted. If I remember correctly, you were determined to race me."

He didn't release her waist, his features a mixture of concern and mirth. "And I seem to remember there weren't hundreds of men on horseback creating an obstacle for you that day."

"Perhaps not." She wet her lips, dry from the winter air. "But he did handle that little escapade quite well, I think."

His eyes drifted to her mouth. "You've perfect lips, lass." He pulled her closer. "Mayhap before you start teaching the—"

She shook her head, stood on tiptoe, and gave him a quick peck on his mouth before he could finish his sentence. Wasting no time, she pulled free from his hold. "No, you can't be serious. We're in the middle of nowhere. And it's snowing!"

He laughed, grabbed her wrist, and dragged her against him again. "So? We've a tent, if the weather bothers you."

"William!" She was well aware of his aroused state and worked hard to ignore her own response. "We really shouldn't."

He made a low, primal sound in his throat, grabbed her backside, and pulled her tighter against him. His lips took hers and made a mockery of her self-control. Just as quickly as the kiss began it ended, and he set her aside. "You're right."

She breathed heavily and puffs of misty moisture erupted into the cold air. Regaining her wits, she stuck her tongue out at him. "You're cruel."

A sparkle twinkled in his eyes. "Am I? It was you who said 'twas time to train the horse."

Tempting blackguard of a Scotsman, he was naught but a tease. She smiled knowing that if she wanted him in her bed this moment he'd not likely deny her; he wouldn't be able to. Turning her attention to Gaiscioch, she wondered where she should begin.

William looked to the horse. "You'll remount and teach him how to not bolt right away."

She nodded and was plunked back astride. Frowning, she quirked an eyebrow at William. "Any ideas?"

He stood, hands on hips. "Well, he likes Scot on your tongue. Perhaps you should try something along those lines."

She nodded, leaned forward, and whispered in Gaiscioch's ear. The horse stomped his hoof and made no movement.

"What did you say to him, lass?"

"Do you mean to tell me you couldn't hear that?" she said.

"Nay, I'll not be in your mind nor eavesdrop while you train. 'Tis for you and the horse to know one another without my intrusion."

"So be it." She patted the muscled equine neck. "I told him I'd like him to trot, not run. Apparently, he didn't like that."

William shrugged. "Mayhap you should be a bit sterner. An order with a promise of a boon. It seems he thinks he's in charge. You are just a wee sprite after all."

She frowned and contemplated the advice. All right. She leaned over and whispered again in the horse's ear. At once, he trotted forward. Not by any means a full-out run. Triumphant, she laughed and cried out, "Well done!"

Gaiscioch appeared pleased with her praise and turned around easily when she told him to. William was leaning back against a tree, his arms crossed over his wide chest. Amusement softened his quicksilver appraisal. "What did you promise him?"

She swung off the horse, too excited to wait for his assistance. "Some of your dried apple slices."

"My apple slices! Damn, lass, I could've summoned some fresh grass for him." He pushed away from the tree and walked over to his satchel.

"How was I to know that? Summon an apple slice then." She took the piece of dried apple and fed it to the horse.

He slipped his arm around her waist; his voice dropped. "It doesnae work that way. I summon directly from the earth. Do you not remember the flowers and grass in the oak grove?"

"Aye." She warmed inside. "That was your doing? I thought it simply Scotland's magic."

"In a way it was, through me." He lifted his hand to her forehead, between her eyes. "And you."

"But I didn't know how to use my magic, then."

He patted the side of the horse's muzzle with his free hand. "I simply shared with you. Let you see what only your soul was capable of witnessing."

She held his gaze, her awareness of him stirring. "I hope we'll be able to go back there someday."

"We will." He brushed a snowflake from the bridge of her nose. "I prom—"

She brought her finger to his lips to silence him, sudden melancholy swelling inside of her. "Please don't make a promise you might not be able to keep."

His tongue flicked the tip of her finger before he took it into his mouth and closed his eyes. She stared, transfixed by the sight and feeling of the intimate gesture. William's eyes opened slowly, and he kissed first her palm and then the inside of her wrist.

An eagle cried overhead, and he abruptly pulled away. "We've little time. Resume your training, lass. And I can summon the grass if need be. Now we've spoiled the horse, he might not want it."

She nodded, speculating. "William, why don't the clans travel magically to the place of battle and avoid the hassle of weather and such?"

"Simple. The amount of magic it would take to transport this many men would not only wear out those of us magically inclined but leave the others weakened as well. And such a state for the clans would be catastrophic moments before a war."

That made sense. She swung back onto her horse and proceeded with training. After an hour, she'd accomplished far more than she could have anticipated. Gaiscioch learned quickly and would not only respond to a variety of whistles but mind commands as well, which totally fascinated her.

At last, they headed back into the woodland to catch up with the clan. She watched William at ease upon his horse. His hair was damp, muting the auburn highlights, his perfect profile intent, every inch the warrior. Such a sight, she wished she rode the horse with him, in front of him.

They hadn't spoken for some time, and the silence bothered her. She knew his mind was on the upcoming war. Understood the significance of what lay before them. Still, she needed to hear the sound of his voice so she spoke useless words knowing full well he could transport them. "Will we be able to catch up with the clans? The snow is becoming deeper."

His gaze slid to her. "Do you really want to?"

"Want to catch up with the clans? Of course."

She wiped the snow off her fur hood.

He brought his horse alongside hers and stopped both mounts. His eyes were rich pewter caught within the snowflakes. "I dinnae. But we will. We'll lay camp just behind their rear flank this eve. I've a mind to have you to myself."

New warmth infused her as anticipation of nightfall and all it offered was made clear. "That sounds tempting."

"It does, doesn't it?"

Without preamble, he reached over and scooped her off Gaiscioch, plunking her down in front of him. His mouth came close to her ear. "I heard that thought back there, sprite. And it pleased me. So you'll ride with me. We'll switch horses on occasion, but I've a mind to keep you close. Unless, that is, you've still an issue with having a Scotsman at your back?"

A wicked throb of need tore through her. She turned slightly, only to slam into the lust in his eyes.

"I do believe we've moved past that, aye?"

William leaned down, his lips brushing hers. "Aye, lass, we have."

Coira twisted more, reached up, and pulled his hood over his head. "Please keep this on. You'll be drenched and miserable when we make camp if you don't."

He leaned down until his mouth was within a breath of hers, his eyes now the same alabaster gray as the fur. "The last thing I'll be is miserable with you to keep me warm."

She twisted forward again for if she allowed another kiss they may not catch up with the clans at all, and both of them knew it. William chuckled and she leaned back, snuggling into his warmth and security.

As they made their way through the forest, her horse following closely behind, she closed her eyes. The sway of the mount and William's nearness brought her to slumber quickly. And slumber brought her no peace.

****

The great white eagle soared high above the snow-covered forest. His keen eye roved the land until he saw them clearly. They were cloaked, riding together, and lost within each other.

That was, until she fell asleep.

Adlin angled his body and dove, swooping down as the dream took her. He caught her spirit easily and brought her into the eagle. Let her feel the wonder of the bird. Flapping his wings he flew upward, circling to the east. When he knew her spirit was at ease and not fighting the dream, he spoke within her mind.

"I want to show you something, child." He covered space quickly through magic and flew down low over the flatlands bordering the North Sea.

"Where are we?" Her voice was soft, confused.

Adlin whipped out over the sea then turned back. "We're flying over your ancestor's homeland, East Lothian."

Wonder and exhilaration filled her, awe and interest. "Really? How wonderful."

The eagle took them lower, allowed her to see the flat sweep and shallow hills of the Scottish lowlands, dove lower until she could see the heavy throng of warriors trudging north. "Can you see them, lass?"

Her spirit lay still for a moment before her voice spoke, a whisper in his mind. "They wear the red and black Broun plaid."

"They are your brethren; they come to fight for you, for Annie, Arianna, and Caitlin."

Coira's awe infused him, her voice tender. "They're lowlanders. They've no part in this war."

"Aye, it doesnae matter. A Broun is fighting. They will come to your aid."

He felt her pleasure at this, her acceptance.

"Thank you, Adlin."

The eagle pumped his wings and flew back the way they came. He had shown her what she needed to see. Understand. Find pride in. He again moved swiftly, let her feel the flight of the bird at her disposal, and then dropped her neatly back into her human form.

With a loud cry, he left the two people upon horseback.

~Sylvan Mist~

Chapter Seventeen

"What is her purpose here? She's but one mere lass thrust into a man's war." William drank whisky from his flagon and tried to bank his rising concern and anger.

Adlin sat across the fire from him. Ferchar, Iain, Hugh, Arthur, and Niall formed the remaining circle eating and drinking in their group. Coira already slept in their faintly glowing tent built not at the edge of the clan as he had wanted but directly in its heart. Even with Fionn's protection and that of now six Highland clans, William's better judgment took hold of him.

"Must we go over this again?" Adlin gazed calmly across the way.

William kept his eyes expressionless. Aggravation stirred beneath the surface; the bloody wizard knew more than he was saying. Always did.

"What of this marriage to Brodick Cochran?"

Niall snorted but said nothing.

Adlin shrugged. "There's naught we can do about that but make her a widow as soon as possible."

All the men nodded their heads in agreement.

William watched small sparks spit into the air. The snow had finally stopped, leaving the forest muffled and white. "And the ring?"

Adlin tensed at this. Apparently, the wizard had not anticipated the loss of the ring. "We must get it back."

Iain sat forward. "What harm can he cause having it?"

"Substantial harm." Adlin took a bite of meat, chewing thoughtfully. "To our clan, not this war."

No one save Adlin knew the reason for the three rings, beyond the fact that they brought true lovers together. William often wondered why there were only three rings. "So we kill Brodick and retrieve the ring."

"Aye," Niall said.

William took another drink. "But what does he accomplish if we dinnae kill him? He wins the war and he's got the ring and Coira? The ring will never glow for him."

His father, Hugh, spoke quietly. "But if he wins the war, takes Coira, and the remainder of our clan, 'twould be a simple thing to say the ring glows for his eyes." Hugh made a pattern in the snow with his finger. "And if it comes to the point that he wins this war, none of us MacLomains with magic would be left to dispute him."

Ferchar nodded and scowled. "Aye, 'twould matter naught that he has no MacLomain blood in his veins. He would not be questioned by any that dinnae carry magic. It would mean their deaths to dispute him."

The men grew silent for a length of time, each lost in his own thoughts.

William looked to the sky. The three-quarter moon was uncovered by a hurtling slip of cloudbank, giving the snow-covered pines overhead an ethereal glow. His gaze fell back to Adlin. "Our other allied clans amass tomorrow, and then we travel quickly. The battle will be under the full moon."

"Aye." Adlin's eyes bore into his. "'Twill be a peak for both our magic and theirs."

"It will be something to see the Broun clan again," Iain said, leaning back and shaking his head. "'Tis too bad the other lasses had to stay behind on that one count."

Iain offered a wry, somewhat giddy grin. "Arianna was not pleased she wasn't able to come, to aid in this war and meet her clan. Silly chit, she's pregnant!"

William swallowed a mixture of emotions. He was glad the other Broun lasses had to stay behind, but it brought him back to why Coira had to be here. Aye, he understood she was somehow an important part of this, but that helped little when it came to his feelings toward her.

He'd rather bundle her up and return her to New Hampshire, never to see her again, than have her involved in this war. William's eyes made rounds over the immediate campsites. Men chatted softly, some sharpening their weapons, others casting a constant, watchful eye to the land beyond, warriors all, used to carrying on a conversation with eyes razor-sharp alert.

Ferchar looked to William. "Coira did well training Gaiscioch, I take it."

William couldn't contain the pride in his response. "She did better than any other lass and most men."

"Amazing horse, that one," Ferchar said.

"Aye." William's thoughts drifted to their time together earlier in the day. How her azure eyes sparkled with mischief when she continued to bribe the stallion with William's dried apples. Her porcelain skin grew rosy in the cold air, and her lips a sweet, swollen pink beneath the kisses he had continued to sneak in, though he promised professionalism.

She was impossible to leave be though he had tried. And when she fell asleep in his arms astride his horse, he nearly didn't return her to their clan. His desire for her was too intense, and William quickly realized that he needed to keep his perspective. He was the leader of one of the most powerful clans in

Scotland, and his clan was leading this half of the war. It was not a position that allowed a wee bit of a lass to be a distraction.

But she was his lass, married or not, and he had every intention of keeping it that way.

He felt Adlin's eyes on him and met the wizard's gaze. When William spoke internally, all others were blocked. "You need not worry."

Adlin's ice blue eyes shimmered in the firelight. "You speak to me, though you try to convince yourself."

"I will fail neither my clan, nor Coira." He kept his eyes locked with his elder.

Adlin was nothing less than ruthless. "And if you find yourself in a position where you must choose between them, William, what will you do?"

William hoped it never came to that. "You know what I would do.

"Do I?" Adlin's eyes narrowed. "I have no use for vague answers or assumption."

William stood and bid his clansmen a good eve. As he walked past Adlin, he gave his answer. "I would choose my clan."

****

Coira wrapped the fur cloak tightly around her and stood facing the southeast. They were coming. A stir rose within the vast sea of kindred clans spreading as wide and far as the eye could see, their plaids a rainbow of checkered colors against the snow.

Niall stood beside her, his light green eyes watching intently. He touched her arm. "Are you nervous?"

Of course I am. "No, eager."

"You really aren't good at fibbing, Coira." He laughed when she glared at him.

"Now I know you didn't just read my mind. I'm becoming very good at masking thoughts."

He shook his head. "One doesn't need to read minds to know what you were just thinking, what you're feeling."

She shrugged a shoulder and offered a small smile. "This is a fairly big deal after all."

William and the other wizards had gone to meet the Brouns. Niall volunteered to stay behind, and Coira was eternally grateful to him for it. He had become a close friend, and she had no desire to meet her relatives, albeit distant, alone.

"There." He pointed to a distant stir in the wood line.

She squinted and saw the haze of movement Niall referred to. William had ordered the MacLomains to make camp so that they were positioned along the southern border of the thousands amassed. The Brouns would wall them in for the eve, allowing Coira to meet her kinsmen with ease.

Eventually, she could make out William. He rode beside a man and a woman. Another woman! How wonderful! As they drew closer, their features became clearer. The man was of a slighter build than William, with glossy dark brown hair and deep-set eyes. The woman was lovely, with long reddish-gold hair and a tall, lithe figure.

She watched in silence as they dismounted and walked the short distance left. Hundreds of Broun clansmen fell in behind, many traveling further to cushion the whole of the MacLomain clan.

William closed the distance and took her hand. "Coira, this is Chieftain Stephen Broun and his wife, Arianna."

Arianna? As in the Arianna who was originally supposed to marry Iain had she not run off with the infamous first in command, Stephen?

~Sylvan Mist~

Stephen stepped forward, took her hand, and kissed the back of it, his eyes nearly the same sky blue as her own. "Hello, Coira, 'tis nice to meet another Broun from the future."

He was several inches shorter than William, perhaps six foot one. So he knew she was from the future. Coira supposed that made sense, after all. The Brouns would have desired an explanation for whom Iain had married when the Arianna from this time period did not arrive at the MacLomains' castle back in 1199.

She smiled and nodded. "Nice to meet you as well."

Stephen turned his attention to his wife. "This is my wife, Arianna."

Coira smiled at the woman and made her greetings. Then as an afterthought, she added, "It's nice to have another woman along."

Arianna offered a wide, intense smile. "I wouldnae have missed it for the world."

Coira grinned not only at the woman's thick accent, but at the strong spirit she possessed. This was a woman that no man controlled, nor would ever. She fell into step next to Arianna as the men spread out, tending to their tents, fires, and hunting.

Arianna eyed Niall up and down, her tone at best civil. "Well, well, we've a Sassenach in our midst."

"He's a MacLomain." Coira stood to her full height, which barely reached Arianna's nose and met her eyes with all the seriousness of a woman leaving no room for debate. "And a friend."

Arianna's eyes fell to Coira's, and a fine eyebrow crawled up. "So be it." She looked to Niall, her expression softening. "'Tis a pleasure to meet ye then."

Niall nodded and wore a bemused expression when he looked Coira's way, then Arianna's. "Would either of ye lasses like a wee bit o' whisky, then?"

Arianna threw back her head and laughed. "Ye've a good dose of humor in ye, Englishman. Aye, I'll take a bit o' whisky."

Coira's lip quivered with suppressed laughter. She liked the woman. Why, she hadn't a clue. A month ago, this female would have struck her as abrasive and crude. Poorly spoken and rude, now she was an ally, of Coira's own bloodline, and someone who Coira knew would fight for her kinsmen with the heart of a true warrior.

The women sat before the small fire burning in the early dusk. Each received their flagon of whisky and kept a comfortable silence for a small time. Coira was brimming with curiosity about what Arianna and Stephen had endured over the years.

"Ye may ask me anything ye wish, cousin."

Arianna's words startled Coira. She knew full well the woman couldn't read her thoughts. So she proceeded with the most obvious question based on what she knew of Iain and her cousin's, nineteenth-century Arianna's, tale. "Where did you and Stephen go when you ran off together?"

Arianna drank deeply from her flagon, her expression giving away nothing of her thoughts. "We traveled for a long time, clan to clan, finding refuge with those that would have us."

Coira bit the inside of her cheek at the thought. All for the sake of love, these two had forsaken the protection of two clans and made their way where fate would take them. Her eyes sought out an absent William, wondering if they would have done such a thing. No. William was a chieftain. His loyalty and pride would keep him from acting in such a way, no matter the woman. He'd already made that clear when the ring glowed for her and Niall.

She returned her attention to Arianna. "But you returned to the Broun clan."

Arianna's face turned bland. "Aye, I did, many years later."

Coira remained silent and drank a small portion of her whisky, waiting. The conversation was Arianna's to lead now.

"Stephen sent me back to our clan and left. He wanted me to be safe, not living the life of a wanderer." Arianna clenched her jaw. "'Twas a hard day, that one, seeing him for what should have been the last time and returning to a clan that would likely not take me back."

"But they did," Coira said.

"Aye." Arianna didn't appear impressed. "Out of loyalty to my deceased father, a man faithful to the king of Scotland until the day he died. He was a hard man, gave me no leave to lead my own life. It would be Iain MacLomain who I married, because of an old agreement made with Iain's father."

Arianna grunted with disgust. "A perfect stranger! And me, a mere lass, with no choice of who I'd marry! Nay, I'd have none of it." She took another swig of whisky. "Besides, I loved Stephen."

Coira scuffed the snow with her boot. What a mess. She couldn't imagine an arranged marriage. Then again, why fight an arranged marriage when you could be kidnapped by a rival wizard and forced to marry?

"Where did Stephen go?" Coira said.

"To the MacLeod clan at the north of Scotland. He spent many years there before returning to the Brouns."

"The MacLeod clan? They're here with us now!" Coira was confused.

"Aye, it seemed he had to go in part because o' one of our relatives." Arianna looked directly at Coira. "A lass named Caitlin."

Coira almost choked on her whisky. Caitlin? Her twenty-first century cousin had made no mention of this. "I don't understand."

"She needed help escaping from the MacLeods, and he had to establish himself within the clan to aid her. He said he owed it to the MacLomains for falling in love with me." Arianna shrugged. "'Tis over now. He came back, made right with the Brouns, and after many trials and tribulations holds the chieftain position now."

"Unbelievable." Coira shook her head. The men had just returned. William, Niall, Stephen, Ferchar, and Iain joined them.

Stephen rubbed his hands together before the fire and smiled. Puffs of moisture followed his words into the cold air. "'Tis a good-sized buck to roast this eve over yonder!"

She eyed the larger fire in the distance. Every eve different men tended the kills roasting on the spit. Apparently, fire was of no consequence when it came to the enemy. This war was a highly advertised, prominent affair. It was no secret the fronts were edging closer together.

William sat down beside Coira and stretched his long legs out in front of him. "Aye, there will be plenty for all." His eyes slid to hers, softening as they did. "Your clansmen are good hunters, lass."

She ignored the thrill his presence caused. He had put more and more distance between them this past week. The eve she trained her horse had been the last time he'd made love to her. She remembered the slow and languid way he had woken her. There'd been no urgency, but slow passion. As though he were trying to erase the combustion between them, fight the obvious.

After that, he merely slept by her side, holding her close each night, pleading tiredness. And he had every right to be tired, between the constant weaponry practice, magical practice, and spending ample time amongst not only his clan but all the others.

That logic didn't stop the involuntary fists she balled within her cloak, the urge to scream her need at him. They'd already had to wait two weeks before she was kidnapped. What happened to being finished with training? What happened to the mutual sentiment that they may not live through this war and intended to spend the time well?

Iain spoke before Coira could which was just as well. "Aye, the Brouns hunt like Highlanders!"

Arianna nodded and met Iain's eyes. "Did you expect any less?"

Coira contained a smirk. She knew for a fact that today was the first time Iain had laid eyes on the woman who should've been his wife. How strange it must be for them. But they soon proved her wrong, another testimony to the way of the Scots.

Iain laughed wholeheartedly and offered Arianna a mocking tip of his head before looking at Stephen. "She has a good way about her, friend. Mayhap I should've charged after you two back then!"

Stephen smiled and looked at his wife when he spoke to Iain. "You would never have caught us."

Arianna returned Stephen's steady gaze and chuckled. "Nay, we would've given him a good turn though, aye?"

Everyone laughed and Coira forgot for a time how frustrated she was becoming with the man at her side. Her attention should have been completely on Stephen and Arianna, on the Broun clansmen drifting in and out, but no. She was completely aware of William's spicy, clean scent beside her, aware of his never-ending banter with his friends. He had the ability to joke to no end yet maintain an aura of impenetrable respect from those around him.

Her gaze drifted to the moon overhead, nearly full. A low roll of dark clouds crashed toward it like a tidal wave of ebony water. Was there another storm rolling in? She smelled the air, leaden already with winter, pine, and chill. They had one more day of traveling before they reached their destination.

Ferchar spoke, making her suddenly aware they were alone. William and Iain had gone to retrieve food, Stephen and Arianna to do the same, and then join their clan. His voice was gentle, level. "Gaiscioch will serve you well in this war."

She didn't smile, couldn't. Talk of the war did not allow such a thing. But with Ferchar, she knew her eyes were warm. Where Iain still took time to teach her new things within magic, Niall continued to be a constant with weaponry training and Ferchar her silent partner while working with Gaiscioch. Not because William didn't want to help, but because of his constant obligations within the traveling war party.

She leaned forward and propped her elbows on her crossed legs. "Yes, I think you're right."

"I am." Ferchar leaned over and handed her another flagon of whisky. "Have this. I saw you gave yours to Niall."

She shook her head at his offering. "No, I've had enough, thank you."

"You've had but a sip, and you've a need for it this eve." He urged her to take it, his sapphire eyes intent. "Please."

~Sylvan Mist~

She couldn't deny her desire to have more than just a sip and leaned over and took it. "Thank you, Ferchar."

He leaned back, his gaze dropping to the fire between them, his words serious. "You're brave, Coira. No one expected this from you. Know that 'tis not just William who cares for you but Iain, myself, and Adlin as well."

A wonderful feeling of warmth and acceptance infused her. Did they really? These four powerful wizards truly thought of her with such regard? She drank the whisky and let the words hang, enjoying an unexpected sense of accomplishment. She, Coira O'Donnell, a woman who once carried no magic, was now kin to the magical Scottish clan she'd heard about all of her life.

And in love with their chieftain.

Just as quickly as the thought surfaced, she pushed it away and looked back to Ferchar. "Why, Ferchar?"

He knew what she spoke of. Knew that she wondered why it had not been Caitlin or Iain's Arianna who should be part of the war. He pursed his lips momentarily before he issued his answer, and his eyes rose to hers. "Do you honestly think I've an answer?"

She shook her head and drank deeply from the flagon. "No. I just can't help but keep asking the question that is on my mind always."

William and Iain returned with food, and Coira ate in silence. She still had so many questions unanswered. So much she needed to understand. She stared at her bare fingers and thought first of the Irish ring. How she missed it! And as a far off, now fading regret, she thought of the beautiful diamond engagement ring James had given her. She honestly

~Sylvan Mist~

couldn't imagine seeing him again. Wondered what she would say to him if she did.

"That you love him but you're not in love with him."

She did not acknowledge William when he spoke within her mind but finished the last of her venison and returned to her whisky. Coira had not closed her mind to him, though she'd been tempted to. Still, she hadn't and doubted she would. She liked their link despite her current distress with him, liked that he was always there, watching, tender, with a caress that didn't go beyond her mind.

Not that she didn't want him caressing her—did she ever—but his presence within her mind was becoming necessary to her everyday existence. And that distressed her more.

The whisky was warming her and William's hands weren't, so she decided to take an unrecognizably brazen approach. The forthright attitude of a woman who understood she might not be alive in a few days but acted as though she would be. "You'll meet James someday. I wonder will you like it when you hear what I've to say to him."

She didn't miss the posture shift in William, nor the terseness of his words. "Aye, lass, I'd better."

Coira stood and stretched her arms, flagon in hand, and smiled down at Iain and Ferchar. "I believe I'll stretch my legs a bit, and then retire."

Ferchar grunted. His eyes glued to William.

Iain's eyes did a similar dance before settling on Coira. "Take care you dinnae wander too far, lass."

She nodded to both men, turned and sauntered into the stretch of speckled firelight that made up the Broun clan.

As far as Coira was concerned, she couldn't wander far enough from William at the moment.

~Sylvan Mist~

Chapter Eighteen

William stood, glared at his fellow clansmen and dared them to speak. Neither man spoke but continued munching on their venison. He knew that as long as he was following Coira, his kinsman would say nothing more.

Damn woman!

He shot one last lethal glance at Ferchar, knowing without a doubt Coira carried his flagon of whisky. Ferchar merely gave him a guiltless shrug and enjoyed his food. Wasn't it enough that Adlin stuck his nose in every aspect of his life, let alone his fellow wizards? As William made his way through the Brouns, smiling here and there, he cursed the whole bloody situation.

He allowed Coira to saunter, for that's what she did, her hips swaying, through the campfires ahead of him. She was in her cups and though not drunk, was not far from it. And she was beautiful, as many Broun clansmen noticed until they saw William, keeping a steady pace behind her, two campfires back. She'd lowered her hood, and her long black hair spun a wave of ebony enchantment on every man she passed.

Eventually, she broke free from the firelight and entered a stretch of moonlit forest. Careless of the danger she put herself in, though he knew Fionn watched, cared. He stopped when she did, mesmerized by her actions. The moonlight poured over her small form as she dropped the cloak to her feet, leaving only

~Sylvan Mist~

the pale gray of her wool gown and the MacLomain plaid.

She removed the plaid and let it fall into a small heap, a shadow against the pool of silver fur cloak at her ankles. He spoke within her mind. "Coira, what are you doing?"

She didn't respond but turned to face him, the fabric shuffling and twisting in the snow. She stood a distance away, but he could see the steel and determination in her gaze. He could also see the flagon of whisky clutched loosely in her hand.

He went to step forward but her hand rose in the air, urging him to stop. Then she spoke aloud. "I needed time alone. Is that too much to ask?"

William watched her newfound magic ignite, glow around her, a silver haze the color of mist and moonlight. He didn't move but waited, as he would when hunting. "'Tis not so much to ask for, lass, if we were not at war."

"We are not at war, William! Are we?" Her gaze shifted, covered the sky, the land, and his face in one sweep.

Damn Ferchar for giving her that whisky. What had he hoped to accomplish? William held his ground, eased both his tone and concern. His words were as wrought with double meaning as hers. "We are not at war, lass. Not quite yet."

She didn't appear to appreciate his response and sipped again from the whisky. "Go to hell. Leave me be."

But she didn't turn away, instead she dared a response.

William decided upon logic. "You're nearly bluttered, Coira."

"And what of it?" She took another sip of the whisky and wiped her mouth with her sleeve, making a wide swipe with her arm. "Do I not deserve to be after all of this? After you!"

He moved with a lightning speed born of magic until he stood in front of her. "You deserve a hundred flagons of whisky, if 'tis your desire after all of this, but not now."

Head tilted back, she narrowed her eyes at him. "But now is now, is it not, William? Now is a mere day before we might die. Why do you push me away? No. Don't answer that. You've your reasons, I'm sure. Perhaps you don't want to become too much more attached to me before I die."

William stopped the endless stream of words coming out of her with his mouth. He pushed hard against her lips, hoping she would fight him so that he could let her know she had no choice. That he had no choice. But she didn't. Her arms came up, encased his face, and deepened the exchange.

He'd been strong up until this point. Well in control of his emotions. The urgency of her whisky-flavored lips had snapped his determination in half, made a mockery of his good intentions. He'd endured the horrible need and want night after night as she had, but knew Adlin was right. His final decision, if it ever came to it, must be for his clan, not her.

Her small hands found their way beneath his cloak, up under his tunic and stroked each muscle. She whispered, urged, pleaded. Her body quivered against his and sharply reminded him of how she shook upon release, completion. He'd not let her die, he wouldn't die, without feeling her heat once more. He groaned and pulled her closer, lifted her, and walked forward until her back pressed against the flat surface of one of many boulders skirting a nearby mountain. With a thought, he encased them in a cloak of privacy. To the common eye, there were not two lovers but merely the dull slate gray of stone.

She murmured endearments in his ear, things he couldn't hear over the roar of his blood. The moon vanished, and a light layer of snow began to fall. He allowed the small flakes to touch them, to wet their skin.

I need you. I've always needed you.

He took no time to admire the picture she presented before he lifted his plaid and her dress, and drove into her, fully clothed.

Coira quivered in his arms, a strangled groan escaping her lips. It was if she sought to pull him further into her body as her slender legs climbed his thighs, as her heels dug into his arse.

His need was too strong, so intense he had no idea if he pleasured her or not. *I need to release inside her. Make her mine this one last time.*

 He had no ability to slow the thunder pounding through him, the desire to own her, body and soul. In. Out. In. Out. *More. More. More. Mine. Mine. Mine. I can't get enough. I can never get enough. Dinnae you know that?* He was thrusting his feelings into her, how much he cared for her, couldn't contemplate her dying, wanted her as his wife.

The snow fell heavier. A light wind blew through the forest, whipping her hair around him. He buried his face in what he could catch of the billowing locks, seizing a piece with his teeth. He brought the thread of hair to her neck and ran his lips down her skin, nibbling the smooth surface cut by ebony curls.

"I love you, William."

Her words shuddered within his mind, and the last of his sanity snapped, blown away on the wind. His mouth found hers, and he knew, somehow, that his moment of surrender and freedom was hers as well.

He cried out and squeezed her so tightly her groan was a mixture of pain and pleasure, bliss and unimaginable release.

The pleasure and throbbing was endless, the absolute bond. If tears fell from his eyes, he ignored them.

There was only this... *them.*

He held her that way, with the rock at her back and the snow blowing around them for an immeasurable amount of time. Well after her breathing evened, he continued to hold her, not wanting to let go.

At last, her small breathy words broke the silence. "So we will have no war between us."

He lowered her and put his mouth close to her upper jaw line, allowing his warm breath to sooth her skin. "No war, lass. Just this."

Her hands skirted his cheeks and ran the length of his neck until they settled on his chest. "This is all I want."

"I know." He whispered and lightly ran his teeth along her chin until he found her lips again. He nibbled her lower lip, murmuring, "Me, too, lass."

She pulled him closer, kissed him again, and then buried her head against his chest. Her words were muffled by his fur cloak. "I wish things could be different. That we weren't getting ready to fight a war tomorrow."

He took his cloak and wrapped it around Coira, sheltering her. Feeling her pain, the silent crying against him that she tried to disguise. He would not use magic to bring them back to their tent, but instead, he retrieved her cloak and plaid, lifted and carried her back.

Not a single Broun clansman lifted his head when he passed, but kept his gaze elsewhere. It was a sign of respect to both their kinswoman and the man who carried her. He knew of their sense of honor and duty, their overwhelming pride in the woman within his arms.

When at last he had her in their tent, securely bound in blankets and nestled close to him, he spoke. "Things will be different. I promise."

****

Coira sat motionless.

Dusk was falling on the eve of the battle. The pristine, alabaster woods were quiet and etched with a dewy purple. Nothing could be heard but the occasional shuffle of hooves in snow and the whisper of wind blowing over the forest floor beneath, whistling around the tree trunks.

The formation of the clans was not what she expected. The MacLomain wizards were located at four points within the massive troop, William in the front, Iain at the northern end of the clans, Ferchar at the southern, and Adlin at the western. Others with magic made up a border surrounding the clans, between the wizards.

Coira was next to Adlin.

The sun sank quickly and left the full moon to its mischief. She looked overhead, feeling easily the magic throbbing from the great orb overhead. What a most unique and petrifying thought it was to know that war lay within moments of one's life. That everything she'd known up until this moment would change.

She tried not to think of William, practiced the magic Iain had taught her, and pushed him to the back of her mind. Still, his mind was there in hers, his essence. Somehow she knew, if he died this night, he would always be there, a part of her no man would ever be able to conquer.

Her surroundings wavered, twisted. Was it time? She tensed and ran her hand along Gaiscioch's warm neck, an automatic response to sooth the horse so that he did not feel her fear.

"Coira."

She stilled her hand at the voice, watching as the men and horseflesh around her froze, as though caught in a block of ice. Fionn? Her gaze fell to the warrior emerging from the ranks of clansmen ahead.

He glowed, his golden beauty blinding as he came to stand beside her. She smiled at him, soothed by his presence. "Have you come to help me through this?"

"No." His serene, earthy eyes held hers. "It is time for me to leave you."

Her throat closed but she pushed past the sensation. "Leave me, now? I don't think that's such a good idea. Please don't do that."

He did not turn to the form of an old woman, did not offer her that sense of comfort, but appeared taller suddenly. "It is time for you to fight, my child. To become the woman you're destined to be."

"Destined to be?" She frowned and shook her head, trying not to panic. "I've only become who I am because of you!"

His voice turned soothing, nearly that of a wonderful melody. "No, you are where you are because of you. I merely helped you along."

"Why leave now?" She made to climb off the horse, but he stopped her.

"Stay." His voice took on a stern edge, and his skin glowed a bit brighter. "You will fight. It is your destiny, your fate."

She offered no false front with him. "I'm scared."

"You won't be. Utilize what you've learned. Be who you are." He handed her a sword the like of which she'd never seen before. "Fight."

Her stallion whinnied and cast an eye to the weapon she'd just been handed. She tested the weight, perfect. Without thought, she handed him the sword she already had, and he nodded.

Before she could voice anything else, Fionn vanished, and the world swung into motion. A massive roar filled the horizon, a sound that could not be compared to either a thunderclap or a two-hundred-foot wave crashing against rock. She looked to Adlin and saw that his features were intent, his gaze unfocused. She pulled into herself, found her center, and became part of the war from a mental aspect.

Power surged through her, whipping the mental eye forward. The magic felt like a massive arrowhead being shot at the enemy. Light pulsated and radiated forward. Those without magic fought a war of bloodshed, while those with magic battled one another and protected their clans. The enemy's power was formidable, unending, searching for weakness.

"Where are you, Coira, my wife?"

As quickly as Brodick Cochran's voice and essence entered her mind, William was there, fighting Brodick within his mind as his body fought those rushing at him. She felt their souls clashing against one another, struggling to get to her, keep her.

Without thought, she protected William, shutting him from her, giving Brodick's mind an open channel. William needed to fight and protect himself. She would handle this evil presence alone. He did not put himself at the forefront of his own war, as William did, but hung back, protected, free to fight her without hindrance.

She felt William's silent roar of defiance deep inside but ignored it. The last few days, she had focused and strengthened; no one was getting into her mind. She felt Iain and Ferchar probing, trying to enter her mind and defend her. Adlin, however, was another story. His aggravation was a thorough thing, humbling. While fighting with magic for the whole clan, his white presence lashed at Brodick, the gleaming teeth of his rage bare and biting.

Brodick fell back, his chuckle vibrating to her soul. "I'll be back soon for you, Coira. Come forward and fight. I've a need to see you in action. See how bold you really are."

His presence dissipated, and Coira again became aware of the surge of warriors ahead of her. With a silent command, she gave Gaiscioch the release he needed, and the two of them burst forth, dodging the full-fledged battle unleashed all around. Explosions sounded in the distance, and she knew they were the sounds of magic.

Men fought with swords, axes, blades, and fists. She disregarded it all and gave Gaiscioch free rein, utterly confident in his ability to carry her where she meant to go. Coira had no idea how far she traveled, how much bloodshed and death she witnessed before the first man came into sight.

He had a small stature and wiry dull brown hair, quite unexceptional really, unless one looked closely. And Coira did. She unleashed her magic, sword in hand, and flew toward him. A bemused expression stole his features mere moments before a scowl. Without any thought but the well-being of William and her clans, Coira drove the sword down and swiped it across the man's throat.

Numb to everything and everyone, she continued on, seeking and doing what needed to be done. For an immeasurable time, she fought, her surroundings a place of blood and snow, cries and roars, highland forest and the stallion between her legs.

When it all fell away and became something else, Coira didn't know. Just that it did. She rode Gaiscioch south, seeking freedom from death. Freedom from the things she'd just done for hours. Knowing she'd never escape them, yet still she rode until the full moon turned to dawn, peach and vibrant against the sky.

"Coira."

She heard his whisper, William's voice, somewhere in her dimmed mind. Felt the tears on her cheeks, hot and endless. But emotion did not feed them, at least not any emotion she could feel.

"Coira."

This time the voice was dark, sinister, eager, and relentless. Close.

"Stop." With Brodick's one word, she was flung from her mount. Coira hit the ground hard, rolling. When the momentum of the fall finally released her, she was far from Gaiscioch. The snow drifts blinded and came mid thigh in some places, knee high in others. She stumbled clumsily to her feet, dumbstruck.

Brodick's amused voice filled her eardrums. "I see you used a bit of magic to travel here." One corner of his mouth inched up. "But you didn't realize you did so, did you? You made me chase you all the way to East Lothian, you little fool!"

Her stallion lay in the snow, his eyes fixed on her. He was fatally injured. She ignored the fact that walking toward Gaiscioch would put her closer to Brodick. All she could see was her horse. All she cared about was the animal. The darn beastie had made his way into her heart.

The enemy's voice grew nearer as she staggered forward. She had to make it to Gaiscioch. Had to touch him, make sure he knew she hadn't abandoned him, even if it meant her own death.

"Oh, my love, such spirit you have!"

She hissed into Brodick's mind. *"Leave me be."*

"Never," Brodick said. Within mere feet of the horse, he seized her, his hands crushing her arms painfully. "Do you know how much trouble you've caused me?"

She didn't bother turning her head from him. She was no longer the passive type. "No, how much?"

His features softened, not a pleasant sight. "More than I anticipated." He smiled, his eyes roving her form. "For such a small thing."

Her blood curdled, but she didn't look away. "Good."

Her forthrightness appeared to intrigue him, and he cocked his head. "I don't want to have to kill you, wife."

A bit of berserker humor bubbled up through her chest, and she chuckled. "I'm sure you don't, but you should. I'll never be much of a wife to you."

He threw back his head and laughed, his humor was a quick and sickening sound. "Oh, you'll be more of a wife than I could ever have expected or hoped for."

She was tired of useless banter and pulled forth the last of her reserves. Crawling inside of herself, she centered, and spat at him every ounce of magical power she was capable of.

He stumbled back, as if stung, a look of first bafflement, then blatant rage swallowed his face. Coira wasted no time but turned away and made to run.

He caught her around the waist and pulled her back against him, his voice thick with disdain. "And to think I thought you soft and yielding, a woman of substance."

She tried to breath, tried to take air into her lungs. When she could, her tongue lashed out instinctively.

"I'll never be flesh and blood to you, nor will I enable you to break me."

At her words, Coira froze. Flesh and blood? *No! Please no!*

Her dream unfolded, just as she remembered it. "Flesh and blood?" The devil chuckled. "You give yourself too much credit, woman."

She had little control over her natural response and didn't bother struggling. "Do I really?"

He leaned in close until the edge of his mouth skirted hers. "Aye, and I've little use for those such as you."

"I doubt that." She remained still.

"Dinnae doubt, lass." He ran his tongue along her jaw until he seized her earlobe with his teeth.

He growled, released his hold, and threw her to the ground. In a flourish of precise, deadly movements, he lodged a knee into her back and withdrew his sword.

Shouldn't she be able to alter the course of this moment somehow having dreamt of it so long? But no, the sounds, smells, and thoughts remained the same, locked within a foretold magic, unchangeable. She felt the satisfaction in the steady draw of his breath, the purr of his domination. So she was to die like this? With a sword driven though her back? A flash of fear flooded, but she tempered it. What good would it do?

Oh, yes, all the same thoughts she'd had in her dream.

He lifted her dress, straddled her backside, and leaned in close. His whisper was more efficient than his blade. "Did you think your death would be so swift?"

To speak would be a waste of time, a means to incite the beast upon her to act more rashly. But fear was not something she was immune to, and it threatened to overcome. And it did as his hands traveled up her thighs and covered her backside.

"Release her."

It was a whisper on the wind.

William! Dear lord, it was him. But she'd known that all along, hadn't she? Denied it, yet known it.

She struggled to see, but the blinding snow kept her vision shrouded. Her teeth began to chatter from the berserker laughter that rang from the man holding her down.

"Interesting that you chose words over action. Do you ken the difference? The result of such foolishness?"

Brodick snickered through his words thrown at William. He shoved her face against the ground as he leaned back. Then his large hands squeezed around her neck tightly and she gasped.

Magic was useless. She was empty from fighting all night. She tried to fight the paralyzing fear of helplessness. The clutch of strong fingers dug deeper into her windpipe and made reasoned thought impossible. The alabaster snow released black flecks into her vision, and panic seized her. Her hands fisted in snow beneath, and she offered her last attempt at a struggle.

It was a pointless venture. She reached out a numb hand to Gaiscioch as the last bit of air drained from her lungs and her body grew heavy, leaden. Milky white ground became foggy gray, then all went dark as death stole her vision and wiped away the last of her arrogance.

****

He had dreamed of this moment!

William roared with rage, closing the distance to Brodick's hunched figure within seconds. The enemy turned fast and rose, raising his arms in the air. A surge of power crashed into William, slowing him a mere fraction.

Brodick cackled, the sound dark. "So much anger, MacLomain." He countered William's magic.

"Over a lass. My lass!"

He didn't let Cochran's declaration faze him but continued his magical assault, inch by inch. The overwhelming desire to wrap his hands around the man's throat empowered him.

The two wizards were nearly equal in strength, but one was stronger at the moment, and Brodick knew it. His gaze narrowed with concentration on the power William threw at him. "I'm surprised you abandoned your clan to chase her. It says much about your leadership skills."

He continued to ignore Brodick's taunts, knowing his useless words were said only to distract William from his enemy's weakening. He pushed all thoughts of both Coira and his clan aside as he fought the archwizard, drawing on all of his expertise and experience.

"I only married the lass so your clan, which will soon be mine, would cause less friction." Brodick's lips thinned and inky mirth doused his eyes. "But it seems she will be of little use to me now."

William faltered at the harsh declaration, felt his magic weaken. Centering his being, he pushed past Brodick's barrier and seized the man. Both men turned from magic to what they were, Highland warriors, fighting hand and fist, weapon to weapon.

But William possessed something Brodick didn't, bone-deep rage and a vicious need for revenge. They fought with claymores, circling one another in a timeless dance. Like William, Brodick liked to wear down his foe, allowing the other to exert his energy too soon. Low sunlight broke through the trees, splintering on the white snow.

A bright green flash caught the corner of William's vision, disabling him for a moment. It was just enough time for Brodick to land a hard blow, dislodging William's claymore from his hands.

The enemy guffawed wildly and made another quick slash with his blade. William dropped to the ground and rolled to where the glimmering light had appeared. His hand closed around the hilt of a gold sword unlike anything he'd ever seen. Coira had been carrying this? Fought with this?

Without hesitation, he rolled over and pushed the sword into the air as Brodick made ready to strike. The blade slid easily beneath his ribs into his heart.

A flicker of amazement brought Brodick's eyes down to the sword embedded in him. Disbelief swam within his eyes as he groped at it. His dying words were not what William expected.

"Again, this bloody sword."

Then he was gone, and his body crumpled into the snow, but not before William swore he saw the blade flash green once more. He swiftly turned his attention to Coira's limp form a few feet away. She lay face down, motionless. A staggering flash of terror overtook as he crawled to her.

No. Please no.

Carefully, he turned her, smoothed her skirts, and pulled her onto his lap. Her ebony hair fell away from her face. Her wide blue eyes stared up at him blankly, her skin a chalky hue. She was gone. Her soul had left.

His lips worked, but nothing came out. Rational thought left, swept away on a wave of such grief he couldn't breathe. No. This was not possible, couldn't be. He'd witnessed much of her bravery and courage as she fought earlier, specifically targeting those with magic.

He'd felt immense pride, knew that she would live through the war, that he would, they all would. When she fled south, he'd followed like a madman, knowing Brodick was in pursuit and would reach her first. But he never expected the enemy to kill her, had assumed Brodick needed her too much.

William shook his head in denial, unwilling to close her beautiful eyes to death, refused. Pulling her tightly against him, he buried his face in her hair and willed her back to life. If he cried, he was unaware, as was he of shaking, trembling, and moaning. Blast his visions. He'd known nothing of this save for the vague dream born of another's magic. Even Brodick had not been completely clear as the enemy, though he should have guessed.

A hand fell to his shoulder. He barely felt it.

Adlin's voice was soft. "William."

He tried to shrug the touch away, but Adlin's grasp was firm. William buried his words in Coira's hair. "Leave me."

Adlin did not, but squeezed his shoulder. "The war is won. We must bring her home."

An insurmountable time passed before he pulled back. Home. Aye. They must bring her back to Cowal. Maybe there was still a way to bring her back to life. Even as the desperate thought tightened his muscles and filled his mind with hope, he raised his shaking hand to her face and ran his fingers over her eyelids, closing them.

They would bring her home.

When he raised his head, William saw that not only Adlin stood over him but also Ferchar and Iain.

Adlin alone was free of blood and the remnants of warfare. His cousin's expressions were like nothing he'd seen before. They'd cared about her, too. Grief, heartache, and love ravaged their faces.

She had fought fiercely for the MacLomains, and they were all proud. He stood, holding her in his arms. "Let's bring her home."

Adlin nodded, his eyes mournful, strong, old, yet young. He raised his arms in the air and started chanting. William closed his eyes, let the magic take him and leaned his head close to hers, whispering in her ear. "We'll take you home. We'll find a way to bring you back."

He breathed deeply and held her tightly. The air turned warmer and brushed his skin with the scent of roses. William jerked up his head. Not to Scotland, but to New Hampshire.

Dread suffused as he gazed at the house they'd visited weeks before in the twenty-first century. But he knew this was not that era. This was Coira's era, nineteenth-century America.

The four of them stood by the oak tree, blood gone from their bodies and plaids clean. Only Adlin wore his robes, the white fabric blowing in the wind. The rope swing swung back and forth, and the leaves overhead whispered a sad welcome.

A petite redhead stood in the doorway to the house, frozen. Eyes wide with shock. A tall, dark-haired man came up behind her. Then there was Annie, peeking past them both.

When had Annie come here?

Adlin spoke and urged William forward. "Marie, Liam, I am so sorry."

William instinctively pulled Coira tighter against him as the three rushed forward. Marie and Annie were crying, Liam looked lost, baffled and horrified. William stopped, dazed. They had brought her home to her family. She would not be coming back to him. New anguish tore through him.

Marie stopped, her eyes wrought with pain as she gazed at her daughter. Her blue eyes rose to his, and a mother's torture met a lover's agony. Marie's eyebrows came together, and she bit her lower lip.

"Oh, God. No."

After that, everything became a blur. Liam took Coira, and the loss of her flesh in his arms numbed him to a point he doubted he'd return from. Where Liam took Coira, William didn't know, couldn't follow. Everything fell away, dissipated, and he stumbled back until his back hit the oak tree. There, he slowly sank to the newly sprouted grass beneath.

She was truly gone. He knew his fellow wizards were still there, knew that the women's crying had entered the house, but nothing else infiltrated his reality. How could this be? He stared straight ahead, seeing nothing, feeling nothing. Not wanting to.

Then, as though the last of his strength had deserted him along with her, William closed his eyes and welcomed darkness.

Chapter Nineteen

"William, where are you?"

Coira's plea echoed off the walls of her subconscious. There was no pain here. Was there pain before? She struggled to remember. Nothing came. Where was she? What was she forgetting?

"Death."

She turned at the sound of the voice. A man stood before her, tall and handsome, with dark brown eyes. His bearing was regal, yet not condescending. He was familiar somehow.

"Do I know you?" she asked, awed.

He took her hand, his warm touch soothing and gentle. "Yes."

His previous statement crashed into her like the remnants of a dream. Death? She shook her head, confused. "Death? I don't understand." Coira tried to pull her hand free, but he did not release it. She frowned at him. "How do I know you?"

He lifted a hand and ran it along her hair, offering a level of comfort a friend would. "Yes, death. You are between worlds right now. You know me as Gaiscioch, Coira, but that is not my real name."

As if being dead meant less, she whispered her more prominent thought. "Gaiscioch, my horse?"

His lips curled on one side, his humor a serious thing. "Yes, your horse. The stallion was but a conduit, a shape shift. My name is Erc. I was the king of Dalriada in Eire."

"Ireland?" She began to tremble. "I don't understand."

"No." He removed his hand, eyes intense. "But now you will. Stay brave and focus on my words, Coira."

He started to walk, taking her with him. Only then did Coira perceive her surroundings, terrifying and living, pulsing around her with need and temptation. She walked again through the nine stones she had dreamt about with William. Overhead was beautiful, the sky, and below that the trees and nature seen from beneath. Every grass stem and tree root visible. When Coira gazed below, she started to panic until Erc's voice cut in.

"You have met my Druidess, Chiomara."

Coira kept her gaze from falling down to what they walked over, startled by his revelation. "Yes, I have."

His voice was soft, soothing. "She was... my queen. We sired many children together. Our firstborn, taken from us when he was but a babe in the womb, then nourished by the gods, was the first of the Scottish MacLomains."

Her eyes again drifted, mesmerized by the fiery serpents swimming at their feet. Erc's grip tightened, and he urged her on. "Do you want to be dead, Coira?"

A shiver ran through her. "Of course not, no."

"Then do not look down, keep your gaze ahead, do not give in to temptation." His tone held the timbre of a king accustomed to being obeyed.

To distract herself from the multitude of oddities below, Coira continue talking. "Can I ask why you, as a horse, preferred the Scottish tongue?"

A shadowed smile graced the handsome king's face. "I thought you needed practice."

"Practice?" She focused on the sweep of his crimson robes and the tree roots overhead.

He looked at her, his gaze piercing. "Practice speaking in the way of the Scots, in the way of your bloodline."

She put one foot in front of the other, her thoughts easily adrift in the onslaught of middle world. "Why are you here now, Erc? Why did Chiomara visit me?"

"Because we love you, Coira."

At that, she looked overhead and felt the warmth of the sun through the bizarre haze of being underground. Such peace filled her, she knew she would not look away, would never look with wonder at the serpents again.

Erc's arms came around her, and blinding white light filled her vision. She had but one thought before everything fell away.

Thank you, Ireland.

****

A pinpoint of white light broke through the distant darkness. William tried to focus, to see clearly the sparkling diamond chip, but it wavered. He reached out, touched nothing but knew there was something.

"Coira!"

She was there, somewhere. Again he yelled her name, praying for a response, nothing. He fell back into the darkness as the brilliant glow receded until it snapped away, leaving him helpless and sad.

A foreign voice sighed into him. "It will not save you. But it will save him."

He tried to sort out the source of the female intonation but lost it. Yet her voice left in its wake pleasure, love, hope.

"William."

His eyes felt heavy, unused, and abandoned when Iain's voice broke through, coaxing him forth. He opened them, struck by daylight. The oddity of bright light receded, and he found he still sat on the ground, his back to the oak tree. He smiled, feeling as though he'd been reborn.

Iain's face came into focus. Ferchar stood behind him, Adlin nowhere to be seen. Both of them frowned at him, obviously assuming he'd snapped.

William jumped to his feet. "Where did they bring Coira? Where is she?"

Iain's hand clamped hard upon his forearm, his features granite. "Into the house, but I dinnae think 'tis wise for you to follow just yet."

His gaze fell directly into Iain's emerald's eyes and held them, dared them. "She's not there."

Iain's regard did not waver, his face showed nothing but intensity. "She is, and you will stay here for now."

He would not challenge Iain, knew that his cousin was stronger than both him and Ferchar, but not nearly as strong as Adlin. He spoke slowly, enunciating each word. "Wait, you will soon see."

At his words, Adlin exited the house, followed by the O'Donnell family. His eyes held a unique tint, one of curiosity, amusement, and intrigue. Iain released William's arm and stepped back.

Excitement grew as William walked forward and directed his question at Adlin. "She's vanished, hasn't she?"

"Aye," Adlin said, surprising both Iain and Ferchar. "She has."

Annie's quivering voice burst forth, her eyes flashing. "Coira was lying on the settee one moment, and then she just faded away."

Marie and Liam appeared confused and fearful.

"Where did she—" Iain ceased talking when realization dawned on him. "How is this possible?"

"My thoughts exactly," William said, though he could really care less. He was so happy, as though his spirit had been returned to him after a long sabbatical.

"I still don't understand what's happening?" Annie allowed Marie to wrap an arm around her waist and continued talking. "Why do you all seem so relieved? How is this a good thing?"

"Because I'm not dead."

Everyone turned at the sound of Coira's voice.

She stood in the lower drive, long black hair blowing in the breeze, face serene and glowing. The look in her eyes was different... wiser.

William didn't recognize the strangled sound erupting from his throat but moved swiftly and took her into his arms. He couldn't catch his breath, couldn't do anything but hold her against him and mold her body to his. Her arms wrapped around him and held just as tightly. She inhaled deeply, her small form shaking.

If anyone spoke, they didn't hear, so lost were they in one another. He stroked her head, neck, back, reveling in the feel of the warm flesh and the beating heart next to his. He mumbled into her neck.

"Thank the gods."

Adlin cleared his throat, the sound magically enhanced. Coira pulled back, her eyes covering William's face one last time before they turned to her family.

"Oh, Mama!" She pulled free and ran into Marie's waiting arms. Liam and Annie gathered close, awaiting their own hugs. As Liam stepped away from Coira's embrace and allowed Annie entrance, his sky blue gaze swung directly to William.

He met the fatherly evaluation and waited. Her father was a tall man, perhaps a few inches shorter than himself. His gaze bespoke intelligence and a natural inclination toward leadership.

While Coira was embraced and welcomed by Ferchar and Iain, Liam spoke to William. "So, you're me girl's Scot then?"

He didn't hesitate. "Aye."

Coira's attention returned to her father and William. "William is the current MacLomain chieftain, Papa. Well, current being six hundred years ago."

"I assumed he was." Liam came to an internal conclusion and strode forward, offering his hand to William. "Welcome to New Hampshire. Thank you for bringing her home."

He shook Liam's hand in the customary American fashion and offered the man honesty. "Thank you, but you can thank Adlin for bringing her home. If I'd had my way, she'd be in my castle right now."

Liam didn't miss a beat but offered sincerity. "Either way, your heart was in the right place."

William smiled at this. "My heart will always be in the right place."

"Yes, I've little doubt of that." Liam's eyes sparkled.

Coira quickly proceeded to introduce Ferchar, the only one of the four wizards who had not been to this time period. Her eyes drifted to William as Iain and Adlin reacquainted themselves with the O'Donnells. He took her small hand in his and leaned down, whispering in her ear. "When can we escape?"

She gave a flirtatious grin and shook her head, her eyes shadowed beneath thick black ashes. "No time soon, my laird."

He shot her a mock glare and brushed his thumb over the inside of her palm. He reveled in the visible shiver his touch caused. How enchanting she was standing there in naught but a white wool dress and his plaid over her shoulders. He wanted to kiss her, feel her skin, and savor its softness.

Instead, he was led into the house. The furnishings were vastly different from what he'd seen in the twenty-first century, the furniture more elegant, the wood richer. A textured paper spun with tasteful burgundy and crème designs lined the walls.

He chuckled inwardly and entered Ferchar's mind. "'Tis beautiful what they did with this place, what happened?"

Ferchar scowled. "I much prefer the way we have it in my time."

Liam led the men into the parlor while the women went to the kitchen to seek refreshments for everyone. William sat down in the same spot where the ring first glowed for Coira and Niall. Now the chair was wider, with curving feet and far less plush.

William and Adlin sat in chairs. Ferchar and Iain stood before a fireless hearth. Iain was the first to speak. "She walked past death as I did."

Adlin nodded once, his expression vague. "Aye."

"'Twas my belief that only MacLomain wizards could do that?"

William watched Adlin's face closely, searching. The old wizard gave nothing away.

"'Twas my belief as well." Adlin offered a loose shrug.

Iain's eyes narrowed and his lips thinned. "So we remain in the dark, Grandfather?"

Adlin made a noncommittal sound. As were William's, his cousins' eyes were trained on Adlin. He still found it hard to believe Coira had experienced the same ancient Viking magic that Iain once had. Back before William was born, in the war of the clans in 1199, Iain had died. Adlin and old magic had walked him through and helped maintain his life in accordance with an ancient MacLomain wizardly right. Where William thought Coira had died, so too had Arianna of Iain at the time.

He closed his eyes, still seeing the bright flicker of diamond glow that had assured William she still lived. It was the ring, her ring. It had glowed for him. As the thought occurred to him, he opened his eyes and looked at Adlin. "The ring, bloody hell, where is it?"

The women entered at that moment. Annie carried a tray of beverages and hors d'oeuvres. Liam took the tray from his daughter and set it down. Coira handed out the mugs and seconded his question. "The rings, yes, where are they?"

William flinched. Aye, rings, there were two.

Adlin's hand rose and he opened his fist. There they were, both of the rings, gleaming gold, one more brilliant than the other, its status a slap in William's face. Coira smiled, took them from Adlin and slipped first the engagement ring on, hesitating briefly as she slipped the large diamond onto her finger.

He sensed her disquiet. She didn't look at him, but he could clearly sense the betrayal she felt wearing the ring now. He dismissed his irritation and watched as she took the other ring. Her slender fingers quickly shoved the ring onto her finger as though she'd been lost without it.

William nearly jumped from the chair when she did. The sudden tension of his body drew her eyes, and her brows slammed together. He looked expectantly at the ring, sure of what he would see there.

He saw nothing.

Her eyes fell to the ring as well, then back to his face. Had she expected it to glow also? How could it not? But it did not. He didn't care and told her as much within her mind. She looked away abruptly, took a glass of her own, and sat on the settee next to the other women.

A strange silence fell over the misplaced group until Adlin broke it, his shrewd gaze meeting Marie's. "So tell us, Coira, who walked with you?"

Good question.

Coira sipped from her glass, blue eyes soft and indirect, as though she treasured her secret and was reluctant to share it. "Gaiscioch."

It appeared this bit of news took no one by surprise.

"Your horse." Ferchar stated, nodding.

She smiled warmly, eyes meeting Ferchar's. "Yes."

They all knew that Adlin had been in the shape shift form of a horse when Iain had died, knew Adlin had walked as a man with Iain through the gateway between heaven and hell. Everyone knew but Coira until it was explained to her.

Ferchar's tone turned whimsical. "And who is Gaiscioch?"

Her eyes left Ferchar and settled on the oriental carpet at their feet. She spoke softly. "Erc, king of Dalriada."

Shock struck William. Erc? Their distant Irish ancestor? His mind roved the recent discussion he and his cousins had had in this very room during the twenty-first century, mere weeks before. Pieces started to rapidly fall in place, Fionn, the druidess, Chiomara, and now Erc.

Hell, it had been made so clear for him! 'Twas the dream he'd had when he'd awoken to find Sarah in his arms, not Coira. The dream showed him Brodick's evil unleashed upon Coira and then her free, happy, and miraculously riding across his castle's field on her black stallion. Not a horse but Erc, King of Dalriada, trying to send him a message. Coira would be delivered from harm to him. She would not die.

His gaze seared Coira. What was her place in all of this?

Adlin's eyes remained on Marie, which William found curious. He looked to the petite redhead. What did these two share? His mind sharpened and entered Coira's. "What does your mother know about all of this?"

Her blue eyes grazed Marie and then rose to his. "My mother? Nothing."

He highly doubted that. "Why would our ancestor walk Coira through? This makes no sense."

Annie, who was normally so talkative, spoke for the first time. "Why not?"

"Why not, indeed, lass," Adlin said, obviously pleased with the blunt, straightforward logic offered.

Annie took her sister's hand and nodded. "It seems logical enough to me. He's dead, of course, but I've seen many strange things since traveling back in time. Heck, I saw plenty of strange things before that. I'm rather glad someone stepped up to the plate out of you MacLomains and made sure Coira survived."

Marie agreed, smiling. "Me, too!"

William watched the whole exchange thinking that both Adlin and Marie had managed to avoid a discussion they had no desire to share. How convenient.

The conversation quickly shifted to the girls' experience in medieval Scotland as William knew it would. He sat back, watching Coira at acceptable intervals. She was an innocent in all of this. That he knew. His gaze fell to Adlin and Marie.

They were not.

****

~Sylvan Mist~

Coira lay in bed, staring at the curtains swaying in the breeze. Her bedroom felt tight and confining. Candlelight still flickered nearby, throwing dancing shadows over the lower half of her bed. She reached out, using her magic, and caught a thread of light, letting it sift through her hands.

How strange it was to be here again. Nothing felt right. The walls were too short and the ceiling too low. She turned her head sideways and stared at the low flame of the candle. She thought of the magic within her, a fire that had not been hers when last she lay in this room. Her eyes traveled to the neatly piled papers on the secretary.

She tore her blankets back, stood, and walked over to them, so neat and tidy, organized and confined, like her, no, like she had been. An English history teacher, oh Lord. That was her. This was her. She ran her hand over the stack, traced a fingertip down the edges of the paper. The perfection of the pile annoyed her. The way she had pushed it against the right hand side of the secretary as she had always done out of habit.

She felt as though she was looking upon the actions of a stranger. A dribble of laughter escaped her mouth and tasted good on her glib tongue. No, not glib anymore! Without a care, she laughed, gripped the edge of the stack and smeared it across the desk top.

One sheet of paper slid too far and sailed to the floor. She turned to retrieve it and found William standing directly behind her. Automatically, her hand rose to his chest and she stared up at him. "How can you dwell in my mind as you do, yet I never sense you sneaking up on me?"

He gave a slow grin, his light gray eyes smoky in the candlelight. His strong hands held her upper arms lightly. "You were lost in thought, love. Not surprising considering your occupation."

His amused eyes fell to the ruined stack of papers before returning to her face. "Have you an issue with your paperwork?"

She glanced down ruefully at the paper at their feet. "I just needed to get organized."

He laughed, his masculine beauty a heady distraction. "Remind me to never allow you to organize anything within our castle, lass."

Coira froze. Our castle? What did he mean by that? She experienced a confusing mingle of delight, apprehension, and fear. She brought her other hand to his chest and felt the hard contours of his muscle beneath the material. "Our castle?"

"Aye, as soon as we return to Scotland, we'll be married."

Her heartbeat stopped. Married? Back in Scotland? Reality came crashing down around her. She was back in New Hampshire. Yes, she'd become a much different person, but this was still her home, wasn't it? How could she leave her parents?

She twisted the diamond-centered ring on her finger and spoke, voice small and timid, completely foreign to her ears. "I thought we could not marry without the gem's glow?"

William's smile vanished, and his brows drew together. His brogue thickened with passion, nearly impossible to understand. "I lost you, Coira, you died. And when you did, I felt I'd lost my soul. I won't lose you again. You will be my wife, regardless what the bloody ring does."

Coira tensed, not much of a proposal. But what had she expected really? Her mouth turned dry, and she could barely breathe. Isn't this what she wanted? Yes, with all of her heart. But there was newness in her, the war and killing, the magic, had changed her once more. Her respect for magic and fate had grown.

~Sylvan Mist~

She thought of Fionn and the sword, the destiny behind its power, and the fact that it had been bestowed upon her.

And Erc, the king who'd kept her alive and cared for her.

She relaxed, sad, yet enlightened, and brought her hand to William's face, tracing the strong jaw and high cheekbones. "No, I won't marry you unless this ring glows. I will not thwart the history or the beliefs of the MacLomain clan any more than you would at one point. How could you ask that of me?"

A low growl rumbled in his chest, and his eyes glittered pale silver, subdued and magically enhanced. "Because I love you, Coira, because 'tis impossible that this isnae supposed to be. I do no disservice to my people by marrying you."

Though caught in his gaze, she fought the sweet heat in her heart. "So you're essentially willing to do the same thing Brodick Cochran intended to do?"

His eyes returned to normal, but he squeezed her arms tighter. "I have no intention of deceiving my people. They would know the truth of it. They already love you, accept you as one of their own, and 'tis clear to all that you're mine. The ring will work its magic eventually."

Oh. But no. She lowered her hand to his collarbone, and the heat of his skin burned her. "And if it doesn't, William? What would happen if one day it glowed for another MacLomain?"

He ran his hands down her arms and his whisper turned deadly serious. "It willnae."

Before she could speak, he shook his head and put a finger to her lips. She felt the twist of emotions within him, apparent only through the firm set of his jaw. He was fighting the logic of her words, becoming once again the chieftain, and releasing the sentimental man. He turned away and walked the short distance to her bed where he fingered her comforter.

When he spoke, his voice was level, less intense, his head turned slowly back to her. "What will you do, Coira?"

She breathed deeply. What would she do now? Where was her place in this life? She couldn't imagine not returning to Scotland with William but realized the peculiarity of such an action were they not to marry. A week ago, she wouldn't have hesitated, would've gladly been his mistress for the rest of her life.

Yet what of his heirs? She wanted children, and they would be bastards. Coira knew the clan would accept them gladly, but she wanted more for her children, more for her future husband. In addition, this intense love she felt for William would only grow stronger with time. If the ring decided he was not for her, the agony of their separation would be devastating.

William deserved more, so much more.

Moisture stung her eyes when she met his. "I will stay here."

His body locked, and the muscles in his long body vibrated with restrained power. "I saw the stone glow in my mind when you were gone. 'Tis how I knew you were alive. It saved me from losing myself. Why would I see such a thing, lass? Why?"

A swallow lodged in her throat. He'd not yelled at her aloud but in her mind, his question as intense as a thunderclap in a cave, laced with sharp anger. It saved him, the ring. Suddenly she remembered the Druidess's words by the stream. *It will not save you, but it will save him.* And it hadn't saved her; Erc had. She tried to speak but was unable.

He moved so fast, she had no time to blink or resist. He sat her on the bed, knelt and grasped her hip bones, pinning her in place. The candlelight flickered and then snuffed out, leaving them in the dull glow of a half moon muted by window glass. Pockets of darkness chiseled his serious face, left shadows between his cheekbones and jaw, and in the area beneath his strong brows.

His well-formed lips flattened, and his eyes narrowed to streaks of moonlit diamonds. "You worry for children we've yet to have and worry for me, yet you forget that all a child needs to be happy is to be loved, as do I. As far as that other thought you had, I would gladly share a year, month, or even one more day with you and risk losing you, than lose you altogether at this moment."

A tear slid down her cheek.

He leaned forward, catching the tear before it slid off the corner of her jaw. Intense longing buried her in white heat, and breathing became impossible. His face hovered so close, his breath scalding hot against her skin. She turned her head slightly and brought his lips closer to hers, left so little distance between them that they nearly brushed.

"No, I can't."

He muffled a curse and covered her mouth, spread her legs, and pulled her against him. She whimpered under the onslaught of pleasure and urgency. He had never kissed her quite like this before, with such a medley of longing and fierceness one moment, and tenderness and tentativeness the next. She buried her hands in his thick, rich hair, while every nerve ending blew apart, stung skin, and shook her body.

Then he was in her mind, his essence wrapping around her spirit. "Goodbye, my lass, my love."

~Sylvan Mist~

Mist crawled along her skin and touched every part of her, wrapped her in love. A forest filled her vision. William filled her vision, tall and plaid-wrapped and perfect. He seemed one with the mist, as if it created the gloriousness of his form and not the other way around. She reached for him even as the mist took him away and left her alone in the moonlit bedroom with but a trace of mist swirling away over the floorboards.

Coira stared at the retreating moisture, felt it suck the last of her heart before it vanished entirely. A wrenching cry tore from her throat. He was gone! Really gone. Just as she knew it had to be. He'd done it swiftly, easily, as she knew he had to. Still, the pain was incredible.

Then Annie was there, sitting on the bed, holding her. Her sister stroked her hair and said nothing. This is how it had to be, Coira knew. This was the only way, yet it didn't ease the fact she'd most likely never find a love so true and pure as that she had with William.

But all the logical thoughts in the world meant nothing. Perhaps by morning they would.

~Sylvan Mist~

Chapter Twenty

Marie sat and waited, a single candle burned beside her. He didn't make her wait long. When Adlin appeared in the attic, his white robes harsh against the lackluster wooden walls and beams overhead, his expression was more serene than she'd expected. The wizard didn't sit but stood silently for a time, his gaze moved gracefully over the darkened corners of the room.

His sapphire blue eyes at last settled on her. "I'm not upset, lass. I was at first, but no longer."

"Good." She flicked her wrist and a trunk appeared. "It's in there."

Adlin looked at the trunk embedded with emeralds, sapphires, and diamonds, the gems reminiscent of the three rings. What a long road wrought with pain, new beginnings, and profound love. The journey had been a lengthy one, but he was proud he'd been part of it.

Marie stood and came to stand beside him. "Will you take it now?"

Adlin's eyes glowed momentarily and the trunk slowly opened. "Aye, 'tis time for it to go home."

She gazed down at the crown of gold, a warm thrum of love and wellbeing filling her heart. "It's beautiful."

The wizard smiled and took her hand in his. "Aye, fit for a king."

She smiled. "I was most honored, you know, regardless."

He nodded slightly, leaned over, and retrieved the crown from the trunk. "I'm sorry it was at such an expense to you."

Marie sighed and offered a wobbly smile. "Truly, how can my family finding true love be a sad thing? It cannot be. I'm too practical to see it otherwise."

Adlin's wise eyes found hers. "Your destiny has been a great one, your sacrifice thorough."

"Aye." She did not look away. "Yet all is not lost in the end. I have been part of a powerful, enchanting circumstance born of magic. And I have Liam." A small wistful smile stole her lips. "My Liam."

The wizard's eyes softened, comforted her. "You will have grandchildren, loving creatures of Scotland and Ireland."

Marie tempered her tears. They would do no good right now. "I would like to meet Caitlin before all is said and done. I know in my afterlife I will help her, but…"

Her words trailed off. How peculiar it was to know that her spirit would come to her future relative's aid. She had read Beth Luken's book titled Destiny's Denial. How could she not? She had mediated it, helped Adlin recount the tale to Beth. Such an odd position, telling of her own ghost; however, Marie understood the grander design, as did Adlin. It was some comfort to know for certain that there was an afterlife.

Adlin gave no answer to the request but pulled her close and embraced her in what felt to be a father's hold. A magic far more powerful than hers suffused Marie and took away the last of her anxiety, transforming it into a great reprieve of peace and goodwill.

~Sylvan Mist~

Then he was gone.

Marie stared down at the empty trunk and smiled, wiped away a useless tear. The story was nearly finished and she was blessed enough to be part of it.

****

"Mmm, tasty tomato, this."

Coira sifted through the bleak colors the vibrant late summer day offered and watched Beth Luken devour a tomato as efficiently as one would an apple if, of course, they were devouring the core as well.

Her husband, Edward Huntington, looked at his wife with adoration. "I've yet to see another eat a tomato quite like you, my love."

Coira couldn't agree more. Beth Luken, her blond hair streaked with becoming wisps of white, had an intense vibrancy about her that encompassed everything she did. Still beautiful, Beth was animated and more alive than most. She had a quick wit and an even quicker tongue. Beth and Edward had arrived mere minutes ago, and everyone was enjoying sugary sweet lemonade.

She giggled like a schoolgirl at her husband before turning her attention to Annie. "You traveled back in time!" Her eyes narrowed, studied Annie's features. "And you met someone!"

Marie made an inaudible sound before she spoke. "It seems my youngest daughter married that someone as well."

Beth's eyes lit up. "No?"

"Aye." Marie nudged Annie, whose face was positively radiant.

Annie nodded. "Aye, a big tall burly Scotsman!"

"Oh my lord!" Beth jumped up and the two women embraced across the table. "How wonderful!"

Liam did not look as pleased, his blue eyes shadowed beneath his brows. "Too soon and without her father's permission, I might add."

"Papa, I was there for six months while only a few days passed here. Besides, I had Coira's blessing."

One eyebrow drew up so high it nearly touched his hairline. "I know of this time-travel business. He could have found his way here had he the inclination."

Coira interjected before her father's Irish temper made its way onto his tongue and into his eyes. "They were two people in love before the onslaught of a massive war, Papa. Tell me you wouldn't have done the same with Mama had you been in their position."

Liam's azure gaze swung to his oldest daughter and his brow lowered in possible defeat. "You might be right about that. It still would have been nice to witness such a thing and meet the man who stole my lassie's heart."

"And it would have been so dear to have my family there as well," Annie said. "Including Calum."

Marie sighed, her eyes sad. "My poor Calum, now he doesn't expect to be home until next spring what with the apprenticeship."

Coira knew her mother felt as though she were losing all of her children at once, which, excepting Coira, she was. There was little doubt that Annie would be going back to Scotland. She couldn't imagine either her sister or Arthur anywhere else.

The thought of the country brought a sharp sting of longing to her breast. How wonderful to raise her children, William's children there, amongst the MacLomain clan. She quickly dismissed the notion, knew it was a fruitless dream.

Beth's gentle voice interrupted her useless ponderings. "And how was your journey back to Scotland, Coira?"

Coira's back straightened. She was still irritated that everyone had answers she did not. Coira couldn't contain the lash of her tongue. "Don't you know already?"

Beth didn't shy away but allowed a smooth smile instead. Without hesitation, she spoke, voice light. "No, I don't."

"No?" Coira was overtired, heartbroken, and in no mood to be less than direct. "Tell me how and when you were able to write two thoroughly truthful, engaging stories about my family and the MacLomain clan."

"My, you have changed," Beth said kindly, obviously not wishing to provoke. Her eyes skirted between Marie and Annie before settling again on Coira.

Coira gave her no chance to speak. "Don't you think I've been in the dark long enough?"

To her credit, Beth was not intimidated by Coira's crisp tone. She wiped her hands on a cloth and stood, her eyes met Coira's. "Come with me."

She didn't hesitate, but stood abruptly and followed Beth away from the table onto the fields behind the house. Their long skirts swept the grass underfoot, no wind blew, and the summer air felt slightly oppressive. Beth waited until they were a good distance away before she spoke. "You have every right to be upset."

"Aye, I do."

Beth didn't flicker a brow at Coira's very Scottish sounding response. "I had no leave to tell you what I had written sooner, and I am sorry."

Coira had known Beth since she was a child, had looked to her as an aunt though she wasn't blood related. Now everything was different, and Beth knew it, yet she appeared undaunted at best. "How did you manage to write two novels about such things on top of the novels you published?" She continued on. "And, how did you know everything?"

Beth slowed her pace and eyed Coira. "I wrote the two novels, *Fate's Monolith* and *Destiny's Denial*, through the aid of Marie."

"So you know of the magic in this family." Coira held up a hand and waved away Beth's next statement. "Of course you do, silly me."

Coira stopped walking and eyed her companion, refusing to draw forth the magic to enter Beth's mind. "Why you? I know you don't carry magic."

Beth cocked an eyebrow. "Ah, yes. And you do now? How fascinating and unexpected." The other woman grabbed her hand quickly, her eyes warm and compassionate. "And wonderful, Coira, truly wonderful."

She ground her teeth, aggravated to realize that Beth meant no harm. How discontented she was! She couldn't be mad at Annie but had expected to be able to vent on her Aunt Beth. And though she intended to be short, she wasn't. "It is wonderful."

Beth's eyes teared and her lips curled in. "I learned about the magic of the Brouns and the MacLomains the night Arianna left. The night Edward and I confessed our love for each other, the same eve Adlin showed all of us, Arianna and Iain, what we could not see clearly."

Coira flinched at the word MacLomain. Lord, William had vanished mere days ago, and the very thought of him spun her mind, made her weak, unpredictable. William. She missed him terribly, missed all of them.

She made no attempt to mask the emotions on her face. Why should she? Coira looked to the clear blue sky overhead, her words to Beth soft. "Why was Annie privileged enough to know all of this?"

"Simple really. She carries magic." Beth sighed. "But that's exactly what you thought I'd say, yes?"

"Yes, exactly." She met Beth's gaze. "And now I'm privileged as well."

Beth took Coira's other hand and held them both. Her eyes fell to the rings on either hand. "I do believe your story will be the most interesting one, Coira."

She bit her lip, barely glancing at the rings. One saddened and the other confused her. She whispered the only response that held a grain of truth. "My story ended with William leaving."

"No." Beth squeezed her hands, released them and turned back toward the house. "Every ring has a tale, and yours will end with a MacLomain."

She looked at Beth sharply. "Do you already know my ending then?"

Beth shook her head. "No."

Coira wasted no time, but entered Beth's mind briefly. The woman was telling the truth. Blast it! As they walked back up the small field, she couldn't help but wonder about so many things. Coming into magic, meeting the Druidess, Erc, and Fionn; what was the bigger picture? What was she missing? There must be a purpose to the ring belonging to her and such help from Ireland.

A slight wind blew up and she stopped abruptly, tilted her head into the air. The sharp tang of sea salt engulfed. She spun slowly, her eyes taking in everything, the delicate sweep of oaks, birches, elms, and pines that dusted the outer edge of the lower meadow. The verdant expanse of grass elongated, and then shortened before everything sharpened.

Coira held her footing when intense magic swamped. She recognized this magic, had felt it before.

~Sylvan Mist~

The world faded and became tarnished, unclear. At last, her surroundings transformed until she stood where she'd once stood in a dream, outside a circle of nine tall stones, evenly spaced. Bright sunlight fell through the tall, encompassing oak branches overhead.

Her pulse accelerated, and her chest tightened painfully. William? She looked around frantically, desperate to see his tall form.

"Coira, my child, come into the circle."

Coira blinked in astonishment as the form of the Druidess appeared in the center of the stones. Her long, white dress glowed in the sunlight, made her appear a glorious, enchanting goddess. Little gold beads sparkled throughout her many braids.

"Why am I here?" Coira didn't hesitate but entered the circle. Colossal power suffused and warmed her soul.

The Druidess, Chiomara, raised her hand to Coira's heart, touch feather light. Her voice held a singing quality. "Because I want you to know who you are."

Coira waited under the powerful gaze of the woman, unable to form a coherent thought.

Chiomara smiled softly. "You are the daughter of the man called Liam O'Donnell."

Coira nodded slightly.

"Liam descends many, many generations from Erc and me, from our foster child."

Coira's breath caught in her throat. What had she just said? No. It couldn't be. Choimara and Erc were her distant relatives?

"In heart and soul, not in blood," Chiomara said. The Druidess kept her hand on Coira's heart as she continued. "Very soon, you will have to make a decision, my child. Listen to your heart when you do so. Trust your instincts."

She had so many questions but before she could voice them, the Druidess and stones vanished quickly, leaving her lost in a blur of misplaced colors and shapes until New Hampshire resurfaced.

"Coira, are you all right?"

Beth's voice went from sounding far away to right next to her. Coira looked at her. They still stood in the same place, at the top of the field behind the house.

"Coira?"

She tested her voice and found it steady. "Yes, I'm fine."

Beth frowned, eyes worried. "You appeared lost there for a moment, as if you'd seen a ghost."

Indeed she had. Coira continued to walk, grateful her legs supported her. As they rounded the corner of the house, she ran straight into James, her fiancé. Before she had a chance to respond, he pulled her into his arms. She brought her hands tentatively to his shoulders. How strange he felt against her now after William's much larger, taller frame.

Actually, James's frame suited her small form. Yet, he didn't feel right, and she pulled away slowly, tactfully. His sea green eyes met hers with concern. "How are you feeling, Coira?"

How was she feeling? Confused, alone, and fearful.

He brushed aside a stray lock of hair that had fallen free from her bonnet. Without thought, she removed the cumbersome thing. Before she'd left for Scotland, she'd worn bonnets often, though never fond of them. Now the cap felt entirely wrong. Her hair remained pinned, but loosely.

William stared at the bonnet, perplexed by her action. "I was told you had fallen ill the day I proposed. I've been worried since."

Ill? Well, that would make sense, a good way to explain both her actions and disappearance the last few days. It was still surreal, the concept of mere days passing here in the nineteenth century.

She touched his face with the friendly affection she'd always had for him. "I'm fine now, thank you."

His keen eyes fell to her hand. "Why do you wear Annie's ring?"

He caught her off guard with that question. Luckily Annie piped up from the table. "I gave it to her."

Not the best explanation. She shot her sister a look that only she would understand. And, as Coira expected, James found Annie's explanation strange.

James cocked his head, his articulate British accent a dim reminder of the woman she'd once thought she was. "Though I've never particularly agreed with you, my love, don't you hold a slight aversion to your natural lineage?"

Something stirred in her, tangled her tongue into a rich Scottish brogue, only lending to his confusion. "Aye, I did, but I dinnae anymore."

Annie made a small choking sound, as did a few other family members. Hex on them! Coira squared her shoulders and toned down the burr, it didn't work. To her utter consternation, her next words were in Gaelic. "I'm exceptionally proud to be half Irish and half Scottish."

She clamped a hand over her mouth. What was this? Her mother and father beamed with pleasure, while Annie and Beth muffled their giggles.

Marie stood and smoothed her day dress. "Pay her no mind, James. The sickness has left her acting most unusual."

James shrugged loosely and smiled at her. "I don't mind at all. The accent and the Gaelic language, I'm assuming, become her."

Coira smiled in return. James was such a good man. "How is everything down at the schoolhouse? Were they able to cover my position?"

The mere idea of returning to her profession filled her with dread.

"Yes, all is well. The students are concerned for you. I will tell them you are better. Will you be returning soon?" James asked.

"I would imagine." She stepped away and contained a sigh of displeasure. Oh, how Scotland had changed her! Inwardly, she knew it was for the better, but that made no difference now. It was time to return to her life, move on.

James stepped forward and leaned down close to her ear. "May we have some time alone?"

Coira momentarily recalled the way she'd felt when William had done the very same thing. How he leaned so close to her ear that his warm breath skirted the lobe and sent shivers of awareness through her. James invoked none of those feelings, never had. A twinge of emotion curled through her; poor James would not be bringing a virgin to his bed on their wedding night. The old Coira may have been horrified by that. The new Coira figured he was not a virgin, so to speak, so fair's fair.

She nodded to him, grateful her accent was behaving again. "Of course, you may have a moment alone with me."

They excused themselves and walked down the drive leading away from the house. The day grew late, and the sun sat just below the treetops casting angled tunnels of sunlight across the roadway ahead. Crickets buzzed and chirped, and the occasional squirrel scurried through last autumn's parched leaves.

They'd traveled just beyond the range of the last oak guarding the house's front lawn, hiding them from the family members, when James stopped walking and turned to her. He took her hand and raised it so that the diamond engagement ring sparkled between them.

He stared intently at the ring before his green eyes caught hers. She was somewhat shocked to see desire in their depths. Had it been there before? It must have been. They had kissed a few times when they first decided to take their friendship to the next level. Never the sort of kisses William had introduced, no, not nearly that kind, but pleasant, friendly ones.

Now she saw the undeniable glint of lust there, and she almost pulled her hand away. He must have gleaned her near intention for his brow furrowed before it smoothed again. "Coira, is something wrong?"

Was something wrong? Yes. No, maybe. She kept her eyes locked with his, unable to look away. The Druidess's words snaked through her mind and ignited a stir of recognition. *"Very soon, you will have to make a decision, my child. Listen to your heart when you do so. Trust your instincts."*

Without doubt, Coira understood that this was likely the aforementioned question leading to her final decision. Is something wrong? Yes, there was. She'd denied William for the sake of both their hearts and potential children and knew she had been wise in that decision, though it broke her heart. Was what she was about to do with James any different? She was not in love with him and knew for certain she never would be.

She would always feel affection for him, love him as a friend, but somehow that was not enough anymore. She would end up doing them both a great disservice in the long run, if she married him. She wanted more for him, for her. Chiomara had said to listen to her heart, and Coira knew her heart did not lie with James, not the whole of it. She couldn't marry him knowing that.

She raised her other hand and covered the one that held hers. "More than anything, I want you to be happy, James. Do you understand that?"

He inclined his head, his eyelashes lowered slightly. "Of course, and I you."

"You will not be happy if we marry, James."

His eyes flashed with renewed concern. "What are you speaking of, love? We will be very happy together. You have my word."

"No." She removed her hands from his. "We have been good friends for a long time, and I dare you to disagree that we both decided to marry for lack of desired alternatives."

"I do desire you, Coira!"

She stood taller and squared her shoulders. "Needs of the flesh are one thing, but do you fancy yourself in love with me?"

"Is that so necessary for a contented marriage?"

His statement answered her question, and she made to remove the ring. He grabbed her wrist and stopped her. "I do not understand why you are doing this! You mean so much to me, Coira, please stop."

She didn't, but removed the ring. "James, you are one of my best friends, and I am yours. That is what you are feeling! Yes, you may desire me physically. It is only natural for a woman and man to feel that, but what we share will be ruined if we marry. Clearly you can see that?"

James's eyes calmed as she held her hand out, the ring cradled in her palm. She didn't enter his mind but hoped with all of her soul he understood her words, that they would not cause her dear friend too much harm. Please, Lord, let him see clearly. Many moments passed, her hand held out to him, before he spoke again. "Perhaps you are right."

A considerable rush of relief tore through her.

He meant it. Thank the Lord, he meant it. Slowly he reached forward and took the engagement ring. When it left her palm, she felt as if a two-thousand-pound weight was lifted from her shoulders.

Why had she worn it so long? It was decidedly wrong of her in light of her time in Scotland. Some part of her knew that leaving it on was the safest place for it, and that the minute she'd laid eyes on William, James's ring really didn't belong to her and never would.

"James, I do love you dearly as a friend. I always will."

A smile touched his eyes. "Come here."

He pulled her into his arms and held tight. She embraced him in return and squeezed her eyes shut, so happy that they would remain friends. After some time, they pulled apart, and gazed at one another fondly.

"I'll be keeping a close eye on you and will expect the man you do eventually marry to be a perfect gentleman and madly in love with you," James said.

She groaned and rolled her eyes. "You will, won't you?"

A wide smile freed James' face from such heavy discussion. "But of course! Shall we return and tell your family the news?"

He held an arm out to her which she readily accepted. "Aye."

"Aye?" He lifted a quizzical brow while they strolled, arm and arm back down the drive.

She laughed. "Sorry, I have really embraced my origins of late, I'm afraid."

He chuckled. "So I see."

She rattled on as they reentered the main yard. "I'm really not sure why..."

Words left her, and she stopped walking. James stopped with her, his eyes staring in the direction that had ceased her easy banter and all movement.

Her family was not alone anymore. Beth, Edward, and Liam still sat at the table, their attention intent, where Annie perched on the rope swing with Marie nearby. None of this was out of place. The one who leaned nonchalantly against the tree was. She saw only his profile from here, tall, muscled, and painfully perfect.

William?

Was she mad? Was she seeing things?

Edward leaned close and whispered in awe. "Am I seeing what I think I'm seeing?"

His words barely filtered through, but her mouth answered anyway. "What do you think you are seeing?"

"A man in a plaid cloak with long hair."

"You see him, too?" Her body went numb. Were they both seeing the same apparition, or had he really returned? Her mind couldn't make sense of anything save the Scotsman across the way.

At her disbelieving words to James, William's head turned in their direction. His silver eyes cut right to hers. Every muscle tightened and bruised her skin with defiance and disbelief. Like a coil of rampant, unchecked sensuality, his pewter survey whipped the blood through her veins and caused instant lightheadedness.

James urged her forward, seemingly oblivious to William's immediate venomous evaluation of his person. As they approached, she worked hard to gather her wits. He was indeed standing there, his masculine potency a formidable thing. Why had he returned? He shouldn't have!

Time slowed as they approached everyone. Part of her wanted to run to William, hold him to her, and never let go. The rational part knew she could not for all the right reasons. Still, seeing him again standing there, watching her intently, she realized how much the past few days had felt like years.

She nearly entered his mind but stopped and spoke aloud instead, voice unsure. "William."

James didn't release her arm, but he stared back and forth between the two. "You know him, Coira?"

"Aye," William answered for her, his burr closing the distance between them. "She knows me."

Coira didn't miss the dry undercut in his tone or the tensing of his stance. She shot him a warning glance. James could not know about any of this. "James, this is my friend William. He is from Scotland."

James nodded to William, yet spoke to Coira with a humor that amazed her considering the Highland warrior standing before them. "I would have never guessed. Scotland, you say?"

William didn't appear pleased. His gaze fell to their entwined arms. His brows slammed together, and his nostrils flared.

Annie nodded enthusiastically. "Aye, one of our Scottish relatives."

Annie's meager explanation hung in the air, while a sudden silence fell over the family. The wind blew the oak leaves overhead, tossing the orange glow of the late sun back and forth through the green leaves.

William pushed away from the tree. His eyes turned a vicious shade of jaded silver. Startled by the fierce expression on his face, James took an involuntary step back when William strode toward Coira.

She held her ground, unable to do anything but stare up at William. His powerful presence consumed, made the rest of the world fade away. *Thump. Thump. Thump.* Her heart beat so hard it hurt. Spice and male assaulted her, made flesh crawl with undeniable anticipation. She licked her lips.

His eyes never left hers as he reached down and gently took her hand. His touch shot new shivers of awareness throughout, scalding her very being. No, William, this cannot be. What was he doing? His thickly lashed eyes fell to her hand where his fingers caressed.

Time stopped when she looked down at their combined hands. His strained whisper sounded a tortured plea. "Please, Coira, tell me you see it."

Emotion choked her. Was she seeing clearly? Oh yes! The diamond in the ring shone so brightly, it nearly blinded her. Seconds or minutes passed, while she gazed with wondrous joy at the stone. Her vision blurred with tears. How long she had waited and prayed for this moment. She had thought it would never be hers to have. But it was, he was, William, her one true love.

His hands touched first her arms, then her shoulders before they encased her face and forced her to look up at him. She saw his spirit clearly then, the excruciating need, the insanity he skirted, if she did not tell him what he needed to hear. "Coira, tell me you see it. I have to hear you say the words."

She brought her hands to his and offered a shaky smile. "I see it, William. It glows so intensely."

A ragged keen erupted from his throat before he pulled her into his arms and wrapped her small form

~Sylvan Mist~

tightly within his much larger one. He mumbled a slew of grateful, endearing, passionate words into her hair and neck. She was lost in him, lost in the magic, felt the earth as it slipped away and the mist come, his mist.

She touched him wherever she could while locked within his muscled cage. He was hers, he always had been. He pulled back and lifted her into his arms, kissed her thoroughly. The mist swirled around, cocooned them yet again in their own private world. His eyes burned diamond bright, as did the mist and the ring, bonding them in magic and love.

Coira couldn't taste him enough nor he her. When at last the mist faded a fraction, twirling them within a forest tall with pines and golden needles beneath, an enchanting sphere of sylvan mist. She smiled and felt Fionn brush her mind. He'd never really left her, had indeed always had so very much to do with this union between her and William.

When at last the mist cleared, they stood alone, her family vanished.

"Scotland," she murmured.

"Aye." He reached around her head and plucked away the few pins still containing her hair. The coil fell free, and he buried his fingers in its thick depths. "You've been away for some time, love."

"Have I?" She was still unable to look from his face, only slightly aware of a warm breeze and the sweet smell of flowers. "How long?"

He leaned in and kissed her again before enlightening her. "'Tis spring, Beltane."

"Springtime! Strange how time passes differently for us. It was mere days since I saw you last!"

"'Twas a far smaller amount of torture for you than me, lass." He sighed heavily. "Every day equaled a lifetime. And this knowing I'd never see you again, and if I did, 'twould not be I who had you."

She caressed his cheek with tenderness. "Why did you come back, William?"

"Och, Adlin sent me, bloody trickster of a wizard. I was sent to retrieve Annie."

"Annie!" Reality landed with a heavy thump on her shoulders. "My family! I just left them there, I never said goodbye, and poor, dear James, oh no!"

"James will be just fine," William said. His statement sounded really more a growl. "As for your family, I suspect you'll see them again."

"I will, really? How is that possible, are we going back?" She shook her head, confused. "And what of Annie? You forgot her!"

William laughed and his dimples blossomed. "So many questions, sprite. You will not be going back. This is your home now. I have it on the highest authority, you will see your family again, and once the ring glowed, I realized I was not sent back to retrieve Annie, but you."

Before she began another round of inquisitions, he put a finger to her lips, pulled her close, and kissed the questions from her tongue. They stood that way for a long time exploring one another until the passion became too much. With a great show of self-control, he released her. "We'll not make love again until you are my wife."

She tempered her desire. "How noble you have become. I see no point in waiting."

He grinned. "Not just noble, sprite, but bloody gallant really. I want you beneath me as my wife."

She shivered at his words. "If you wish."

He took her hand and they began walking. She cast him a sidelong glance, curious. "William, would you live in New Hampshire if I desired such?"

He didn't hesitate. "Aye." His expression was unreadable when he looked down at her. "Is that what you want, Coira?"

"No." And she knew it to be the truth. She would miss her family terribly, but Scotland, this Scotland, was where she wanted to be, had to be. "I want our children to be raised here, amongst the mountains and the loch. I want them to play in that beautiful castle of yours... ours, and speak the Gaelic tongue."

"Be kind, I'll not make it to our wedding night, if you speak of our children." He winked, pulled her closer, and wrapped an arm around her shoulders as they walked.

She laughed. "And when will our wedding night be, my laird?"

"This eve."

She stopped short. "Tonight!"

He spun easily, lightly dragging the arm that had been over her shoulder around slightly so that while he still held her, he now faced her. How graceful he was for such a large man. Only a well-trained warrior could pull off such a move with casual fluidity. "Aye, this eve. How long did you think I'd wait?"

Incredulous, she put her hands on her hips. "Long enough to plan a decent wedding!"

"Hell, lass, we Highlanders dinnae plan a celebration. Such things come rather naturally to us."

"What about poor Euphemia, the cook?" She shook her head, astonished.

"She'll manage. I've little doubt that when I left, Adlin nudged her along some." His hand wandered to the side of her neck.

"There's no room for debate, is there?"

"Nay." His thumb grazed her lower lip. "You'll be my wife by nightfall."

~Sylvan Mist~

Chapter Twenty One

William had never been so happy.

As they left the forest and stepped onto the wide field, he squeezed Coira's hand. Two massive bonfires burned in the middle of the meadow, a fiery foreground to the castle beyond. The sun was a bright, golden orb in the lower sky, casting a brilliant veil of light over the spires.

How he'd dreaded traveling forward in time to retrieve Annie. Although Arthur had requested to go, Adlin forbade it and gave no logical reason why. No one questioned Adlin's reasons for he always knew something everyone else didn't.

When he first saw Coira walking arm in arm with James down the drive, he'd longed for a weapon. He'd wanted to dismember the man in a hundred different ways for touching her. She was so beautiful and fragile with the wind blowing random wisps of ebony hair around her face. A rose-hued blush had graced her high cheekbones, and her eyes mesmerized, bright with life. He looked down at the ring and wondered. He'd not probed her mind too thoroughly, only wanted to be there to share their love.

He'd almost closed the distance between them and hauled her from James's grasp, until he remembered why she had stayed in New Hampshire and not returned with him. Nothing had changed, and he knew her resolve would be the same, until he'd seen the ring glow. The wonderful, fickle, undecided ring that had made his life a living hell.

"Coira, what happened after I left you and returned to Scotland?"

"What do you mean?" She frowned.

"Something must have transpired, because the ring glows now for us."

She shook her head. "The only monumental thing that happened was that I gave James back his engagement ring."

He looked down at her other hand. Indeed, the ring was gone. How had he managed to miss that? He knew full well how—nothing at all mattered except Coira, once the other ring glowed, period. He grinned in wry amusement. He would have to be careful in the future. This lass took coherent thought and observation from him, made him think only of her when she was near.

"So all along the one ring didn't glow, because I wore the other?" she asked.

"It would appear so. I can think of no other reason. My thought is that Adlin may be able to tell us why."

She nodded. A confused expression on her face until her eyes took in the crowd.

"The Broun clan is here!" she said, excitement bubbling over.

"Aye, many of them." William pulled her closer, wished instead he was carrying her, better yet, lying with her. "They didnae want to miss this wedding."

Her face shone with delight. "Oh, how wonderful." She pondered. "So you won the war obviously. Brodick is dead. I suppose I just assumed that when you, Adlin, Ferchar, and Iain came to New Hampshire with me."

"'Tis an accurate assumption." He stopped again, brought her small hand to his lips, and kissed it. "We were all very proud and grateful to you, Coira. You fought bravely."

Her lips quivered, then became stern. "I killed men."

He wrapped his arm around her waist, pulled her gently against him, and tilted her head back with one finger, brought her eyes in line with his. "You protected your clans and killed very bad men. Your soul will not suffer for such acts."

"How do you know?" Her blue eyes transformed to the exact shade of the sky behind her.

He caressed her chin and filled her mind with peace and love. "Because they were evil. You only helped your god."

She made no mention that they did not share the same god. It seemed she had already figured that out and made peace with it. Coira nodded and they continued to walk. "Were many on our side wounded and killed?"

"Aye, fair amounts were wounded but not as many killed as we had expected." He contemplated the long months after the war, caring for those wounded and burying the dead. The snow fell heavily and slowed their progress, but in the end, the allied clans returned home with the certain knowledge and comfort that a major Highland threat was defused.

They entered the masses of smiling clansfolk eager to welcome Coira back. Many were Brouns, their black and red plaids mixing with the blue and greens of the MacLomains. He reveled in the delight on her face as he pulled her through; she still maintained the countenance of a lady, a noble presence surrounding her. Yet now she was more relaxed with a touch of rebellion and free spirit just beneath the surface.

It was a combination William knew he'd never get enough of.

~Sylvan Mist~

****

Coira walked beneath the first portcullis with William and stepped onto the drawbridge. She'd never been so happy in her life. It felt right to be back here, as though she were returning to her long-lost family, which in some regards, she was. She thought of the first time she'd crossed this drawbridge, her stallion racing mere feet ahead of William's.

So much had transpired since that day.

As they walked beneath the next portcullis and entered the courtyard, she stopped in amazement. Everybody was here that shouldn't be, beyond the crowd in the inner compound. Her mother, father, Annie, Beth, and Mildred!

And, naturally, though they'd just seen each other, Annie came barreling at her until she was wrapped in a gleeful embrace. "Welcome home!"

Coira laughed and pulled away. "What on Ireland's green earth is everybody doing here? Not that I'm not thrilled."

Annie pulled her toward everyone else. "Your family's here to watch you marry, Coira. They couldn't be here for mine due to the impending war, but Adlin ensured they'd be here for this one. He says this is a rare occasion."

"A rare occasion?"

The others stepped forward to greet and hug her, her mother first in line. "Oh, isn't this grand! I can't believe we're here!"

"Neither can I!" Coira laughed as she was pulled first into her father's embrace and then Beth's. "Why didn't you all just travel back with William and I?"

Beth made a dismissive gesture, her gaze raking William with polite admiration. "You two needed some time alone. Besides, your future husband gave us little choice. He just whisked you out of there."

William made a noncommittal grunt, eyes sparkling with mischief. Liam spoke up. "Yes, shortly after you vanished, Adlin appeared and bid us all to travel back to witness your wedding. Why we weren't able to do the same for Arianna and Iain's we've no idea."

"What of James?" Coira asked.

Her father's eyes twinkled as an enchanting smile lit his face. "Have no worries, my girl. Adlin will see him through, lead him in the right direction. James will be fine, as will your schoolchildren."

She nodded, knowing her father would not lie, and all would be well.

Arthur appeared beside Annie and wrapped his big arm around her waist. Coira watched her parent's reaction and saw nothing but smiles. Apparently, all the introductions were made, and Marie and Liam approved.

She turned her attention to Mildred, Caitlin's grandmother. "So good to see you again, ma'am."

Mildred's eyes held the young delight of a twenty-year-old embarking on her first adventure. "And you, my dear, such a grand occasion it is, too!"

"It is beautiful here, isn't it?" Coira smiled.

"Yes, I never had a chance to see the MacLomain castle before. What a sight!"

Coira was startled. "You've been to medieval Scotland before?"

Mildred patted Coira on her arm and offered a ravishing grin. "Of course, child!"

Coira shook her head. No doubt, one of the novels Beth wrote mentioned that. She just naturally assumed that Mildred was in the book, because Ferchar and Coira had traveled to and remained in the twenty-first century.

"Come," Marie said. She grabbed Coira's hand and pulled her up the steps. "Everyone else is in the castle, and we need to prepare you."

Coira looked back at William only to behold anticipation and happiness on his face. One eyebrow rose along with one corner of his lips. He appeared positively devious when he wore that expression.

What did he know that she did not?

When they entered the hall, it was free of clansfolk save a few servants and all the people she'd come to know and care for. Caitlin and Ferchar sat side by side, their baby nestled in Ferchar's arms. Iain and Arianna, her belly quite swollen with pregnancy now, were in chairs across from Stephen and his Arianna. Caitlin's brother Shane and his wife Catherine sat at the same table, as their daughter leaned over Ferchar's shoulder and crooned to the baby. Adlin stood before the fire beside Niall.

"She's arrived!" Marie declared, leading Coira toward the stairs to the second landing. "Let's go, ladies."

She barely had time to register the welcoming feeling of the castle's great hall again before all the women hurried after them save Catherine and Stephen's Arianna. Before she knew it, the small throng of women had her up the next flight of stairs, down the hall and into William's chamber, now her chamber. The thought shot a rush of excitement and eagerness through her. Darn him for wanting to wait until their wedding night!

She gazed at the familiar furnishings with contentment. A tub of hot water sat by the fire, and steam rose from its surface. The air had cooled, and a small fire crackled invitingly on the hearth. All four torches lining the walls burned and gave the late day chamber a uniquely medieval ambiance.

"Well, now," Marie said, very much in control of the situation. "Let's get out your wedding dress!"

Coira smiled with delight when she spied a trunk unlike any she'd seen before. It twinkled with diamonds, and she saw William's eyes in each precious gem. Eyes meant for her, eyes of diamond brilliance when ignited with magic and passion, and as silver as mist in their natural state.

Marie made a gesture with her hand. "Come, Coira, you weren't supposed to have this on the first day you traveled back to Scotland, but you are now."

Coira knelt down before the trunk, enchanted by the way the firelight ignited the diamonds. Annie and Marie were on either side of her. Arianna, Coira, Caitlin, Mildred, and Beth stood nearby. She knew she would always remember this moment, these women who watched her and waited. Caught within the magic of love that they'd all experienced with the men they were meant to be with.

She leaned over and placed her hands on the metal rose petals on either side of the trunk. They turned to soft petals in her hands, stroking her palm with velvet as the clear ring of a bagpipe filled the room. It filled her heart, mind, and soul, reminding her of the night William played for Iosbail, his mentor. For just a moment, she knew the woman stood there alongside the others, young and beautiful, remembering as well.

Iosbail's spirit slipped away when the trunk clicked and opened of its own accord. She gazed down at the gown and knew it was the wedding dress that had been in her family's possession for countless generations.

She reached down and lifted up the exquisite garment. The long, elegant sleeves tapered to triangular points that would fall over the hand and stop at the base of the index finger. Beyond this point were circles of petite pearls meant to anchor the sleeve in ring fashion. The same pearls ran along the low neckline and the deep point where bodice met skirt.

Parallel to every polished line of pearls was a glorious stream of glistening diamonds. Right before the pearl rings, the ends of the sleeves hinted at the exotic and mysterious with their unusual star shapes woven with diamonds.

Coira knew the tale behind this dress. Every single pearl was hand selected from oysters born of the North Sea long ago by a distant Broun relative.

"So beautiful," she murmured.

"Aye," Arianna said, her eyes somewhere else, yet still focused on the dress. "'Tis the same dress I wore, save the diamonds were emeralds, the very night I nearly married—"

Arianna looked to Beth, her best friend so long ago, their eyes connected in understanding. She continued. "The night I nearly married Edward." Her eyelashes fell, heavy with nostalgia. "But ended up with Iain."

"Thank goodness," Beth said. "After all, you were married to him!"

Arianna laughed, the two long-lost friends shared another kindred gaze. Coira did not know all the details of Arianna's story but knew that she had ended up with the right man as had Beth.

Coira leaned over the chest and removed the veil. From a crown of heavy diamonds, silky crème gauze hung in a sheet of velvety softness. A mere three inches from the bottom, thirteen fragile Celtic crosses of pinpoint diamonds were sewn across the width, touching arm to arm.

She ran her fingers over the diamonds. "How utterly lovely."

Marie laid her hand over her daughter's. "As lovely as you, my child."

Overwhelmed with emotion, she stood, helpless as the women worked with swift efficiency. Arianna removed the gown and veil from her arms. Marie urged her to remove her clothes and climb into the tub. Not embarrassed in the least by the women present, she did so. While the women chattered in excitement, she bathed in rose-scented water and used lilac soap.

As though she were a queen, her hair was wrung out. She dried off and was sheathed within the velvet softness of the gown. It was too long and loose. Before she could implement her own magic, Marie ran her hand down the side of the dress and the hem magically shortened while the waist tightened. Mildred plunked her down in a chair before the fire, while Annie combed through her hair.

Caitlin slipped shoes onto Coira's feet, uttering a few select curses about their turn shoe style, while Beth smoothed out the veil, releasing any twists in the fabric. Arianna eventually took the comb from Annie and muttered something about long, even strokes. When at last the moisture was free from Coira's hair and curls fell in soft waves down her back, her mother took the veil in hand and came to stand behind her. Carefully, she placed it on Coira's head and pinned it securely.

Marie studied her handiwork. Pleased with what she saw, she nodded once and made a demand to the rest of the women. "Och, most of us are witches. Cannae one of you summon a bloody mirror for my lassie?"

Coira chuckled and stood. She'd never felt so regal and feminine. Before they had a chance, she flicked her wrist and a tall, oval standing mirror appeared. Marie met her eyes, an impressed yet wistful look creeping into her blue eyes. She said nothing but turned Coira to face the mirror.

She gazed at her reflection and barely recognized the image. When was the last time she'd gazed in a mirror? It had been her visit to the twenty-first century at Caitlin's home. The woman who looked back at her was a perpetual stranger to the reflection she'd seen then. Now she not only held the stature of a woman far more relaxed but something else. Something so distinct and radiant she did not know what it was.

Her mother leaned close and whispered in her ear. "It's the mixture of magic, true love, and who you always were inside, my daughter."

Coira stared at the brilliant sheen of diamonds contrasting with her black hair. Something passed through her. William. He touched her mind, his essence grabbed hers, swirling through it like mist caught and twisted up into a band of retreating thunderclouds. She watched the mirror in amazement as her eyes ignited and turned the color of a pure blue loch shimmering under a high noon sun.

The women around her vanished, and he stood behind her, gazing into the mirror at their combined reflections. He was not cloaked in plaid but wore his black robes. The contrast of their two forms entranced her. His was tall, broad, and incredibly masculine, whereas she stood petite, fine-boned, and feminine.

Power poured off him and stirred her magic anew.

He touched her only with his deep Scottish brogue. "You are of the moonlight, so thorough in your beauty, it nearly cripples me."

She tried to move but couldn't. Tried to speak but couldn't.

He continued. "Open your eyes, your soul, look to the mirror, my love. What do you see?"

Coira watched, dreamlike, as the mirror became water, and the water became steam. Wraithlike, it wrapped around two nude forms, one tall and muscled, the other slight, a woman. As she gazed intently, their features became obvious. It was her and William! The two of them lost in each other, twined together through the steam and mist. He kissed her deeply and held himself within her.

His strong form caressed her slighter one. She watched as his large hands fanned over breast, then her stomach. Felt everything his talented touch did. Groaning, she watched in the mirror as his curious hand disappeared down below, watched as his eyes went half-mast as his tongue slid down her neck, as his hand slowly began to investigate. She groaned as sharp pleasure washed over her. At last... finally.

Watching them, she shuddered and staggering release found her mortal form instantly. Dear Lord! She would have crumbled to the floor had he not caught her arms from behind. Suddenly, another orgasm ripped through her and she moaned, so needy it was hard to stand. Gripping the wall, she struggled for breath.

As sanity returned slowly, he spoke softly to her. "You're taking too long up here getting ready. Come down and marry me, lass."

Before she could respond, he vanished. The mirror returned to its original form, and the women stood once again in their places.

Arianna took one look at her flushed face and shook her head. "Impatient wizard of a Scotsman!"

Coira blushed furiously. This was the downfall of being surrounded by witches. Magical secrets were a hard thing to keep. Everyone, save Coira, giggled at Arianna's remark before she was ushered from the chamber and led back downstairs.

~Sylvan Mist~

She reflected that it was not such a bad thing going to one's wedding sexually sated, not at all. The hall below was completely clear, save Adlin. He was immaculate as always, his long white robes pristine and his white hair soft and combed.

When they reached the bottom of the stairs, the women walked ahead and left Coira and Adlin to follow at a more leisurely pace. He offered his arm, and she took it as they left the great hall behind and stepped out the door.

Adlin paused a moment, and she stopped with him. His wizened light blue gaze swept over everything, the inner compound, now nearly empty as well. His regard passed over the kitchen, armory, stables, and warrior's quarters. Then they traveled beyond that to the distant mountains and surrounding loch, swathed in the early rays of what would prove to be the most spectacular sunset Cowal had ever seen.

Gold, crimson, and melon slid down the monolithic peaks and turned the water to a rainbow of riotous color. His voice sounded wistful. "Do you truly love this land, lass, with all of your heart?"

She heard the serious undertone in his voice. "Aye, with all of my heart, Adlin."

The old wizard turned his eyes to hers, and she felt not magic but the simple regard of a mortal man who well understood human nature. A short time passed before he spoke again. "Aye. You do then, very well."

They continued down the steps, arm in arm. When they reached the last stair, Adlin gave an answer to a question not asked of him. "The ring didnae glow, because of your engagement ring. It was never in your nature to remove that ring until you had finished with James. And it was not in William's nature to ask you to. The ring of Ireland will not glow until the heart is completely free from whatever may bind it."

She gave no reply, understood the truth behind his words. Though her love for William was and had been a thorough thing, James had always remained there. Someone she'd made a commitment to. They crossed over the drawbridge, beneath the second portcullis and onto the field.

"What of the ring glowing for Niall, Adlin?"

"Aye." He cast an unreadable sidelong glance. "An interesting twist of fate, that."

Coira waited while Adlin remained silent. She was unsure he was going to answer at all until at last he continued. "A MacLomain wizard cannot be bound to one that does not carry magic, yet you traveled back in time, drawn by a dream and William himself, who never knowingly called you. As a mortal, your fate would be with Niall; as one with magic, it is to be with William."

She frowned, not quite comprehending most of what he'd just said. How could Niall have been the right man when it had always been William she wanted, though at first she didn't admit to such? "But what of our instant attraction to one another?"

"'Twas all part of your destiny, lass. I can tell you no more."

She continued to walk with him and had the good grace to let the matter drop. She would get nothing from Adlin he did not wish to give.

Two great Beltane bonfires flared crimson against the blazing skyline beyond. Over a thousand clansfolk filled the field with life. Bagpipes played and people danced. But there was more to this eve than her wedding. She could feel it in the deepest recesses of her being.

Adlin asked her one last question. "Do you wish to be married in the chapel or betwixt the fires, Coira?"

Her immediate response shocked her. "Betwixt the fires."

Why had she said that? She'd always desired to be married before God, in a church. Coira again thought of the Druidess's advice. She would be asked a question, and she should answer with her heart. And though she knew Chiomara's words were in reference to James, she couldn't help but wonder if the Druidess had not helped Coira to free her heart in all things.

She wasn't disturbed at all that William worshipped the old pagan gods and she the new god. She understood that all of their gods would be there to witness the marriage, whether they were in a chapel or betwixt the fires.

William materialized through the crowd and stood before her. He now wore the MacLomain plaid and a black tunic. His hair was free of braids, the auburn on black highlights catching in the firelight. He held out his hand.

Set free from Adlin, she took William's hand. Nothing was said as the crowd parted, and he led her forward. A cleric stood between the two great fires, his brown robes long and his hood pulled back. A warm feeling filled her. William was willing to be married in the eyes of the church, in the eyes of her God.

She could feel them all, her family and friends within the vast circle of people surrounding the fires. How perfect to have everyone here for this moment in her life.

Adlin took one of Coira's hands and one of William's, pulled them together and wrapped a swath of MacLomain plaid around their wrists, joining them together. He stepped back and the cleric stepped forward. The holy man led his sermon, pulled forth the words of the church between the rising sparks of the monstrous fires on either side.

At last, the cleric's gaze fell to William, who was already gazing deeply into her eyes when he spoke the words.

"I, William MacLomain, tak thow Coira O'Donnell to my spousit wyf as the law of the Haly Kirk schawis and thereto I plycht thow my trewht and syklyk."

Coira swallowed, lost in the love and words he offered. She would savor this moment for the rest of her life. With great care, she repeated the vow and stared intently into his silver eyes. "I, Coira O'Donnell, tak thow William MacLomain to my spousit husband as the law of the Haly Kirk schawis and thereto I plycht thow my trewht and syklyk."

His hand squeezed tightly around hers as the cleric said his last few words, and Adlin stepped forward. He raised his arms in the air and flung his head back, his white hair flowing over his robes. "May you forever be united in the eyes of the old gods and the new, and in the eyes of Scotland, may you begin anew."

Coira did not see the wild white roses that sprouted at their feet, nor the blaze of a pentacle emblazoned in the green grass around them; she only saw him. William. Her husband. With a move born of magic, he unwound the tartan at their wrists and pulled her into his arms.

When his lips crashed down on hers, nothing else existed but him. They might have levitated, might have spun in the air, all Coira knew was she couldn't get close enough. She wanted to meld their skin, crawl inside of him, and be one forever. The feeling was so powerful, so complete, she knew it would never fade, never be less than it was at this moment.

It would only grow stronger. How that was humanly possible she couldn't contemplate, but it would. The years ahead would blend them so thoroughly, she knew that even in the afterlife, they would be one.

Soft feminine laughter drifted over them. "There is a priest present."

They pulled from each other reluctantly, their kiss ending in a private smile. She was the first to turn her head away and look at Muriel, William's mother. Hugh, his father, stood beside her and beamed with pride. Lord, she had completely forgotten about his parents!

Muriel strode forth, her eyes wet, and took Coira into her arms. "I'm so pleased, Coira. Welcome to the family."

"Thank you."

Next she was pulled into Hugh's strong embrace. After that, she was swamped by family and friends wishing both William and her well. After all of the congratulations were offered, the celebration resumed, and they had a moment of privacy.

William sat down on a bench and pulled her onto his lap. The vivid sunset had given way to a dusky lavender twilight. His eyes glowed with admiration. "You look truly breathtaking this eve, lass."

"Do you think so?" She preened at her husband's compliment.

"Aye." He whispered and cupped the back of her head. "My wife."

William lowered his lips to hers and kissed her thoroughly, his lips warm and promising over hers.

"Hey, save it for later, you two! Come dance and celebrate!"

Coira groaned and pulled away. She scowled at Annie. "I have saved it for later. Now is later."

Annie laughed, grabbed Coira's hands, and pulled her from William's lap. He followed close behind the women as they commenced celebrating. The wine, whisky, and ale flowed, while couples danced and celebrated the wedding on Beltane's eve. The crowd was boisterously alive. She danced with many Broun clansmen as well as MacLomains as the eve wore on. Eventually, she ended up dancing with Niall.

He looked down at her with warm affection. "I suppose this means I've really lost you."

"No." She smiled. "You've not lost me, Niall. In many ways, you've gained me as a sister, for I love you as I do my brother, Calum."

A swift ache rose in her. Would she ever see Calum again?

Niall leaned in and kissed her on the cheek. "I am honored then, my sister."

William appeared from nowhere, and Coira smirked at the look on his face. It seemed her chieftain was a mite jealous. Just as William was ready to claim the next dance, her family appeared. Their expressions alarmed her.

"What's wrong?" she asked.

Marie teared up. "It's nearly time for us to return home, my daughter."

William took her hand, gave it a reassuring squeeze. She'd known they couldn't stay, that this moment would come eventually. It didn't make it any easier. She shook while she embraced her mother and father tightly, not knowing whether she'd see them again.

Caitlin and Ferchar came next. She embraced Ferchar longer. She was quite fond of him, though it was more likely she'd see him again due to his position amongst the four wizards.

When Annie stepped forward, Coira smiled. "You can hug me later, sister. We've plenty of time."

She froze when a tear slid down Annie's cheek. Why was she crying? A clenching sensation surrounded her heart. No. "You're leaving too, aren't you?"

Chapter Twenty Two

Annie nodded slowly and confirmed Coira's fear. "Aye, I have to leave."

"Why?" She looked from Annie to Arthur. She couldn't imagine these two anywhere but Scotland. "You belong here!"

"No," Annie said, shaking her head. "I belong back in New Hampshire, as does Arthur."

Coira reined in her misery. "I don't understand."

"You see." Annie looked at the women by them. "Mildred and Caitlin descend from Arthur and me."

She choked on this information with disbelief. Caitlin and Mildred both nodded in confirmation and looked fondly at Annie.

"My Lord," Coira whispered. "You knew this all along?"

All three nodded. How well they had hidden it! Her eyes narrowed at Annie. "This knowledge is in one of Beth's novels, isn't it?"

Annie chewed the corner of her lip and nodded. "You couldn't know, Coira. I'm sorry I lied to you, really! It was crucial that you knew nothing about it. Adlin did not want your destiny affected in any way by the past."

Bloody meddling wizard! She dismissed her irritation and tossed a dry glance at Beth. She wasn't completely innocent either.

~Sylvan Mist~

Beth put up her hands and shook her head. "Hey, I'm merely the writer. I pen what I'm told and have every right to remain silent under the strict orders of a wizard!"

Coira couldn't fault her for that. Without further ado, she released William's hand and pulled her sister into her arms. The two held each other for many minutes. When she pulled back, she accepted the scrap of tartan Arthur offered and blotted Annie's tears away before drying her own.

She sighed deeply and drank in the sight of each beloved face. "So this is goodbye."

"Not quite yet, my child." Adlin's low voice cut through the night, young and full of magic.

The crowd had ceased their merriment at some point and surrounded the two bonfires again, leaving a path from where they stood back to where she was married hours ago.

The clansfolk appeared curious, fully aware something important was happening. Very rarely did Adlin enter so many minds and compel them to cease their celebration. Even the wizards looked confused as Adlin took Coira's hand. Adlin must've entered his fellow wizards' minds and made a request, for in the next instant they wore not their plaids but the robes of their calling.

Coira didn't miss the avid curiosity radiating from the men. Adlin pulled her forward and urged William, Ferchar, and Iain to follow until the five of them stood between the fires. He spoke softly, allowing only their small group to hear. "I must explain to you now why you three were summoned when Coira woke from her month-long slumber after having traveled back to Ireland and our distant relative."

The air shifted when the three younger MacLomain's magic stirred to life with slight unease.

~Sylvan Mist~

William's eyes took on a diamond intensity, Ferchar's sapphire, and Iain's emerald. She'd never been in such close proximity to all of them at once when their magic erupted. It was a powerful, humbling feeling.

Adlin met each of their eyes individually as he continued. "As you know, I've lived for a very long time, but none of you know just how long."

The men's faces were chiseled into stern masculine perfection, all of them unmoving and stiff.

"I was born in what is now known as Scotland in the year 487 A.D. I was the first MacLomain," Adlin said.

She was sure her mouth hung open and gave credit to the other three that they appeared so unaffected by the news, when she could clearly feel their inner awe and turmoil.

Adlin continued. "The king of the Dalriada was my father and the druidess, Chiomara, my mother, neither of whom I ever met in person but know well within my heart."

Iain was the first to speak. "So, because we are closely related to you, our blood has a good dose of Irish then, much more than our kinsmen."

"Aye." Adlin nodded. "I have fathered other children over the decades, the last being around the year nine hundred. Since then, there have been none until your father, Iain, who is William and Ferchar's grandfather. It was a time between times, when the old pagan ways merged with the new Christian religion. The Irish goddess Brigit is at the heart of us four wizards. She desired back then to keep the old ways from completely dying. She believed above all things, that the old ways and the new could remain for all time within our hearts."

Everyone waited as Adlin went on. "And, of course, Brigit was a goddess of love, amongst other things, and believed in true love, that every soul was one half of another in this world. It was her desire, for her love for the druidess and the kingdom of Dalriada was so great, that their lineage remain strong and knew that eventually it would be annihilated in Ireland. So she sought Fionn to bring forth three rings. These would find three great loves that would ensure the lineage always."

Ferchar spoke, his sapphire eyes flashing. "What of the Broun clan? Why are they the connection?"

The fire spit sparks into the air on either side of them, and Coira realized the clansfolk around them were blurred and inactive, as though they were frozen in time as the wizards spoke.

"That would be because of my foster sister." Adlin's eyes clouded briefly.

"Foster sister?" Iain asked.

"Aye, that's right, my sister was not of my blood."

"Iosbail?" William asked. His brows lowered in confusion.

"Aye." Adlin offered a rueful smile. "Iosbail was the foster child, younger than Erc and Chiomara's blood-born children. She had a restless spirit from the day she could toddle. She was a young woman when she began the lineage that would lead to Liam O'Donnell. Shunned by a society that believed in children only within marriage, she left the babe behind with his father, a wealthy man, and left Ireland, compelled to come to the land of the Scots. She knew nothing of me, the brother who never set foot on Irish soil. The moment she arrived here she was interwoven into the fate of the MacLomains, and she became immortal as did I."

Coira was completely enthralled at this point and saw the others were as well.

Adlin sighed. "Her wanderings took her through Scotland into Britain, over the water into what is now known as the European continent where she settled in Romania for some time. There she met a man whom she loved dearly and began a family. He passed away, as did countless others descended from them. But she held their clan together as the centuries unraveled, traveling north slowly with them, through France, England, and back into Scotland."

Coira was speechless. Romania? Wasn't that where her mother had mentioned at some point her clan derived from? No, it couldn't be.

Adlin was not finished. "In what is now England, she bore a child who stayed behind. That child is Niall's distant relative, though he believes her to have been his great grandmother. Eventually, her clan settled in East Lothian where they remain. She learned of me somehow over the many long years and eventually, when the old gods spoke to her of her immortality eventually coming to an end, she knew it was time, left her clan and came to me to spend what she knew would be her remaining years here."

Coira and Iain spoke at once. He stopped and urged her to have her question answered first. "Her clan was the Brouns, weren't they?"

Adlin smiled. "Aye, and Iosbail loved them dearly and the goddess Brigit loved all of Chiomara and Erc's children. She desired that the MacLomains and the Brouns, my clan and Iosbail's, and all our love, must come together and unite."

Silence fell for many moments before Iain murmured, "Why three rings, and why us?"

Adlin shook his head slowly. "Even I do not have all the answers. Some things must be left to mystery, left to the old gods."

Iain could not entirely contain his distress when he addressed Adlin. "You and Iosbail began to age. She was told her immortality was coming to an end. Now she has passed away. Why? What does this mean for you, grandfather?"

"And so we arrive at the crux of it, my children," Adlin responded.

The veil of blurriness dropped and the huge ring of clansfolk became animated, listened, waited, unaware of the wizards' previous conversation.

Adlin raised his arms in the air and turned slowly as if he engulfed the whole of both clans present. "'Tis been a glorious eve, my clans. 'Tis been a glorious celebration. You are my family, my heart."

His words carried over the field and entered the souls of all. The fires lowered, and the stars overhead shot shards of white light down upon them as though they were a million different moons. He completed his circle until he again faced Coira and the wizards.

Adlin lowered his arms and held his hand out to Coira. His voice continued, carried far and wide. "Your ancestors wish to give you something. I wish to give you something."

Coira felt Adlin's magic surround and engulf her, his voice entered her mind, soft and soothing. *Dinnae fret, lass. You have been given a great gift. Let Scotland and Ireland have you, let the MacLomains have you. Always follow your heart and never doubt what you know to be true.*

The overwhelming smell of flowers surrounded and covered her skin in velvet softness. Incredible knowledge filled and connected her to something so great and wondrous she nearly fell to her knees. Trembling, she closed her eyes and welcomed it, became it.

~Sylvan Mist~

When the feeling passed, she opened her eyes slowly and knew that her life was again completely altered. The crowd was silent. She looked immediately to William. His silver eyes registered shock and sadness, then pride. Her gaze traveled to Ferchar and Iain. Their expressions were similar.

Why were they looking at her like this?

William's tender words slipped into her mind.

"You're one of us now, Coira."

Adlin kept her hand and smiled widely to the crowd. "My family, my clan, I give you Coira, the fourth MacLomain wizard."

She gasped in astonishment. What? Instantly, she looked down and realized that the wedding gown was gone. Instead, she wore the same white robe as Iain and Adlin. She tried to speak but could not.

How could she be the fourth?

The crowd roared, shocking her even further. She gazed at the faces, men, women, children, and saw only pleasure and acceptance.

As before, they fell away somehow and left the five of them alone. Adlin did not speak aloud but entered their minds individually, likely telling them different things. Coira knew that she heard what she was meant to hear.

"You are the fourth MacLomain wizard now, Coira. You are not immortal, nor are the others or any generations to come. It will be a wonderful life you lead with William and the clan. You'll have many children and protect them well. Now that you are a wizard, your family is not lost to you and you can visit them at will, but always remember time passes differently between your time and this one. Never forget that."

When he pulled free from her mind, he did so with the other three. She did not miss the moisture in any of their eyes, nor the heart-wrenching expression on Iain's face. Adlin stepped forward and embraced each of them one last time, his eyes memorizing their faces.

At last, he turned and walked to where her family stood at the edge of the circle. The crowd was still frozen, misplaced in time, as she stood with her fellow wizards. Ferchar would leave soon but not yet.

Now she knew her family was not lost to her, she was able to offer a teary smile. Marie, Liam, and Annie returned her smile, their watery gazes locked on hers as Adlin summoned his magic into a spill of twisting starlight and Scotland. They faded slowly, like ghosts in the night, until they were gone.

William's arms came around her and pulled her close. He said nothing but held her against his chest, soothed with his steady heartbeat.

When they pulled apart, the clans had returned to their celebration, she knew that Adlin had crawled within all their spirits and eased his departure. There was no pain of loss, only love for a man who had created and worshipped them for their entire lives, a father to them all.

Ferchar and Iain still stood with them, their hearts laid bare in the silence.

Iain raised his eyes after some time and eyed his fellow wizards. "So begins a new era for us all."

"So it does," Ferchar agreed.

"Welcome, Coira." Iain's emerald eyes were direct and kind.

"Aye," Ferchar said. He smiled, obviously content with her new position within the clan.

A wave of relief passed over her. They accepted her and did not hold any animosity. She was one of them now, a MacLomain, yet still a Broun. Everything felt exactly right, and she knew her fate was fulfilled, that from now until the end of her days, these men would be her brethren, her circle.

And as was his way, William offered a bit of humor. "Who would have thought my prim little English-loving sprite would be a wizard?"

She rolled her eyes and laughed up at him, once again caught within the love and desire she saw there.

Ferchar looked to the western horizon. "I must go now, but I'll see you all again."

He shook hands with the men, arm to elbow, the way of the Scots, until he came to her. Holding her at arm's length, he looked into her eyes. "'Twill be an exciting life you lead, lass, and I'm proud to count you as a sister of magic. Stay strong, and keep your husband under control."

Her lips twitched with amusement. "You ask a lot."

He laughed and pulled her into his arms. "Goodbye."

Ferchar pulled away, turned, and walked into the night, the Highland darkness consuming him.

Iain approached. "Well, lass, you've learned much, but I'll teach you even more. You will do well with the three of us, I promise."

"I'm sure I will." She smiled warmly.

Iain leaned in closer. "I have to be honest about something."

She cocked her head in question.

"Arianna didnae have her ring on when she traveled back in time. As I learned later, only Adlin knew that our meeting would be the first of the three great loves. As Adlin has just explained, Marie never had the emerald embedded in Arianna's ring. The emerald had been there all along unseen until the day Arianna and I gazed upon it together."

"Why did you not tell me that on the wall walk that day?" Coira asked.

~Sylvan Mist~

"I wanted you to keep hope. I wanted you to be with William. Had I told you the entire truth, you might have countered by telling me that the ring likely would've glowed for Arianna and I from the start had she been wearing it."

He was right. "Thank you, Iain, for both your honesty and friendship."

His famous lopsided grin erupted. "Aye, my fellow wizard, you shall have both always."

He embraced her then looked to Arianna, who stood nearby. His gazed roamed her swollen form with appreciation. "I've other matters to attend to now. Enjoy your wedding night, lass."

Iain's last declaration erased the night and everything that had transpired and left only thoughts of William. Before she could turn his way, he seized her wrist and whipped her against him. Her hand rose to his chest, sandwiched between them. He wrapped one arm around her back and the other around her shoulders.

"Aye, your wedding night," he said.

Before she could respond his lips covered hers, worshipped them with a blaze of heat and urgency. She met him evenly, eagerly, shouting into his mind that he'd best get her to privacy soon.

He pulled back a hair, pewter gaze dark with want. "I think it might be time to take you to our chamber."

She played coy, raised one eyebrow, and offered a dainty frown. "Do you really think so? After all, the night is still fairly young."

William leaned forward. His eyes twinkled. "I do believe I'd like to see something."

It was good he held her so tightly or she would have melted into the grass beneath his gaze. "Oh, and what is that?"

He offered a devilish smile and a wicked flash of white teeth. "You in my plaid with nothing else on."

Coira couldn't contain a burst of laughter, remembering the day she'd flirted with him about the obvious comforts of a plaid versus a dress. She leaned as close to his ear as she could manage and whispered softly. "I'm quite sure, my laird, that I would like to see you look upon me in nothing but your plaid."

William gave a chuckle mixed with a passionate groan. "My lady, I live to please you."

With that, he swung her up into her arms and strode through the crowd. Another whoop of pleasure arose from the clans as they cleared a path. When they broke free from the throng of people and entered the quiet, dark place between the celebrations and the first portcullis, Coira took her gaze from his beautiful face for a moment, compelled to look at the dark forest beyond.

There, glowing softly but clearly for her eyes, they stood. Chiomara, Erc, and Fionn were together, watching. Chiomara, druidess, wore her long white robes, King Erc, tall and cloaked with a crown of gold, and Fionn, golden and perfect, one with the forest. She raised her hand to them. In kind they did the same.

Just before they left the field, the three vanished in white light dusted with sylvan mist. Coira snuggled closer to William, so in love with him it hurt. Her heart was full and absolute.

She was home.

~Sylvan Mist~

Epilogue

Salem, New Hampshire, Present Day

Mildred finished the last sentence and closed the book, running her fingers over the cover, such a lovely love story, as they all were. Carefully she set the novel, *Sylvan Mist*, on the small table at her side.

Spring had just given way to summer and flowers were still in early growth. A hummingbird danced at the feeder hanging from the porch overhead. She loved this bench just outside her front window, where she could watch nature unfold at her feet.

"Annie did a wonderful job writing this novel," she said.

"Aye."

"William was given no visions throughout. The poor lad never even called her back, sinfully wicked and very lucky victim, in my opinion."

He chuckled. "No, this was in Ireland's control entirely. 'Tis no small task making a love match of two wizards, I would imagine."

The hummingbird left the feeder and hovered between them before it flitted off.

"And Brodick was actually Eoghan, an old enemy of Chiomara and Erc's, reincarnated? I would have never supposed such a thing."

~Sylvan Mist~

He received a hard candy from her and popped it in his mouth. "'Twas a minor detail in the story. Insistent evil spirits don't typically get far."

A van rolled down the drive past the house and they both waved. Caitlin and Ferchar had their hands full with little Logan.

"Why did they choose Coira for a wizard, a lass without any magic at all to start?" Mildred waited eagerly for the answer.

His handsome face unraveled with delight. "As a wise woman once said, I believe she was your great, great grandmother, Annie Broun O'Donnell, when asked why Erc, a king, would save Coira from death, said, 'Why not?' " He grew wistful. "Why not indeed? As we now know, she was a MacLomain wizard, therefore Erc could save her. So, what don't we know now that makes the question to your answer obvious?"

Mildred cocked her head, relishing the game. "Pray, tell."

He cocked a brow and issued a rakish grin. "Mayhap, 'tis merely because she carried no magic, and her heart desired it so. Mayhap her magic was hidden by Ireland. Lord, woman, we've the rest of our lives together. Do you expect me to give all of my secrets away?"

She threw back her head, laughing in delight. "I would hope not!"

His eyes roved her face with appreciation.

"Will they all fare well?" she asked.

"Aye, all will be well, both clans will go on, and magic will always be at the heart of them."

A warm breeze caressed her cheek. Mildred smiled and gazed at the man seated beside her. "I never expected this, you coming here."

"Well, you wouldn't live with me there, so it was only natural that I come to you in the end."

~Sylvan Mist~

He took her hand in his, eyes sparkling and mischievous. "I love you, Mildred."

She moved closer and leaned her head on his shoulder, content with life at last. "And I you, Adlin."

A word from the author...

If you enjoyed *The MacLomain Series* and want to follow some of its characters (especially head shaman, Adlin), keep your eyes peeled for my upcoming *Calum's Curse Trilogy*. Yes, this is a trilogy entirely devoted to Calum. You might remember him vaguely from *Fate's Monolith* (he was the babe in Marie's belly) and *Sylvan Mist* (he was the brother overseas). Well, Calum was a very bad boy and got involved with dark magic. Now he's a ghost with a curse upon his shoulders and three modern day super-sexy ghost hunter descendants to watch over.

Did I say watch over?

I meant to say Calum's managed to cause a world of trouble for his distant offspring. Three haunted houses. Three creatures of the night set to destroy all. No, I'd say Calum and his are truly cursed.

The Victorian Lure (Calum's Curse-Ardetha Vampyre) is available now. Coming soon, The Georgian Embrace (Calum's Curse- Acerbus Lycan. .

About the author…

Award-winning New Hampshire native, Sky Purington writes a cross genre of paranormal/fantasy romance heavily influenced by history. From Irish Druids to Scottish Highlanders many of her novels possess strong Celtic elements. More recently, her vampire stories take the reader to medieval England and ancient Italy. Enjoy strictly paranormal romance? Sky's latest novels follow three haunted houses and the sexy ghost hunters determined to make sense of them. Make no mistake, in each and every tale told you'll travel back to another time and revisit the romanticism history holds at its heart. Sky loves to hear from her readers and can be contacted at Sky@SkyPurington.com.

Find out Sky's latest news at SkyPurington.com
Twitter @ Skypurington
Facebook *Sky Purington*

~Sylvan Mist~

Made in the USA
Lexington, KY
10 February 2012